I awoke to find myself lying in a big motel bed without any clothes on, with a naked woman for company. Morally speaking, it was no doubt very shocking, but we don't do too much moral speaking in this line of work. I was more concerned with the professional aspects of the situation.

"What's your name, darling?" Libby Meredith's voice interrupted my wandering, early-morning thoughts. "And I don't mean Grant Nystrom."

I turned my head to look at her. She was being very casual about security.

"Relax, darling. I'm a very important person in the organization. They still trust me implicitly; they don't suspect a thing. I'm sure they wouldn't bother to put a microphone in my room."

It was a naive little speech for anyone as deeply involved with a lot of unpleasant people as she seemed to be.

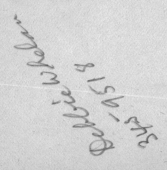

The Interlopers

DONALD HAMILTON

FAWCETT GOLD MEDAL • NEW YORK

A Fawcett Gold Medal Book
Published by Ballantine Books
Copyright © 1969 by Donald Hamilton

ISBN 0-449-12907-1

Manufactured in the United States of America

First Fawcett Gold Medal Edition: May 1969
First Ballantine Books Edition: December 1983
Second Printing: February 1986

The
Interlopers

1 *I GOT TO THE RIVER BEFORE DAWN,*
as instructed, and nursed the Chevy pickup cautiously off
the dirt road and down along the bank to the safe and
solid place I'd selected late the previous afternoon when
I'd scouted the area by daylight. Of course, I'd done a
little evening fishing afterwards, to make it look good, but
what I'd mainly been after was the assurance that, come
morning, I'd be able to find the rendezvous in the dark.

Now, having found it, I switched off the headlights and
went around to the rear of the vehicle and opened up the
camper to let the pup out. He was still young and naive
enough to take me for a dog-lover just because I fed him
once a day. He paused briefly, therefore, to give my face a
couple of wet licks before racing off to take care of various
items of urgent dog business. I could hear him out there in
the dark but I couldn't see him since he was all Labrador
and just about as black as a dog can get.

I wiped my face with my sleeve and looked across the
faintly gleaming water toward the Hanford Atomic Ener-
gy Reservation. According to the map, it occupied a considerable area of the state of Washington off in that direction—northwest, if it matters—but at this hour of the
morning, from where I stood on the opposite bank of the
Columbia River, I could see only a few mysterious lights.
I wondered if whatever they did over there had anything
to do with what I was doing over here.

In any case, I hoped they knew more about their
present business, whatever it was, than I knew about
mine. It was one of those super-security capers that seem
to develop every time agencies other than ours get into
the act, and as usual I was supposed to go out and save
the world with blindfold and earmuffs on, seeing and hearing nothing of a sensitive or classified nature.

I reached inside the camper and turned on the light and
pulled out my fishing rod—well, it was mine now, the
previous owner having no further use for it. I explored

7

some tricky little tackle boxes and found a metallic lure that looked suitable, meaning that it looked heavy and compact enough to cast easily, and to hell with what the Columbia River steelhead trout might think of it. After some fumbling I managed to attach it to the practically invisible monofilament line by means of a little swivel-and-snaphook gadget. I leaned the rod against the truck, pulled off the cowboy boots I'd been wearing, drew on some heavy socks, and fought my way into a pair of rubber hip boots.

I switched off the camper light, picked up the rod again, glanced toward the lightening sky to the east, and headed for the wide expanse of grayly shining water to make like Ike Walton. The pup thought this was a fine, exciting project. He abandoned his business up along the shore and went racing past to splash into the water ahead of me.

"Hank," I said, "get the hell out of there. I'm doing the fishing around here, not you. Hank, heel!"

I reached for the whistle hanging by a thong around my neck, but I didn't need it. He was kind of a special dog. At the moment he was operating under the alias of Avon's Prince Hannibal of Holgate—Hank for short—but his real name was equally impressive, and he'd come to me complete with as many instructions as an expensive camera. These included a list of authorized commands which, to my surprise, he usually obeyed.

I mean, I'd known hunting dogs before, but they'd been wide-ranging pointers and setters mostly, with a few hounds thrown in for good measure: all homegrown canine geniuses of a fairly independent nature. I'm sure the idea of walking docilely at heel had never occurred to any of them. Their job was to find game, not to show off their party manners. If you wanted one of them to stick around, you attached one end of a husky chain to his collar and got a good grip on the other end.

But this was a retriever and a real gold-plated pup, professionally trained. At the command he came back out of the water. He came reluctantly, but he came. He shook water all over me by way of protest—apparently there was nothing in the rules against this—and then he followed me along the bank, walking exactly level with my left knee. When I sat him down on a dry spot and told him to stay, he stayed. Somebody'd obviously put in a lot of work on him.

I left him sitting there obediently and waded out into the river, wondering if my contact was watching my antics through nightglasses, perhaps from the high ground behind me. I also wondered how long he'd make me play angler before he showed himself. There wasn't a sign of a fish in the water ahead of me. The evening before, some big stuff had been breaking the surface out there from time to time, but this morning the river was perfectly smooth except for the shifting patterns of swirls and eddies caused by the heavy current. I heaved my spoon in the general direction of the other shore, let it sink too far before starting the retrieve, and promptly got it snagged on the rocky bottom.

Maneuvering to free it, I reflected that this was a hell of a complicated identification routine to have to go through just to receive a little secret information from some guy who wasn't supposed to have it. However, certain people were interested in uncovering that guy and a lot of others like him up here in the Northwest, not to mention being also interested in preventing the stolen information from being used to our disadvantage.

So for the time being I was a gent named Grant Nystrom, a real sporty character, mad about fishing tackle and guns and Labrador retrievers—black Labrador retrievers, if you please. None of your offbeat yellow Labs for friend Nystrom, or your lousy Chesapeakes or Golden retrievers, either.

Just black Labs and fancy spinning and fly-fishing tackle and expensive sporting firearms for friend Nystrom, plus a rugged little sleep-two camper on a long-wheelbase half-ton chassis—a miniature house on wheels—to take him to where the fish were swimming or the birds were flying, or to where a piece of illicit data was waiting to be collected from an undercover operative and passed along to people somewhere on this continent who had the facilities for passing it along to people somewhere on another continent, people we'd rather didn't get their hands on it,

9

at least not before we'd had a chance to make a few judicious alterations—or substitutions; they hadn't told me which—to render it useless and perhaps even downright misleading.

It seemed as if Nystrom had picked a pretty good cover for a courier operating out here in the great open spaces where everybody loves the outdoors or pretends to. After all, there was no real reason why contact couldn't be made beside a trout stream as well as in a bar; and a man who likes dogs tends to be accepted as a sterling character, above suspicion.

It had been a sound enough plan, with some nice, imaginative touches, and it should have worked out well for friend Nystrom. But instead, for reasons still unknown to us, something had gone wrong. He'd met with difficulties of a fatal nature and so had his young black dog. We were callously trying to profit from their misfortunes.

In other words, my young black dog and I were taking over Grant Nystrom's courier route where he'd abandoned it due to circumstances beyond his control. At least that was the theory as it had been explained to me in San Francisco a few days earlier by a very important counter-intelligence type from Washington who'd told me graciously that, if I had to call him something, Smith would do. One of these days I'll meet up with one of these coy characters who'll have picked on some family other than the poor, abused, overworked Smiths, but I haven't yet.

"So this is the man," Mr. Smith had said, looking me over suspiciously after the introductions, such as they were, had been made. He was a tall, ascetic-looking individual with deep-set X-ray eyes. At least he looked as if he thought he could see through my flesh and bone right down into my probably corrupt and subversive soul. I wondered how Mac had come to get us stuck with him. Well, it's a big government and you can't duck all the kooks. Mr. Smith frowned dubiously and said, "The resemblance isn't really very close, is it?"

Mac said coldly, "According to the computer, it's the best match you're going to get if you insist on a trained U.S. agent with proper clearance. Of course, you could try Central Casting, Hollywood."

Mr. Smith said hastily, "I didn't mean——"

"If you're not satisfied," Mac went on, "just say the word. This man has plenty of work to do without pulling your people's chestnuts out of the fire just because he bears a faint resemblance to a corpse in which you happen to be interested."

"No, no," Mr. Smith protested. "I just . . . actually, the height and weight are very good, indeed excellent. The eye color is acceptable, and the hair can be taken care of. There is, of course, a certain age difference, and a certain grimness of expression. . . ."

"I am sure Eric will agree to change his expression if the necessity is explained to him," Mac said, using my code name as always. My real name is Matthew Helm, but that's beside the point. Mac went on, poker-faced: "I'm afraid we're going to have trouble making him any younger, however. Our rejuvenation techniques are still in the experimental stage."

Mr. Smith didn't seem to realize he was being kidded. He said, unruffled, "Also in our favor is the fact that your man is an outdoorsman, at home with guns and fishing tackle and such. Isn't that right?" He looked at me for the answer.

"Guns, yes," I said. "It's been a while since I handled a fishing rod, however."

Mr. Smith dismissed this objection. "It's not something a man forgets, I gather. You'll be briefed on the latest angling techniques, of course, as used by the man you're to impersonate. How do you get along with dogs?"

I shrugged. "We have a nonagression pact. I don't bite them and they don't bite me."

"Well, I'm sure you'll do a good job, Eric. You have an impressive record and we're glad to have your help." Mr. Smith regarded me benevolently for a moment; then his expression hardened. "Of course you'll keep in mind at all times that security is paramount on this assignment. Absolutely paramount. My people will supply you with the information you need to do your job, no more. Well, I must start for the airport if I'm to make it back to Washington today."

That had been in California, last week. Now I was

standing knee-deep in the Columbia River, a couple of states to the north, all made up like a fisherman, with my hair bleached almost white and a black dog watching me expectantly from the bank. Daylight was upon us, and a sporty-looking coupé—one of those glamorized compacts with slanting rear decks and fancy wheel covers—was nosing its way off the dirt road and down through the brush to where my truck was parked.

It stopped there. A tall, blondish girl in jeans got out, opened the trunk, and began to climb into the kind of chest-high waders that look like baggy rubber pants with feet in them.

2 *I WASN'T SUPPOSED TO DISPLAY*

any curiosity, of course. In fact, I was supposed to do nothing whatever except present myself, complete with dog and whistle, on the riverbank at dawn. Perhaps because—in my Nystrom incarnation—I was so easily described and so readily identifiable, the approach was to be made by the other party.

If this leggy female was my contact, the next step was up to her. And if she wasn't, the less interest I displayed, the better. If I ignored her, maybe she'd go away. I just glanced at her rather coldly, therefore, like any angler finding his private fishing spot invaded by a stranger.

Then I went back to heaving my lure, which I had freed, out into the wide Columbia and cranking it back again. On the next retrieve, as it came into sight flashing erratically in the dark water, the biggest fish in the world made a lazy roll right behind it. I mean, for a trout, if it was a trout, it was a monster. Any red-blooded American boy would have found his heart beating faster at the sight of such a fish. I had no trouble doing a reasonably convincing job of impersonating a fisherman, therefore, for the next half hour or so, as I dragged everything in Grant Nystrom's fancy tackleboxes past the spot where I thought the giant was lurking.

Nothing happened. No more fish investigated my lures—if that's what the big one had been doing—and no humans made contact with me, either. When I looked around for the girl, she was standing in waist-deep water a couple of hundred yards upstream, swinging a heavy, two-handed, steelhead-type spinning rod with the ease that comes only with years of practice.

I cast some more, gaining skill but losing enthusiasm as the morning wore on. Finally I gave up on fish and waded ashore to make myself a little more available to people. My watch said that the contact deadline was getting close. If nothing happened by seven, my instructions were to leave the place and try the alternate rendezvous that had been provided for later in the day.

I went back to the camper, poured myself some coffee from a thermos jug, and got a doughnut out of a paper bag. Munching and sipping, I stood by the door looking out at the river. Another car had come down to join us: a rather elderly white Plymouth station wagon. The occupants, two men, were fishing downstream from my spot. Nobody seemed to be catching anything.

As I turned to reach into the camper for another doughnut, having had no breakfast, I became aware that the girl had left the water and was coming toward me. The pup, whom I'd given permission to run, was romping along behind her; obviously he'd found a friend. I felt the familiar tightness come to my throat. No matter how long you're in the business, I guess you never get over that slightly breathless feeling just before the first card is dealt to open the game. Of course, it still remained to be proved that this blond kid was in the game. She could just be a friendly female who liked fish and dogs.

She stopped in front of me. The baggy rubber waders, held up by suspenders, did nothing for her figure, but I could see that she was the reedy, rather fragile kind of tall girl: a little girl stretched out long rather than a well-proportioned Amazon. Everything about her was rather small and delicate except for the long bones, and they looked as if they'd break rather easily. She had a small, tomboy face, framed by streaky blondish hair that was parted on one side, combed down straight all around, and whacked off level an inch or so below the ears. Her eyes, I saw, were blue and innocently direct, as if she'd never heard about fluttering eyelashes and maidenly reticence.

"Is this your dog?" she said. "He's perfectly beautiful."

It wasn't exactly what she was supposed to say, and it wasn't exactly the truth, either. I mean, a Labrador isn't really a beautiful dog like, say, an Afghan hound or an Irish setter.

I said, "He's a good pup. Would you care for some coffee and a doughnut?"

"No, thanks. Well, yes, if they're handy, I guess I will, please." She waited until I'd brought her the stuff. "Are you having any luck?" she asked after a bite and a sip.

I shook my head. "No. I saw a big one roll out there, but I couldn't interest him further. Of course, I'm not an expert on the tastes of your local fish."

"What are you using?"

I showed her my current lure. It didn't impress her. "Well, they sometimes take that," she said. "But I have more luck with this rig, usually. A brass spinner and a single hook with a grasshopper on it. Of course, you've got to use a sinker to make it cast right. Here." She showed it to me.

"Where do you get the grasshoppers?" I asked. I was trying hard to show the proper interest, but I wasn't really interested in grasshoppers or even in big steelhead trout. I hadn't been sent here for any fish, no matter how spectacular, and the interview wasn't going right. There were certain things she was supposed to say in a certain way, if she was the right person, and she hadn't said them. She'd been close, but in our business close isn't good enough. The actual, specified words are supposed to be spoken.

"The grasshoppers?" she said. "Oh, you can chase them in the daytime, but I generally just pick them off the leaves after dark. What's his name?"

Her mind wasn't on angling either, I saw. She obviously was more interested in the pup.

"Hank," I said.

"No, I mean his real name."

"Oh. Well, officially he's Avon's Prince Hannibal of Holgate." I grinned. "If you want the works, his sire was

14

Field Champion Avon's Prince Rufus, and his dam was Holgate's Black Donna. . . . What's the matter?"

There was a funny look on her tomboy face. "He doesn't look like one of the Avon dogs. I've seen pictures of them in the magazines, and they're all built like greyhounds." She laughed quickly. "Not that I'm running down your dog; I like the small, stocky type of Lab myself. After all, if you're going to have a retriever, it ought to look like a retriever and not a racehorse, don't you think?" She hesitated but went on before I could speak. "Of course you have papers on him."

"Sure," I said. She had me baffled; I couldn't guess what she was driving at. I tried another grin. "But I'm afraid he's not for sale."

"Oh, I wasn't thinking of buying him. But I have a little bitch who's just come into heat and the dog to which I was planning to breed her . . . well, it didn't work out, and I was wondering . . . could I see his papers?"

We'd considered all kinds of possibilities, setting this up, but the pup's love life hadn't really entered into our calculations.

I said, "Well, he's pretty young to be used at stud, and I'm only in town for a day or two."

She gave me a nice, unselfconscious grin. "How long does it take, actually? And I shouldn't think it would hurt him to learn the facts of life." She looked down at the black pup. He'd got wet again, visiting with her upriver, and now he was on his back, rolling himself happily in the dirt. In that position it was rather obvious that he was a little boy dog and not a little girl dog. The blond girl laughed. "He seems to have all the necessary equipment. He might as well learn how to use it."

She was kind of a refreshing young lady, but if she wasn't the person I'd come here to meet, I was wasting my time on her; in fact, she was an obstruction I'd better dispose of fast, before her presence scared off the real contact.

I said curtly, "I don't really think——"

"Please," she said softly. "I really want to get a good litter out of Maudie before she's too old. She's been . . . she's been pretty great." She stopped and cleared her

15

throat. "Where are you staying in town? Or are you camping out?"

"No, I got tired of pioneering. I'm staying at the Thunderbird Motel, but . . ."

She said, "Please. I'll pay any fee within reason. Your dog is really lovely. He's just what I've been looking for. They'll be beautiful pups. How about twelve o'clock? I'll buy you a lunch and we can talk it over, and I'll take you out to see Maudie. Of course I have to keep her penned up right now. She's a very good Lab. You'll like her . . ."

Ten minutes later, I was driving away, pretty well committed to officiating at a canine love-in. The time was up and the right words hadn't been said to make the contact official. Either she wasn't the one, or she was stalling for some reason, perhaps suspicion. Well, if she really knew dogs—and she seemed to—she had good reason to be suspicious.

3 I'D TOLD MAC FROM THE START that Mr. Smith from Washington was a damn fool, having me go to all the trouble of making my hair an exact match for the dead man's but giving me a pup that, aside from being black and a Labrador, hardly resembled the dead dog at all.

Mac had called me into the San Francisco office he was using temporarily, to ask for a progress report. This was at the end of the third and final day of indoctrination and general remodeling, designed to make me think, look, and act like Grant Nystrom. More study would have been useful—on other occasions I've taken weeks, even months, to work up a character properly—but Nystrom's schedule didn't allow it. I had to be on the banks of the Columbia on time.

As always, Mac had managed to pick an office with a bright window behind his chair, but after working with him for quite a few years, I didn't need to see him clearly. I knew what he looked like, crisp gray hair, black eyebrows, and all. I knew his business expressions by heart. He doesn't have too many that he uses in the line of duty. You could call him poker-faced and get no argument from me. What he's like at home, if he's got a home, I wouldn't know.

"Well, Eric?" he said.

"Just a minute, sir," I said, and turned to the pup, who was showing signs of wanting to investigate the office, perhaps with ulterior motives. "Hank, sit! Now stay there. *Stay!*"

I sat down and looked across the desk apologetically. "I'm supposed to take him everywhere I go. He even sleeps in my hotel room. It plays hell with my love life—or would, if they gave me time for a love life."

"I gathered they were keeping you pretty busy."

"Yes, sir," I said. "They're trying hard, all those bright young characters working for Mr. Smith. But it isn't going to work, sir."

There was a little pause. When he spoke, the tone of the voice told me that the black eyebrows had lifted a fraction of an inch. "Why not? They seem to have done a good job on your hair. It's a close match for that of the man we were taken to see in their private morgue. And I gather they have been able to give you a thorough knowledge of the late Mr. Nystrom's likes and dislikes, his personal habits, and his current identification routines and itinerary."

"Yes, sir," I said. "They know more about Grant Nystrom's private life than seems quite reasonable; more than they could possibly have got from simple surveillance, and they won't tell me how they got it. Another thing they won't tell me is why the guy was killed, although it's a subject in which I have, I feel, a legitimate interest."

"Maybe they don't know."

"Maybe," I said. "But maybe they do know and just aren't saying. They're very selective about telling me things. The story I got was that the agent tailing the guy heard a couple of rifle shots. He'd been waiting in his car out of sight while Nystrom worked at training the pup out in the country somewhere. Hearing the shots, the agent decided he'd better drive up and take a look. He found them lying out in the field dead, man and dog both. As he got out and hurried over to them, a guy took off through the brush, jumped into a car, and drove away."

Mac grimaced; he dislikes inefficiency. "Maybe Mr. Smith should teach his people a little more common sense and a little less security."

"Yes, sir," I said. "It was a pretty sloppy performance, all right. Maybe the agent in question couldn't keep his subject from getting shot—maybe he wasn't even supposed to—but he could at least have refrained from barging in clumsily until he'd got a good look at the murderer and learned what the guy was up to. Incidentally, the rifle was a .243, a pretty small caliber for a pro. It may be significant. I don't know."

"It seems to have been a professional enough job of shooting, Eric. Two shots; two dead bodies."

"Yes, sir. But most pros would prefer to stack the deck in their favor by using somewhat bigger bullets. That six-millimeter rifle is pretty light. You've got more leeway with, say, a seven-millimeter or thirty-caliber gun. You've got some extra power in reserve, in case you don't put the shot in exactly the right place." I shrugged. "Anyway, after letting the murderer get away unseen, the agent started behaving with reasonable intelligence for a change. He quickly bundled both stiffs, human and canine, into Nystrom's pickup camper and drove it out of sight. Then he came back for his own car, taking time to clean up the premises. So the only people besides us who know Nystrom is dead, we hope, are the people involved in having him killed. At least we're gambling that the outfit we're trying to get the goods on—the Communist spy ring for which he was playing courier—hasn't got the word."

"Of course there's always the possibility they did the killing," Mac pointed out. "Couriers have been eliminated by their own people before now, when they turned unreliable or somebody thought they had. What evidence is there that this did not happen here?"

I said, "I asked the same thing of Mr. Smith's young man."

"And the answer?"

"Well, there's the little amateur gun that was used." I grimaced. "And then there's some classified information, the source of which does not concern me, to the effect that our Communist friends are totally unaware that their courier is dead. I just love classified information the source of which does not concern me," I said sourly. "Particularly when my life depends on it."

Mac was frowning thoughtfully. "Then it would seem that you have two distinct adversaries, or groups of adversaries: the professional espionage ring and the amateurs —to judge by the rifle used—who killed Nystrom."

"If this inside dope from mysterious sources is correct," I said. "Well, it had better be. Otherwise I'm going to have a lot of fun trying to convince these Communist snoopers that I'm the ghost of their courier, the one they liquidated themselves."

"You are also, of course, taking a considerable risk of meeting someone who knew the real Nystrom. Has this been taken into consideration?"

"Yes, sir. I've been assured that I've got a good chance of pulling it off because Nystrom never ran this northwest route before. Well, that's what Mr. Smith thinks. Personally, I don't think I have much chance of getting away with this impersonation even with people who never saw the real guy."

"Just what is the problem, Eric?"

I said, "Well, aside from the normal risks and all the security crap I've got to put up with—hell, they won't even tell me the nature of the earthshaking information this spy ring's after—there's the dog they insist on my using. Look at him!"

The pup thumped his tail on the carpet as we both looked at him. Mac asked, "What's the matter with him?"

"Remember that poor beast we were shown with a bullet in his head? If you recall, that was a long-legged ridge-runner, sir, a tall, lean, rangy dog for a Lab. So what am I supposed to impersonate him with? Look at this low-slung little canine bulldozer—yes, I mean you!—built like a barrel, with only about half the road clearance of the dead dog. Oh, he's a good pup, bright and well-trained, but——"

19

"Maybe that's the point," Mac said. "The training is very important, perhaps more important than the appearance. Nystrom's retriever was known to have been professionally trained. If you appear with a dog that simply won't mind you, that will give you away instantly." He paused for a moment, and went on: "Besides, it is really Mr. Smith's problem, is it not?"

I looked at him sharply. "I thought it was mine, too, sir."

"Of course." His voice was bland. "But essentially you are dependent upon the briefing and equipment supplied by Mr. Smith. If they should be faulty in any way, you can hardly be blamed for it. Or for the resulting failure—if failure should result. Of course we sincerely hope it won't."

I studied him for a moment, but his lean, expressionless features didn't give me much help. However, it had already occurred to me to wonder just why he'd hung around here on the Coast for three days as if I required a chaperone, instead of just turning me over to our associates and heading back to Washington.

Well, I had my answer: we were going to be clever. It wasn't going to be a straightforward impersonation job after all; it wasn't just a friendly favor our outfit was doing for the brother-organization run by a nice man named Smith. We had, apparently, some problems of our own that could be solved by my making like a dead man named Nystrom, although of course we wouldn't admit it for the world. I grimaced wryly, but I must admit I felt relieved in a way. I hadn't really been comfortable in the role of the good guy in the white hat, riding to the rescue of my fellow government employees.

"Yes, sir," I said. "Sincerely."

"You have, of course, protested officially to Mr. Smith's representatives. You have informed them that, in your opinion, the dog they have supplied will not do."

"Yes, sir."

"Then, if they stubbornly insist on your working with this animal, you are not responsible if your mission is unsuccessful due to such an obvious defect in your cover."

"No, sir."

There was another little pause. He was waiting for me to ask the question, and I was waiting for him to tell me the answer without being asked. Rather to my surprise, I won.

"Do you remember Kingston?" he asked. "You worked with him on a couple of occasions, did you not? Well, he was killed—knifed to death—last week in Anchorage, Alaska. And that is one count too many against the man who killed him, Eric. I think it is time you took care of Hans Holz. Permanently."

I looked at his expressionless face for a moment longer. "Holz, eh?"

"Holz."

"Okay," I said. I rose. "If you say so, sir. Come on, pooch. We've got to go kill a guy named Holz."

"Eric, sit down."

"Just a minute, mutt," I said. "Sit and listen. The gentleman has more to say to us."

"You don't approve, Eric?"

"No, sir," I said. "I don't like these damn vendettas. So Kingston went and got himself killed by Holz, and we're sorry about that, but so what? I've done jobs with quite a few guys who died later, without charging out heroically to settle accounts with the guys who killed them. If Holz is threatening the welfare of the universe, the world, the United States of America, or even the state of Alaska, fine, I'll be glad to look him up and dispose of him, if I can. But if all he's done is kill somebody, hell, I've done that myself. Besides, haven't you heard, sir? The man is dangerous. He's one of their big guns, perhaps the biggest they've got right now. He's been coming up steadily since we first heard of him back in the late fifties. I mean, going after him is apt to be, you know, kind of risky."

Mac eyed me coldly. "Are you afraid of Holz, Eric?"

Now he was being ridiculous. I said, "Sure, I'm afraid of Holz. I'm afraid of any experienced pro who knows how and when to kill. He's been around quite a while now, too long for it to be just dumb luck. He's survived a lot of guys who've gone against him. That means he could

21

survive even me, outlandish as such a thought might seem."

"You've survived pretty well, too," Mac pointed out.

"Yes, sir. And I've done it by never seeing myself in the part of an avenging angel or of some movie dope trying to prove he's the fastest gun west of somewhere. Of course, I work for this outfit, and if you order me to go after the guy with the horns and the tail, I'll step right out and have myself fitted for an asbestos suit. If you order me to hunt down Hans Holz, that's that, and I'll be on my way to Alaska or wherever. But I'd kind of like a better reason than an agent named Kingston who was old enough to take care of himself."

"Well, I wasn't exactly thinking of having you hunt down Mr. Holz," Mac said deliberately. "I was rather thinking of having him hunt you down, if you know what I mean."

I sighed. For once I was, if not ahead of him, at least not too far behind. "Yes, sir. It's becoming clear to me, gradually. So that's why you encouraged this masquerade."

"Precisely. I am glad to hear that the dog is not all he should be. And I am happy to see that you do not really resemble the dead man very much, except in the basic dimensions. Do you understand, Eric?"

I said, "Let us say that outlines are appearing through the fog. But perhaps you would care to blow the mists aside a little farther, sir."

Mac nodded. "As far as our associates are concerned, you are impersonating the dead man to the best of your ability, as of course you are. You will endeavor to carry out the mission they have assigned you. You will do your best to keep your cover intact, such as it is. However, you know and I know that your best will probably not be good enough. This type of impersonation is inherently improbable anyway; it's a television gambit that's very unlikely to succeed in real life."

"Yes, sir," I said. "So you expect my cover to be blown, sooner or later. And then what?"

"That," he said, "is a very foolish question, Eric."

"Excuse me. Of course. When my cover is blown, they'll kill me. Or try."

"Precisely. And whom will they call upon to perform this distasteful task? The average spy is a specialist at gathering information; he is not required to be particularly brave or skilled with weapons. For violence, he calls in a specialist in violence. And it happens that the murder specialist assigned by the Communists to this particular espionage ring for this particular mission is Mr. Hans Holz. As a matter of fact, it was through his current associates that we finally managed to locate him so that we could send Kingston after him. The details don't matter. I mention it only so that you will understand that this is no vendetta, as you called it. We were looking for Holz long before he killed Kingston."

Obviously, I was supposed to ask why. I asked, "Why, sir?"

"Because we have learned, never mind how, what his next assignment is to be." Mac paused. It occurred to me that he was being pretty evasive himself, but I didn't say so. He went on, "We have learned that Holz's superiors have decided to capitalize on the recent political murders in this country by staging an assassination of their own, calculated to create more political chaos here. Holz is the man they have chosen to carry it out. As you said, he is the biggest gun they have at the moment."

"And who's to be his target?"

Mac said, "It should be obvious. In an election year, who would you pick for maximum effect, Eric? Essentially, Holz has been marking time in Alaska on this other, relatively unimportant assignment. His big job must wait until he knows of the outcome of the presidential race this fall. He has orders to strike as soon as the U.S. electorate has decided which candidate to elect."

I whistled softly. "Yes, that might cause us a spot of bother, as our British friends would say."

"Precisely. So you must get him, and it had better be soon. If he follows his usual behavior pattern, he'll go underground well ahead of the target date in November."

"I'll keep it in mind. Do we know how he's planning to do the job? I mean the big job?"

23

"Like two of the other recent killings, it's to be a long-range-rifle job. If the American people wish to note the resemblance and attribute it to a gigantic conspiracy of extremists, right or left, I'm sure it will make our friends in Moscow very happy. And like you, Holz is quite as good with a rifle as with a knife. Incidentally, do you still carry that little knife our ordnance people disapprove of?"

"Yes, sir," I said. I reached into my pocket and brought it out to show him. It looked like a slightly oversized jackknife. "If they had their way, I'd be lugging a junior-grade machete. The knives they specify are great for fighting, but where do you hide them? This looks like a pocket knife and does the work."

"Keep it handy. You may have need of it, going against Holz. Now you'd better visit the recognition room and get our latest information on the man. Report when you can."

"Yes, sir." I put away the knife and got to my feet once more. "Come on, stupid, wake up. I mean, excuse me, Prince Hannibal, please arise and follow me."

4 THE TOWN WAS CALLED PASCO AND didn't like dogs. At least Hank and I had had to try three hostelries upon our arrival the previous day, before finding one that would take us in. One prim-faced motel lady had informed me that little dogs were all right, but she couldn't possibly see her way to admitting a great hulking beast like a Labrador—a piece of logic that baffled me, since I'd been under the impression since childhood that the smaller the dog the more persistent the noise and the sharper the teeth.

The place that had finally saved us from having to camp out was a pleasant two-story motel with swimming pool, coke machine, ice machine, and all other customary facilities except a restaurant—a lack that was filled by a cafe a block away. Returning from the river, I stopped at this eating place to put a little substantial nourishment on top of the coffee and doughnuts. Then I proceeded to the motel to shave, shower, and dress in slightly more respectable clothes than Grant Nystrom's weatherbeaten fishing costume. I stuck to the cowboy boots, however, since they had been his preferred footgear under practically all circumstances.

I had a little time to spare, so with the pup comfortably asleep on the wall-to-wall carpet, I stretched out on the rumpled bed and thought about two presidential candidates, one of whom was marked for murder. This was no fun, so I let myself think about a tall blondish girl named Patricia Bellman, Pat for short. At least that was the way she'd introduced herself; whether it was her real name remained to be seen. Thinking about girls is always pleasant, and I'm partial to the outdoors type, but I couldn't form any conclusions about the kid. There wasn't enough to go on. She could be an innocent bystander or she could be involved up to her little ears in conspiracy and intrigue.

I sighed and got up from the bed and dug some objects out of my fishing vest: her parting gifts—a brass spinner about an inch across the blade, equipped with a single, businesslike hook; a good-sized lead sinker; and a little plastic bottle with some holes punched in the cap for air and two grasshoppers stirring sluggishly inside. Pat Bellman had showed me how to assemble these components for proper casting, and told me to give them a try the next time I got out, perhaps this evening. The middle of the day wasn't much good for steelheads, she'd said.

I frowned at the stuff; then I grinned, thinking of how much fun Mr. Smith's young men could have, analyzing a couple of live grasshoppers for secret messages. It hadn't been a satisfactory contact in several respects, but my orders were clear: all materials I obtained were to be submitted for quick examination. We couldn't risk letting any information go through intact.

I glanced at my watch to check the time, and put the stuff in a cute little plastic box equipped with a magnet— very tricky. I added a small note in cipher describing the person from whom it had been obtained and the circumstances—although this was only a precaution, since there were supposed to be agents watching me at all times, and making notes on everybody who approached me. By now, if they were on the ball, they knew more about Pat Bellman than I did.

Then I snapped my fingers to arouse the pup, went out to the truck, and drove to a specified gas station a few blocks away. Why my motel hadn't also been specified, since there seemed to be only one in town that would take dogs, I didn't know, but nobody's planning is perfect, not even ours, so I won't complain about Mr. Smith's.

While the attendant was filling the tank, I went over to the phone booth at the side of the lot and dialed a number which, as it was supposed to, didn't answer. I let it ring seven times, as instructed, and hung up disgustedly, retrieved my dime and went back to the truck, leaving the ducky little plastic box magnetically attached to the underside of the metal shelf in the booth. It was a nice routine, and it made me feel just like a real secret agent, Hollywood division.

"Where can I buy some fishing tackle around here?" I asked the attendant as I forged Grant Nystrom's signature to the credit-card slip.

"Right down the street about a block," the man said. "Just across from that supermarket—you can see the sign. Leave your rig here if you like. Just drive it over against the fence."

If he hadn't suggested it, I would have. I thanked him, parked the truck, stuck my head into the camper and told the pup to behave, and went off. I spent five minutes walking to the store, and twenty minutes picking out some spinners and sinkers more or less like those the girl had given me, and pumping the salesman for steelhead-fishing advice. That still left me twenty minutes to kill of the forty-five I was supposed to stay away; and I crossed the street to the supermarket and bought a bag of dry dog food, and some bread and salami for human-type sandwiches. That took another fifteen minutes. The five-minute walk brought me back to the telephone right on time. I dialed the same number. This time I got an answer.

"What's the big idea?" asked an aggrieved male voice. "Grasshoppers, for God's sake!"

"That's what was handed me this morning," I said. "They didn't have microdots for eyes, or anything?"

"You got them from the girl you met on the beach?"

"That's right. I'm glad your snoopers are keeping their eyes open. Have they learned anything about her?"

"Name, Patricia Bellman. Degree from Berkeley, currently working in Seattle. That's all to date; more will be supplied as forthcoming. If required. But she's either pulling your leg, or she's just a generous lass who passes out angling equipment to handsome strangers. Live bait and fishing tackle is all you've got."

"That's what I wanted to know," I said. "Thanks. I'll do some more work on it and get in touch again when I can."

"If you get any more 'hoppers, check them out yourself. I'll be happy to lend you a microscope. Be careful."

I retrieved the magnetic capsule from under the shelf, where they'd returned it after examining the contents. I got into the truck and drove away, wondering if we were fooling anybody with this nonsense. I headed back to the motel, and hesitated momentarily before turning into the driveway. A sporty little fastback Ford Mustang, maroon in color, was parked in front of my ground-floor room, a tall, slim girl in jeans was knocking at the door. I drew a long breath, completed the turn, and parked the camper unit beside the pony-Ford. Pat Bellman looked around, recognized me, and came over.

"I was just getting some gas," I said. "Sorry to keep you waiting. But you're kind of early for our lunch date, aren't you?"

She laughed. "I was on my way out to the ranch, to change for the great occasion, but I couldn't resist stopping by to show you something. Come over here."

She walked to the sloping rear of the Ford and yanked the trunk with a flourish. Inside lay the biggest trout I'd ever seen at close range, steely-dark and impressive-looking even in death.

"God, what a beauty!" I said. "How big is he?"

"Around thirty inches and twelve pounds," she said happily, closing the trunk again. "I feel a little guilty about it, Mr. Nystrom. It's really your fish. After you left,

I waded out where you'd been standing, and on the third cast, wham! He went halfway across the river on his first run. It took me fifteen minutes to land him. Well, I thought you'd like to see him. Now I'd better go get cleaned up."

I glanced at my watch. "It's eleven-thirty and I'm hungry again and you look all right to me. Of course, you know the town better than I do, but I hadn't noticed anybody being particularly formal around here."

"Well, my hands are pretty fishy——"

"Come on in and wash up while I hunt up the pup's registration certificate and pedigree." When she hesitated, I said, "We'll leave the outside door open, if you're worried about your reputation or something."

She flushed slightly. "Don't be silly, I just . . . All right. Just let me get a comb and lipstick out of the glove compartment."

Any room with an unmade bed tends to create a certain awkwardness in a newly formed man-woman relationship, no matter how platonic. As yet we had nothing in common but fish and dogs, but when the girl paused just inside the door, it was clear that other possibilities were occurring to her—whether favorably or unfavorably I couldn't tell. It didn't really matter. The situation obviously called for me to behave like a perfect gentleman, for a start. Later, if necessary, I could easily break down and become a lecherous heel.

"That door over there," I said. "There are clean towels in the rack over the john."

"Thanks."

I grinned as she disappeared into the bathroom. Her voice had been just a trifle cool. As usual, the gentlemanly approach had given me a slight psychological advantage. No lady, no matter how virtuous, really enjoys having it demonstrated that she's so undesirable in a strange man's eyes that she's perfectly safe alone with him in his motel room.

By the time she'd finished in there, I'd found the necessary papers. We spent lunch, at the nearby café, discussing Hank's pedigree in detail—well, the pedigree of the true Avon's Prince Hannibal of Holgate, deceased. The girl knew her hunting dogs. She concentrated on the field champions, working retrievers proved in field trials, in action against stiff competition. She practically ignored the dog show champions, pretty dogs who'd proved only that they could trot around a show ring without falling over their feet. If she was a phony, she was a good one.

Well, I'd been pretty well briefed too. I managed to discourse knowledgeably about the various illustrious Labradors featured in the pedigree, and the kennels that had produced them, and the trainers who'd trained them, and the events in which they'd performed most notably. Maybe my days in San Francisco hadn't been wasted. Afterwards, having come to terms—I stood to make a hundred dollars on the deal, if Hank proved his virility in a satisfactory manner—we went out to our vehicles, parked at the curb.

"Just follow me," she said. "It's only about seven miles. The place belongs to my aunt and uncle. I'm a city girl myself these days—I live in Seattle—but an apartment's no place to keep a big dog when you go to work every day, so I leave Maudie here and come down weekends."

I watched her get into her car. Girls in jeans leave me pretty cold as a rule, but I'm not unreasonable on the subject; I'll accept a good excuse like hunting or fishing. The kid was very convincing and I was beginning to like her, neither of which was good. I mean, if she really was what she claimed to be, I was wasting my time with her, and in any case my personal likes and dislikes were totally irrelevant to the job at hand.

Well, there was obviously nothing to do but officiate at the proposed canine nuptials and see what, if anything, happened besides canine sex. If she made no further move to give me what I'd come here as Grant Nystrom to get, I'd have to break away to reach the alternate drop in time for the scheduled contact at four-thirty and see who turned up there.

The ranch to which she led me was a rather shabby place in the bleak, rolling hills north of Pasco. No expert on the U.S. northwest, I had visualized the whole state of Washington as a land of lush wheatfields. This looked more like the arid range country of my native New Mexico, where you figured on forty acres to support one cow.

There was a small ranch house, a windmill, an old pickup truck with a flat tire, some tired farm machinery, a barn, and a battered outbuilding or two. A few scraggly trees tried to shade the house but gave no protection to the bare, trampled yard.

Pat Bellman parked beside the house and got out and looked around. "Well, their car's gone; I guess there's nobody home," she said as I came up to her. "You might as well turn your dog loose; he can't get into much trouble around here." She watched Hank give me a couple of slobbering licks before taking off across the yard. "He's pretty fond of you, isn't he?"

I shrugged, wiping my face. I got a leash from inside the camper and tucked it into my hip pocket in case it should be needed. "I wish he'd find some other way of showing it," I said. "Where's the blushing bride-to-be?"

"We've got a kennel of sorts out behind the barn. This way." Pat laughed, walking beside me. "We don't usually keep her locked up around here, of course, but with a female dog—particularly a pedigreed female dog—there are a couple of times a year when you've got to be careful. I'd hate winding up with a litter of half-coyote pups. . . . Oh, damn!"

She hurried forward. I followed more slowly around the corner of the barn to the dog run, an enclosure of fence posts and hog wire with a little wooden doghouse at one end. There was a door in the other end of the run. This stood ajar, and there was no Labrador bitch in sight.

"Damn, damn, *damn!*" Pat Bellman said. "They must have had her in the house and forgot to wire the latch down when they put her back . . . Now where's your dog got to? Let's not lose both of them."

I blew the whistle. After a moment, Hank came charging around the barn and romped up to me where I stood at the kennel door. He sat down beside me automatically, as he was supposed to, and looked up, obviously wondering why he'd been summoned. I gave him a pat for his obedience.

"He's all right," I said. "He sticks around pretty well.

What do we do about yours? We'd better get her back quick, before she meets some virile male."

"Well," she said, "well, if you don't mind helping——"

"Just tell me where to look."

"There's a house over that ridge," she said, pointing. "They've got a kind of collie-looking mutt that plays with Maudie; she could have headed over that way. Why don't you take a quick look, while I take the car and drive around a bit; I know the back roads better than you do."

"Sure," I said. "Okay, pup, off we go to find your lady love."

As I walked slowly through the brush toward the bare, open ridge ahead, with Hank cruising back and forth in front of me, I heard the Mustang start up and drive away. I didn't glance around. I was busy trying to find the rifle, without seeming to look, and presently I had it located by the glint of light off the telescopic sight—a big one by the looks of it—on a little brushy knoll some hundred and fifty yards off to the left, from which the sniper could easily cover the entire hillside.

Well, it wasn't a bad trap, or wouldn't have been if the girl had known as much about dogs as she'd pretended to.

5 WHEN YOU'RE HUNTING AN ANIMAL

that can smell you, you've got to figure your approach very carefully according to the wind; when man is the quarry you can forget such refinements. The wind was right, anyway, blowing gently from the sniper to me, and there was good stalking cover the whole way—if I could only break away to take advantage of it without getting shot first.

I mean, if I could see him up there through the intervening brush, he could undoubtedly see me down here, and he was presumably doing his looking through the rifle-scope, with his finger on the trigger. I was gambling that he wouldn't try to drive a light, high-speed, easily deflected .243 bullet through a mess of twigs and branches

as long as he had a good chance—or thought he had—of catching me in the open if he waited. But the minute he guessed that I was aware of the trap and trying to get out of it, he'd undoubtedly shoot rather than risk losing me.

Of course, it didn't have to be a .243 and he didn't have to be the mysterious marksman who'd killed Nystrom and his dog with two well-placed shots for reasons still to be determined. But that sharpshooter was the most likely candidate, and I wanted badly to get out of his sights before he chalked up two Nystroms—one real and one phony—to his credit.

Luck helped me out, in the form of a rabbit that took off in front of Hank, who was too young to resist the temptation. He was gone in a flash, right on the bunny's heels. Running rabbits is a serious crime for a bird dog of any kind, and it gave me an excuse to blast fiercely on the whistle and shout loud imprecations that I hoped carried well against the wind to the man with the gun while I stumbled clumsily after the chase—until it carried me out of sight into a brushy gully.

Crouching there, I continued to whistle and yell until the pup came slinking back, very guilty and ashamed of himself. I spoke to him severely and used the leash to tie him to a tree, letting him think that was part of the punishment. Then I drew a long breath; I'd made it out of sight, and there were no bulletholes in me, and my adversary was not alerted. At least I hoped he wasn't. Leaving the pup tied, keeping low, I made a quick circle of the little knoll, slipping up behind the rifleman without further trouble. When I got within a couple of hundred yards of the spot, I could see that he was still there.

I had a good view of the sole of a boot sticking out of the brush, and from this angle I could see about half a bare head above the undergrowth. It had a lot of hair on it, but sexwise that means nothing these days, and as far as I'm concerned, no double standard applies to people who hide in bushes with rifles, anyway.

With a rifle of my own, I might have tried the shot, but all I had was Grant Nystrom's choice of sidearms: a short-barreled Colt .357 Magnum revolver with the butt trimmed down for concealment purposes. It wasn't a bad

gun as revolvers go—it was a lot more gun than the .38 Specials we're usually issued—but it was no long-range weapon, and I'm not much of a long-range pistol-shooter, either. The long-range capabilities were all with the opposition, which made my problem clear if not simple: I had to get close enough for one good shot before he spotted me, since I probably wouldn't be given time for a second should the first one miss.

I looked around. The ground rose to the left toward another bare hillside—bare of brush, but there was some scraggy grass that I thought would give me at least partial cover. I worked my way up there, using my knees and elbows, until I was above the sniper and about eighty yards away. Instinct warned me that was as close as I'd better go.

I slipped the .357 out of its trick holster inside my waistband, and cocked it, muffling the click under my jacket. I made myself steady and comfortable, flat on my stomach. Parting the screen of grass in front of me, I tried the square, target-type sights against the prone figure below me, with both elbows firmly on the ground and both hands on the gun. One-handed pistol shooting is mandatory in target matches, but this was simple homicide and there are no rules for that.

The man down there—if it was a man—stirred uneasily, obviously wondering where I'd disappeared to and what I was up to. Well, it was about time. He lifted his head from the rifle stock and glanced over his shoulder as if he'd sensed my presence, and it was nobody I'd ever seen before in real life or in photographs, just a hippie-looking youth sporting longish hair, a droopy moustache, and long fuzzy sideburns.

I drew a long breath, realizing that, hair or no hair, small rifle or big, I'd subconsciously been expecting to see a man I knew—well, a man whom I'd never actually met, but whose dossier I'd studied very carefully, a man who was supposed to be good both with knives and rifles. Without quite realizing it, I'd been looking forward to finishing right here the principal part of my mission, the part assigned me by Mac. Somehow I'd convinced myself it was Holz I was up against already, although why Holz

should be shooting down Nystroms wholesale hadn't been quite clear in my mind.

Still, as Mac had pointed out, couriers had been eliminated before by the people for whom they'd worked. Mr. Smith's mysterious source of information to the contrary could be all wet. It still wasn't totally out of the question that this espionage ring we were after had first summoned their kill-specialist to handle a personnel problem, and then sent him on to deal with an obvious impostor. But the man in front of me was not Hans Holz.

I sighed and lowered the gun, wondering who the hell the young marksman was and what to do about him. Of course, he had been trying to kill me, which was naughty of him. It even prejudiced me against him rather strongly, but we're not supposed to act on prejudice. Dead men are awkward to have around. They tend to get the local police all upset, and I still had work to do in Pasco that would be more easily done without police interference. Reluctantly, I started to let down the hammer of the Colt. Regardless of their age or importance—or unimportance— I don't like leaving behind me, alive, people who've clearly indicated their eagerness to shoot me dead, but sometimes it has to be done.

The young man in the bushes stiffened suddenly, watching something out in front of him. He put his face to the stock of the rifle once more, peering through the big telescopic sight. I looked where he was aiming, and there came the black pup, loping across the hillside straight toward us, pausing every so often to check his radar. I mean, he wasn't tracking me; he wasn't following the roundabout way I'd come. He was no ground-sniffing hound. He had his nose in the air, as a bird-dog should, and he was reading my scent on the gentle breeze, and making straight for the source of it.

A foot and a half of chewed-off leash dangled from his collar. Well, nobody'd told him not to chew his leash in two. Nobody'd really told him to stay put, either. Orders, he might have obeyed, but a little leather string had been only a momentary hindrance to be disposed of with the nice, sharp, adult dental equipment that had recently re-

placed his puppy teeth. A couple of good chomps, and he'd been on his way to find the boss.

I looked bleakly at the boy in the brush below me: he had the rifle ready, he was preparing to shoot. I remembered that the real Hank had been shot, we still didn't know why. I knew a funny little stirring of anger: the juvenile son-of-a-bitch was going to shoot *my* dog. This was sentimental and irrelevant, but professionally I was just as concerned, because the pup was essential to my Grant Nystrom cover. It occurred to me that I might have got hold of an important idea here, but I had no time to develop it.

I just recocked the .357 and brought it back into line and put gentle pressure on the trigger. The drop-your-gun-and-stand-up-with-your-hands-above-your-head routine looks great on TV, but with a pistol at eighty yards I needed my target perfectly still. If I started shouting silly orders and gave him a chance to roll aside, I'd probably muff the shot, and that would give him a crack at me with his high-powered rifle. At this range, with that outfit, he couldn't possibly miss. So I just steadied the coarse revolver sights on the widest point of the target and increased the trigger pressure until the piece fired.

The .357 made an ear-splitting racket, rearing up in recoil in spite of the two-handed grip I had on the skimpy butt. For a moment, it blotted out the man in the bushes. When I got it recocked and lined up once more, he was lying exactly where he had been. The only difference was that all the sharpshooting tension had gone out of his body, and his head had dropped slightly, resting peacefully on the rifle stock as if on a pillow.

6 **THE ADDRESS I'D BEEN GIVEN FOR** the afternoon rendezvous, to be used if the morning contact should fail for any reason, was out at the edge of the town's business district, in the middle of an incompletely developed block containing several vacant lots. Diagonally

down the street from a convenient corner drugstore—well, convenient for me—it stood by itself: a flat-roofed one-story building that wasn't very wide across the front, but ran back some distance from the street. There was a neat sign above the door:

PASCO ANIMAL CLINIC
ARTHUR WATTS, D.V.M.
OFFICE HOURS
9:00-5:00 (Weekdays)
8:30-12:00 (Saturdays)

I couldn't actually read the sign from the drugstore telephone booth in which I waited, but I'd got a good look at it, driving past. As I watched through the front window of the drugstore, a big yellow Cadillac convertible with California plates drew up in front of the building. A dark-haired woman with a figure that was youthful but not really young, if you know what I mean, got out deliberately.

It was quite a production. She was wearing a yellow silk pantsuit—tailored jacket and slim trousers—plus yellow sandals and a white blouse with a million ruffles. At least that was the impression I got from a distance. A white froth of lace encircled her neck, spilled down her bosom, and dripped from her wrists. It was quite a tourist costume to spring on a backward little town like Pasco; or any town for that matter.

She walked around to open the curb door of the Cadillac and brought out a big, gray poodle, clipped and brushed to perfection. They disappeared into the veterinarian's office together.

"Yes, sir," I said into the phone. "It was a big disappointment. No Holz."

"There was no reason for you to expect him, Eric." Mac's voice lost no crispness traveling three thousand miles from Washington, D. C. "Not yet. Who was the man you shot?"

"Just a fuzzy-faced punk with a fancy rifle. He's not in our files, I'm pretty sure. Oregon driver's license issued to Michael P. Bird."

"Bird?"

"Like with feathers." I said. "He was using a heavy Douglas barrel on one of the good Mauser actions with a custom stock. Mesquite or some such light wood with caps and inlays of horn or dark plastic. A three-to-nine power variable scope cranked up to maximum magnification. I guess he wanted to see which button of my shirt he was going to perforate."

Mac's voice was dry: "The young man seems to have gone to a lot of trouble with his murder weapon."

"I doubt that it was originally designed as a murder weapon, sir," I said. "With its small caliber and that big telescopic sight, it's the kind of outfit you'd have made up for varmint-shooting, as they call it: accurate long-range popping at nuisance rodents like groundhogs and prairie dogs. It's a hobby with some people, and most farmers and ranchers are all for getting rid of the little pests and the holes they dig. Our lad just switched to a heavy big-game bullet instead of the light varmint type. So loaded, he could take anything up to deer easily, not to mention man. Hell, a .243 is considered heavy artillery these days. They've been using a lousy little twenty-two in Vietnam."

"Very well, Eric. What about the girl?"

"You have the description and the name she's going under and the car she's driving. Mr. Smith's boys have been checking her out, but I should have known all about her from the start—all I needed to know, anyway. Any girl who has an automatic transmission handle masquerading as a sports-car gearshift lever, and stick-on hubcaps pretending to be instant wire wheels, is bound to be kind of a fake herself."

"Still, it seems her trap didn't catch you totally by surprise."

"I can't take the credit for that, sir," I admitted. "She had me pretty well convinced she was on the level; she's a very convincing young lady. If the pup hadn't tipped me off, I'd probably have walked right into it."

"You haven't made it clear just how he tipped you off."

I said, "Why, he's a retriever, sir. A good nose is part of the package. Also he's a male dog; a little young but

very definitely masculine. And still he sat there calmly grinning at me within three feet of an enclosure that was supposed to have held a bitch in heat! Discipline or no discipline, if there'd recently been a receptive lady dog in that kennel, he'd have made some kind of an attempt to investigate those fascinating female smells, wouldn't he? When he took off with me into the brush without even a sniff in that direction, I knew our Pat was lying like hell."

Pausing, I grimaced at the Cadillac half a block away, wondering if it had anything to do with my problems. I hoped not. One woman in pants was plenty for one assignment.

When Mac didn't speak, I said into the phone: "Well, it's too bad the girl didn't return to the scene of her unsuccessful crime. I'd like to ask her a few questions, and doing it over her partner's dead body might have given me a certain psychological advantage. I waited up there to the last minute that would still let me down here with a little time to spare, but she didn't show."

"And the man? He said nothing useful before he died?"

"No, sir. The bullet got the spine; death was instantaneous. Just plain dumb luck with a pistol at that range. Good or bad depending on the point of view. Something will have to be done about him fairly soon or I'll have cops coming out my ears."

"That is, of course, if we decide it's worth our while to have you stay and continue with the job according to plan—according to Mr. Smith's plan. But this girl and her marksman friend are turning into a serious complication. Apparently we're dealing with a gang of interlopers playing a game of their own; a gang that first shot the real Communist courier and then tried to murder you for taking his place. The question is———"

"Just a moment, sir," I interrupted. "Just one moment. I believe the answer to your question is coming up the street."

I stood in the booth, strategically located at the front of the drugstore, and looking slantingly out through the big window, I watched myself approach. Or maybe I should say I watched Grant Nystrom approach, complete with dog and whistle and cowboy boots. At least, a tall man, in

high-heeled footgear that made him seem even taller, was heading for the animal clinic, accompanied by a black Labrador on a leash.

The man was younger than Grant Nystrom had been, by about the same amount that I was older, but he was the right, tanned, lanky outdoors type. The dog, I was interested to note, was a better impostor than my Hank in some respects. He was taller and rangier, more nearly the size and conformation of the dead dog.

On the other hand, he was not a very good Labrador. His coat was a little too rough and shaggy for one thing, and his tail was too pretty; a great, waving black plume. A good Lab should have a smooth coat and kind of an otter tail. Don't ask me why; that's what it says in the breed specifications. Furthermore, the stranger's dog wasn't particularly well trained. Even on leash, he didn't walk properly at heel, but surged ahead, half dragging his master along the sidewalk.

"Eric?"

"Yes, sir," I said softly. "A man calling himself Grant Nystrom is just going into the vet's office, sir, accompanied by a black Labrador retriever he calls Prince Hannibal of Holgate. At least I'd be very much surprised if those weren't the names he was using."

The telephone was silent for a second or two; then Mac spoke quietly: "Indeed. So now we know the game they're playing."

"Yes, sir. The same one that we're playing or trying to play. Obviously Mr. Smith wasn't the only one to think of having somebody take Nystrom's place. Only these kids, or somebody doing their thinking for them, thought of it first and killed the guy to do it. Mr. Smith's agent interrupted them before they could dispose of the bodies properly, human and canine. When there was no publicity about the murder, no public report of Nystrom's death, they gambled on being able to carry out their impersonation regardless. And then, when they found me here ahead of them—a second Grant Nystrom—they tried to put me out of the way, too, so that their Nystrom Number Three could move in to make the pickup."

I paused. Mac's voice said something in my ear, but I

wasn't listening. A short, rather plump man in a business suit was approaching the clinic, carrying a brown glass screw-top jar. I recognized him at once, although he'd been dressed more roughly when I'd seen him last.

I spoke into the phone: "More fun and frolic, sir. Here comes the other party to the rendezvous. At least, it's one of the fisherman I saw on the beach this morning. It could be coincidence, his coming here at just this time, but it doesn't seem likely."

"No." Mac's voice was thoughtful. "If you saw him, he presumably saw you."

"Yes, sir."

"Then, when he sees the tall individual inside the clinic, he will know it's not the same man. Or the same dog. He will know there are two Grant Nystroms competing for the information he is about to deliver."

"Yes, sir."

"If your Miss Bellman is in charge of the independent operation that conflicts with ours, she should have anticipated this."

"Not necessarily," I said. "I didn't know those other fisherman had anything to do with the job; probably Pat Bellman didn't either. It's apparently a favorite fishing spot for a lot of local people. What probably happened is that Bellman and her impostor arrived at the river just a little late and found me there ahead of them. She had to think fast. Obviously there was no sense in putting two phony Nystroms on the beach; that way neither of us would get anything. The only thing she could do was pray that the other party to the morning contact simply wouldn't show up, giving her a chance to make friends with me and get rid of me before the afternoon appointment."

"It was a long gamble to take," Mac said.

"What else could she do?" I asked. "Sure, she knew the two guys with the station wagon *might* be the people for whom we were waiting, the people with the stolen information. In that case they'd seen me and my dog and she was out of luck. But as long as there was a faint possibility that they were just innocent fisherman, and that the real contact had overslept or had a flat tire, she had to

act on it. Hell, her impostor and dog were ready, she'd come a long way to use them, she might as well shove them into the action and hope for the best. Even if it meant having me and Hank murdered to give them a clear field."

"I doubt that killing a dog is murder in the eyes of the law, Eric."

"Sure," I said. "Sometimes I get the impression that killing an agent is just a minor misdemeanor. But then, there's a theory to the effect that we're not quite human, either."

He ignored this. "Can you stop the man, Eric?" he asked.

"Are you sure I should, sir? Suppose he does go in and learns that there are two Grant Nystroms; he still won't know which is the right one. But he'll most likely assume that one of us is. It probably won't occur to him that both of us are phonies. With a little luck, I can work it for me instead of against me."

"What do you have in mind?"

I said, "Suppose I take a crack at selling myself as Nystrom Number One, the real thing, victimized by these other characters who're trying to impersonate me. We've got a little time. The guy isn't going to pass the stuff over yet, whatever it is; not until he gets us sorted out."

Mac thought it over for a moment. "Use your judgment. Maybe it's worth a try. But before you hang up: do you still want me to take care of the body and the rifle you left out at that ranch?"

"Not yet, sir. Hold off for a little. I may need that death scene, undisturbed, to corroborate the story I'm going to tell. . . . Well, he's inside. Here I go. Eric, signing off."

I hung up and slipped out of the drugstore and around the corner. I made a circle of the block, back in the direction from which the last man had come. It didn't take me long to find what I was looking for: a white Plymouth station wagon that had seen better days. It seemed to be empty.

There was nothing to be gained by being tricky. I just walked up to the car, opened the right front door, and got in. I didn't have long to wait. A shadow moved at the

edge of my field of vision, outside the car. A gun barrel touched the side of my head through the open window.

"Don't move," said a man's voice. That would be the second fisherman of the morning.

"Cut it out," I said without turning my head. "You know who I am. You saw me at the river less than ten hours ago."

"Maybe I saw you. That doesn't mean I know who you are." There was a pause. "If you are who you're supposed to be, you should be in that office down the block."

"Yes, sir," I said. "At four-thirty sharp. But the damn office was getting crowded. I figured two gents six-feet-four with black dogs would be overdoing it." The man with the gun didn't speak or move. I went on angrily: "What the hell is going on around this town of yours, anyway? I burn up the roads getting here to make contact on a certain hour of a certain day and nobody shows up with the right words, just a female making ga-ga noises about my pretty dog—a female who sets me up for murder. I manage to get out of that and head for the alternate rendezvous and damned if a double doesn't show up complete with pooch. . . . I hope your pal has eyes in his head and doesn't slip anything to the wrong person just because the guy is towing a mutt behind him."

"Mr. Stottman knows what he's doing."

"Well, I'm glad somebody does, because by this time I sure as hell don't. And neither do you, or you wouldn't be waving guns at me. Do you have to keep massaging my scalp with that thing?"

"We'll wait," said the man, getting into the back seat cautiously. "We'll wait until Mr. Stottman gets back here. He'll know what to do with you."

Neither his voice and words, nor the gun at my head, were particularly reassuring. We waited. Presently the plump man came out of the clinic, carrying the same or another brown glass bottle containing, presumably, some kind of dog medicine. He looked our way, hesitated at the sight of two men in the car, dropped his right hand casually into his coat pocket, and walked deliberately toward us.

7 THE RANCH LOOKED AS BLEAK AND

deserted as it had the last time I'd driven into the yard, with Pat Bellman. The pickup with the flat tire stood exactly where it had been, and there was no other vehicle around. I stopped the camper rig in the same place as before, and the station wagon pulled alongside, driven by the surly gent whose name I still did not know, who'd turned out to be a chunky, dark individual with flat Indian features and coarse black hair.

The man called Stottman, who shared the truck seat with me, opened the door on his side and backed out cautiously, keeping me covered.

"All right, slide out this way," he said. "Careful, now."

He wasn't so pretty, either, with a round white face, mean little eyes, and an unattractive pug nose that had a kind of a lump at the end. But I wasn't concerned with his unprepossessing appearance at the moment, but with the gun he held: a .25 caliber automatic so small that it practically disappeared in his pudgy hand. The .25 isn't much of a gun—it has less power than a kid's .22—but people have been killed by it, and I preferred not to join their company. I got out carefully and turned toward the rear of the camper.

"Where are you going?" Stottman demanded.

"I just thought I'd let the pup out. He's been cooped up in there quite a while."

"Never mind that. Leave him where he is."

I grinned. "Very few people have been torn to bloody shreds by savage retriever puppies, if that's what you're afraid of," I said, seizing the opportunity to polish my image as Grant Nystrom, dog expert. "Well, you might get yourself bitten by a Chesapeake if you really work at it, but a Lab's more likely to lick you to death in a burst of affection."

"Never mind the pup." Stottman's voice was flat and

unamused. "We've seen your pup. Now show us this man you claim to have shot."

"Right up on that point to the left," I said, waving my hand in that direction. "Like I just told you, the girl sent me off across that open hillside to look for a nonexistent dog—well, bitch, if you want to be technical. I spotted the rifleman lying in wait for me up there, and sneaked around behind him with my trusty .357 . . . ."

"Show us."

There was a certain amount of suspense as we worked our way up the hill through the brush. I could think of several good reasons why Pat Bellman might want to remove the body of her accomplice, but apparently they weren't as good as they seemed. Or maybe I've seen too many movies with disappearing corpses. Anyway, when we got there the fuzzy-faced young marksman lay exactly where I'd left him on top of his fancy weapon.

"There he is," I said. "You've got my gun. I haven't had a chance to reload; there's an empty shell in the cylinder. Smell it and you'll know it was fired within the last few hours. Take a look at the bullet hole and you'll see that the calibers match."

"Keep him covered, Pete."

Stottman put his little gun away, and bent down to examine the wound. He straightened up, rubbing his hands together. "One bullet hole looks pretty much like another, Mr. Nystrom. But say you did shoot this man, what does it prove?"

"Well, you can see it was a trap. They were trying to put me out of the way so they could ring in that substitute you saw at the clinic with his dog—although who could mistake a shaggy, ill-bred, badly trained mongrel like that for a real Labrador, I can't imagine."

"We're not all experienced dog men, Mr. Nystrom." Stottman studied my face for a moment, showing no expression. Then he glanced down and kicked the body hard, so that it rolled over on its back. I made a quick sound of protest. Stottman said blandly: "What's the matter? The punk's been dead for hours; he's not feeling anything."

He was obviously testing me, checking me against what

he'd been told of the courier he was to meet. Grant Nystrom, I reminded myself, had been just a politically minded sportsman type—a dilettante at intrigue—not a hardened killer.

I made a show of swallowing. "Okay, be hard-boiled," I said irritably. "Maybe you're used to dead bodies. It happens to be my first."

Apparently it was the right response. At least it disappointed him slightly. He asked, "Where'd you shoot him from?"

"Up there," I said with a jerk of my head. "That clump of grass up there."

"Check it, Pete."

The man with the Indian face went off up the hill. Stottman frowned at the dead youth on the ground. "Anybody you know?" he asked me.

"Never saw him before in my life."

"Why'd you shoot him?"

"I told you. He was waiting to murder me."

"You could have slipped away and left him waiting for nothing."

I said, "All right, it was the pup. I had him tied, but he broke loose, caught my scent, and came loping this way. This creep saw him coming and got ready to shoot. He was going to kill my dog!" I put indignation into my voice. "So I just let him have it with the .357. Anybody who'd shoot a good hunting dog in cold blood, well, there's just no damn reason for him to keep on living, the way I see it."

Stottman said, "Unfortunately, dead men cause more trouble than dead dogs. Now you've killed this fellow, just what are you planning to do with him, dry him out for jerky?"

I let myself look kind of sick at the suggestion; then I recovered and said angrily, "That's your problem, isn't it, Mr. Stottman?". .

"How do you figure?"

"This is your territory. I'm just a messenger boy traveling through. You were supposed to have things under control around here. Instead you let me walk into an ambush I had to shoot my way out of. Now, if you're satis-

fied with my credentials, just give me what I was sent here to get, and I'll be on my way. Cleaning up the premises is your job, not mine. And you'd damn well better be sure the body gets buried deep so nobody bothers me about it on my way north. Otherwise I think our mutual employers will have a few harsh things to say about the way things are being run here in Pasco."

Stottman didn't seem particularly intimidated. He was still watching me in an appraising, calculating sort of way; he might not have heard what I'd said. He turned as the man Pete came back.

"Well?"

"Somebody was up there, all right, and fired through the grass."

The plump man studied the distant clump of grass thoughtfully. He glanced at me.

"That's pretty good shooting. How come you're wasting your time as a lousy courier when you can shoot like that? It isn't everybody who can cut a man's spine in two with a handgun bullet at a hundred yards."

I said, "That's no hundred yards, and firearms have been my hobby for years. I'm a courier because I like the job, because I've done enough traveling so that nobody asks questions about it any longer, and because certain people trust me and figure I know enough about guns so that in an emergency, like this, I can take care of myself and make sure the mail gets through. But I've got no ambitions to be a professional assassin."

"They trust you, do they?" Stottman grimaced, and spat on the ground beside the corpse. "I don't like it, Pete," he said. "I don't like this character. He's too damn cool, and that's too neat a job of stalking and shooting for an amateur messenger boy like he claims to be. It's got a pro smell to it. What do you think?"

The dark-faced man said, "I don't know, Mr. Stottman. What happened in the vet's office?"

"Another guy was there. Tall, like this one. With a dog, like this one. But he wasn't the right man. When I got the negative sign, I just walked out again with my mutt-vitamins without making the switch."

"Well, if he wasn't the one, this one's got to be, doesn't he?"

"Logic is not your strong suit, I'm afraid, Pete. Just because one man isn't, it doesn't follow that another man is. I wish I'd asked Meredith to stick around."

He said this very casually, as if it were a remark of no importance. He was carefully not looking my way when he said it. You'd have thought that whether I caught the name or not didn't matter the slightest.

Fortunately, I'd heard it before, during the briefing. I'd had to dig for it, and for what little I knew about it, but I'd finally got it, from one of Mr. Smith's fresh-faced young men, pink and sweating as they always get—those well-tailored, well-educated young agents—whenever you crowd them on matters relating to sex or security. This matter, apparently, had involved both.

It had started very innocently, I'd thought. I'd simply asked, "What about girlfriends?"

"What do you mean, Mr. Helm?"

I'd said, "Here's a healthy, tanned, virile-looking outdoors character I'm supposed to impersonate and you've told me everything about him except the most important thing: whom does he sleep with? Does he like the girls, or the boys, or does he just take the damn dog to bed with him?"

That was when the young guy had turned pink. He'd said stiffly and rather disapprovingly, "As far as we know, Nystrom's sex life was perfectly normal."

"Fine, fine," I'd said. "In other words, he liked girls. What girls? Since he was so damn normal, by your standards, he was probably concentrating on one, currently, so let me rephrase the question: what girl?"

"It doesn't matter, Mr. Helm. You won't meet her up north where you're going, so there's no sense in cluttering up your mind with irrelevant . . . "

I'd said, "Who's doing this impersonation, you or I? Suppose you let me decide which irrelevancies I want to clutter up my mind with and which I don't. Who's the girl in Grant Nystrom's life—my life, now?"

"Well," he'd said very reluctantly, "well, there seems to

be a wealthy society lady with radical inclinations, named Elizabeth Meredith. . . . "

Stottman was waiting. I could feel him waiting. He was waiting for me to ignore the name he'd mentioned. It would have been a mark against me, since no man, under these circumstances, would be likely to let pass even a casual reference to his lady love. Or he was waiting for me to betray myself completely by asking who Meredith was, or by referring to the possessor of the name as masculine instead of feminine. He was a bright guy, for all his piggy looks, and he had the instinct for something wrong that makes a good agent.

"Meredith? Libby Meredith?" I said quickly. "Is she here? Where'd you see her?"

Stottman turned to me slowly. If he was disappointed again, he didn't let it show. He said, "You ought to know where I saw her. Even if you didn't get there in time to spot her going into the clinic, her car was parked right in front. I'm surprised you didn't recognize it, Mr. Nystrom."

My mind was working fast. "That yellow Caddy? Hell, Libby trades Cadillacs like some people trade stamps; I'd never seen this particular boat before. You mean that was hers? What's she doing here, anyway? I left her down in San Francisco, and she didn't say anything about coming up this way. Where is she now?"

"By this time, I suppose she's well on her way back to Seattle. At least that's where she came from, when I called Command and asked if there wasn't somebody handy who'd check your identification for me. After watching you play footsie with that blond girl on the beach this morning, when you should have kept yourself available to take delivery, I wanted to be absolutely sure before I handed you the stuff."

"You made absolutely sure, all right!" I said sourly. "You gave me a hell of a check. You never even let Libby see me! If you had, she'd have told you right away——"

"How did I know there was going to be a ringer waiting in the clinic, instead of you? We just set it up that she'd borrow a fancy dog to make it look good and be there when you came. She'd give me the signal, one way or the

other, and go on back to her business in Seattle, whatever it is. There was no need for us to take the risk of talking together, or I didn't think there was. By the time I realized there were *two* guys to identify, she'd got back into her car and driven off."

I hesitated, frowned, and said, "Well, there's an obvious way to settle this. How far is it to Seattle? Do you know where she's staying?"

"She was at the Holiday Inn. At least that's where I called her, setting it up over the phone. Room twenty-seven." He hesitated. "It's a couple of hundred miles to Seattle. But . . ."

I said, "If Libby gives me the okay, will you condescend to make delivery like you're supposed to, and let me get on with my route. Or will you just think up a bunch of new reasons for not following orders?"

The dark-faced man called Pete said unhappily: "It's a long drive, Mr. Stottman, and it's getting late. Hell, he's all right, he knows about Miss Meredith, he knows about everything. He's got to be the right man. Can't you just turn it over to him and——"

"Nobody's got to be anything," said Stottman coldly. "You take care of this stiff, Pete. Take care of it good, and then join me at the Holiday Inn, in Seattle. I'll ride along with this guy." His small, suspicious eyes studied my face. "I think he's bluffing, Pete. I think he's bluffing like hell."

The trouble was, he was perfectly right.

8 IT TOOK US NEARLY SIX HOURS TO reach Seattle. The roads weren't bad and I could have made it faster if I'd wanted to—the new pickups handle better than a lot of passenger cars—but I wasn't really in a hurry to get there just so I could have the rug yanked out from under my feet and the boom lowered on my head, to mix a couple of metaphors, if that's what they were.

We entered the city from the east after crossing a

mountain range or two in the dark. I had a hunch we'd missed a lot of beautiful scenery by making the drive at night, but at the moment I had other things to worry about besides picture-postcard views I hadn't got to see.

The sudden, unexpected emergencies are one thing: you can do nothing about them except deal with them as they come. It's the ones you see approaching a long way off, the ones that are neither unexpected nor unavoidable, that cause a lot of wear and tear on the mental gears.

In this case, I was obviously walking, or driving, straight into serious trouble. The minute Miss Elizabeth Meredith saw me and opened her mouth, I was dead—well, maybe not instantly, on her motel room rug, but at least as soon as I could be transported from there to a suitably discreet and private place. I wouldn't even have the satisfaction of getting myself killed by Hans Holz, as we'd planned. Stottman was clearly willing to attend to it personally, and to hell with the imported talent. Mac's theories in this regard seemed to be springing a few leaks in practice.

The question I had to answer, then, was how far to carry this doomed masquerade, hoping for a miracle. Obviously the safest course was to extract myself from the mess right now, before we ever reached the woman. I could probably handle Stottman at the moment. He was suspicious, but there were undoubtedly some questions on his mind about the correctness of his suspicions; there had to be. It had been a long drive and I'd made no false moves. The chances were good that his guard had slipped a little. Furthermore, he was alone.

If I acted decisively now, before his partner rejoined him, and before his suspicions were confirmed by the Meredith woman, I could probably take him. Later, the job would be a lot harder, perhaps impossible.

On the other hand, I had established contact after a fashion, and I hated to break it now. Making a bluff and backing down on it, I told myself, was bad poker; better to play the hand through. Hell, the woman we were driving to see might slip in the shower and kill herself or drink herself senseless before we reached her door. She might even take off for parts unknown in her yellow

Cadillac. If she proved unavailable after I'd indicated clearly my willingness to meet her, Stottman couldn't reasonably pursue his suspicions much farther. All I needed was a little luck. . . .

The Holiday Inn was located on the southern edge of Seattle, which meant we had to circumnavigate a good deal of the town to reach it. We'd already spent a little time checking me out of the motel in Pasco, and now we got lost twice trying to follow the sparse highway markers through the streets of the big coastal city, which seemed to be almost as badly loused up with waterways and bridges as Stockholm or Venice. As a result, it was well past eleven by the time we drove into the parking lot—and the yellow Cadillac convertible was there. So much for luck.

Stottman motioned to me to park beside it. Then he got out and again covered me as I slid over to join him on the pavement. I turned toward the camper.

He said, "Never mind."

"To hell with you," I said. "You don't have to clean up the mess."

"You're stalling, Nystrom. You're afraid of what Meredith is going to tell me about you."

I shrugged. "Think what you like. The pup's taking a walk or you're shooting me right here. Make up your mind. . . . Out you go, Hank. Don't bite that man, he'll give you indigestion."

The black pup didn't even take time to lick me. It had been a long haul, and he just skittered off across the parking lot and dove into the bushes to keep an urgent appointment with nature.

"*Now* what are you doing?" Stottman demanded.

"I'm feeding him," I said, reaching into the camper. "Dogs eat, you know. . . . Okay, Prince Hannibal. Back inside you go." Returning, the pup leaped into the camper eagerly. He was attacking the bowl of dog food before I had the door closed. I turned to Stottman and said, "See, that wasn't so bad, was it? Not a bite. Not even a snarl. And you thought you were going to be torn limb from limb! Now that the livestock's been taken care of, let's go see Libby and get this settled. Where's room twenty-seven in this flossy joint?"

"Probably somewhere in this wing, since her car's here. I'd guess the second floor from the number."

"Brains!" I said admiringly, and preceded him up the stairs at the end of the building, and along the hall to number twenty-seven, which unfortunately wasn't hard to find.

"Knock!" said Stottman, holding his gun steady.

I knocked. There was a long silence. I was strongly aware of the .25 automatic in Stottman's hand. There are stories of the feeble little bullet being turned by a heavy overcoat, but I wasn't wearing an overcoat. Stottman jerked his head in a peremptory way. I started to knock again, and the door swung open, away from my knuckles.

The woman who stood in the doorway was moderately tall, very nicely put together, and expertly preserved, so that you could safely say only that she was over twenty and under forty. I happened to know, having pried the information out of Mr. Smith's young men, that she was almost exactly halfway between those ages. Her hair was dark and rather short, cut almost boyishly, if the term means anything in these days of shaggy young males, but there was nothing boyish about her face or figure.

She was still wearing the yellow silk pants and the lacy blouse and the yellow silk jacket, open now as if she'd been about to take it off when interrupted. The elaborate, fragile costume had put in a long day on the road, and showed it, and so did she. She'd probably been heading for a bath and bed when we knocked on the door. But even tired, and slightly soiled and rumpled, she was a very good-looking woman, and normally I'd have been happy to meet her. Tonight, however, I'd have preferred a diamondback rattlesnake.

There was a little frowning crease between her eyes as she looked from me to Stottman and back again. Then she stepped forward impulsively and threw her arms around my neck.

"Grant!" she cried. "Oh, Grant, darling, I've been so worried about you. . . !"

9 THERE ARE ALL KINDS OF ELIZA-

beths, and you can pretty well determine which variety you're dealing with by the nickname your specimen wears. At one end of the personality range are the sweet, shy Beths—I was married to one, once. It was at a time when I'd quit all undercover activities and was earning a peaceful living with typewriter and camera, but things happened, as they do to people who retire from this profession. She learned about my dark and bloody past the hard way. It broke her up and our marriage as well. A typical, sensitive Beth. She went to Reno and I went back to work for Mac, but ever since I've considered myself something of an authority on Elizabeths.

In the middle of the personality spectrum you'll find some wholesome, normal girls called Betty. At the far end are the tough and sexy ladies who go by the nicknames Liz and Libby. I don't say it always works this way, but I've found the correlation pretty good.

Libby Meredith did nothing to make me revise my conclusions, Elizabeth-wise. She might be tired from all the driving, but the kiss she gave me showed me no signs of it. By the time she'd finished, I'd been made uncomfortably aware that there was a healthy woman inside the slightly wilted silk-and-lace outfit that something drastic should be done about, and if a bed wasn't handy, the wall-to-wall carpet would do. Of course, it wasn't a very practical idea at the moment, but I couldn't help having it just the same.

She drew back slightly to look at me. There was a hint of malice in her greenish eyes, letting me know that she was well aware of the biological effect she'd produced; but from where he stood, Stottman couldn't see her eyes. Her voice, which he could hear, was tender.

"Oh, darling!" she murmured. "When I saw that strange man and that crummy black dog trying to impersonate you and your Hank in that funny little pet clinic, I was so

afraid ... I figured he must have killed you, or at least had you kidnaped, so he could take your place. I wanted to stay and find you, but you know how they are about following instructions. Are you all right?"

"Sure," I said. She'd given me time to get my brain working again, and the role I was expected to play was pretty obvious. I went on, "Some crazy kids tried to run me into a deadfall, but I managed to shoot my way out of it."

I made my voice carefully casual, the way a man like Grant Nystrom might, after having for the first time proved his manhood with a gun. Libby Meredith looked aghast.

"*Shoot* your way?" she gasped, and of course she was acting, too.

Her mocking eyes told me she knew quite well that shooting guns at people was nothing new in my life. It was fairly easy, now, to guess where she'd learned this. I was beginning to understand from whom Mr. Smith's young men had extracted so many intimate details of the late Grant Nystrom's life; although her motive in spilling all this information to the authorities, and in coming here to help me act the part of her dead boyfriend—if that was why she was here—was not yet apparent.

"Shoot your way!" she repeated, sounding shocked and horrified. "Oh, darling, you're supposed to be just a courier, not a gunman. If I'd thought for a moment, when I talked you into it, that there was any danger in the work our people needed you for. . . . " She paused. Her expression was, for the moment, odd and unreadable. "Did you . . . did you have to kill anybody?"

"I got one of them, a punk with a fancy rifle who was drawing a bead on Hank." I was still Grant Nystrom, trying to work out the proper attitude for discussing his first homicide. "It was pretty much like shooting fish in a barrel. I've worked lots harder stalking deer and elk. I don't know what's so tough about killing a man—he can't smell you coming, and he seems to die fairly easily."

Libby gave a nice little feminine shudder. "Don't! If I'd thought you'd really have to use a gun, ever, I'd never have dreamed of asking you to work with us. . . . But

54

anyway, you're safe! And I suppose Mr. Stottman is taking care of . . . of the evidence, so you'll have nothing to worry about from the police."

I said, "Sure, Mr. Stottman is being a big help. A great big help. Incidentally, what happened to the car you were driving when I last saw you? If I'd recognized that gaudy yellow bucket as yours in Pasco, we wouldn't have had to chase you clear to Seattle."

On the assumption that she was on my side, for reasons still to be determined, I was warning her not to ask me any embarrassing questions on this particular subject. The slightest, briefest hint of a frown let me know that I should have recognized the yellow Cadillac. Chalk one error to Mr. Smith's closemouthed lads and their compulsive security. I guess I was lucky to have got the name of the girl out of them, let alone the brand of her transportation. Well, we could hope Stottman wouldn't check the auto-registration files for the date of purchase.

Libby said quickly, "Why, I told you I was getting a new convertible. You just don't listen, darling! And you haven't said *why* you had to come here—not that I'm not awfully glad to see you."

I jerked my head toward the door. "Ask our friend over there. He's got a problem. You may be able to help him with it."

She looked at Stottman. "What can I do for you, Mr. Stottman."

The plump man hesitated, and asked formally: "Do you know this man, Miss Meredith?"

"Know him?" She frowned. "Of course I know him! Why, I was the one who recruited him down in San Francisco, when we were asked to supply a courier with a background that would let him do a lot of traveling without being questioned. You know I know him. That's why I was picked to run down to Pasco and check on his double for you!" Libby glanced my way. "Darling, what *is* this, anyway?"

I laughed. "Mr. Stottman has doubles on the mind, Libby. He figures if one guy was trying an impersonation, two might be. He wants to be absolutely sure I'm me. Am I?"

"Of course you are. Don't be silly!"

"Don't tell me," I said. "I know who I am. Tell him. . . . Go on, tell him... Put it on the record officially."

Libby looked coldly at Stottman. "I don't know what this is all about and it's perfectly ridiculous. . . . Oh, all right! I hereby certify and depose that this man is Grant Nystrom himself, not a substitute or imitation. Okay, Mr. Stottman? Or would you like for me to make out an affidavit and have it witnessed and notarized and recorded at the county court house?" The stout man didn't answer. Libby turned back to me. "Has he made delivery yet, Grant?"

"Hell, no," I said. "That's why I had to bring him here, two hundred miles in the dark, for God's sake! It's like pulling teeth to make Mr. Stottman turn loose of anything, but maybe if we both plead with him, we can get hold of whatever lousy little scraps of information his cell has managed to scrounge up around here, so I can get back on the road in time to pick up the important stuff waiting for me up north."

It worked. My belittling of his contribution hit Stottman in his professional pride, and he said quickly: "Lousy little scraps of information, indeed! I'll have you know I have the key to NCS right here"—he slapped his coat pocket—"and without it, whatever data you get farther north will be absolutely meaningless."

The initials meant nothing to me. I had been briefed about no organization, system, or object known as NCS, but on this murky mission, that was just about par for the course. Obviously it was something, like Libby Meredith's name, that was supposed to be quite familiar to me—that is, to Grant Nystrom—but on the other hand, it didn't seem to be anything I was expected to comment on, so I just said, "All right. It's great stuff if you say so. Now, if you're satisfied I'm me, hand it over."

Stottman hesitated. His little brown eyes were unhappy and uncertain. He glanced toward Libby, who said sharply: "What is it now? If you're still not convinced, we can have somebody else flown up from San Francisco to confirm my identification. Of course, it will cause enough delay to throw Grant's schedule completely out of kilter,

but I'm sure nobody'll mind that as long as it makes you happy, Mr. Stottman!"

I felt rather sorry for the victim of her sarcasm. He was, in spite of his unprepossessing appearance, a good agent: good enough to respect his own hunches. His hunch was that I was a phony no matter who vouched for me. However, he'd run his protest as far as he could without making a lot of trouble for himself if he was wrong. He might be a good agent, but he was also enough of an organization man to know when to stop pushing. He shrugged his plump shoulders.

"Very well," he said, and took from his pocket a familiar brown-glass jar which, I could see now, was full of large tablets of some kind. "Here you are, Nystrom. . . . Wait a minute. Just how was the delivery supposed to be made?"

I sighed, like a man nearing the end of his patience. "I was supposed to be sitting there in the clinic with my dog on leash, waiting to see the vet. You were supposed to say: 'Isn't that a Labrador retriever? He's a beauty. What's his name?' And I was supposed to say: 'Yes, he's a Lab. His name is Hank.' "

I looked sharply at Stottman. "And what was your next line?"

"I was supposed to say: 'No, I mean his full name. He's pedigreed, isn't he?' "

I said, "And then I was supposed to tell you that the pup's registered name was Avon's Prince Hannibal of Holgate. My God. The people who dream up these long-winded identification routines ought to try them in the field sometime."

Stottman didn't smile. "And then, Mr. Nystrom?"

"Then you were supposed to turn away and raise hell with the nurse about that bottle of dog-vitamins, saying that you'd got them there yesterday but she hadn't given you the brand you'd asked for. The girl would presumably apologize and start to get you the right stuff, and I'd get up quickly and say, 'Are those Pet-Tabs, miss? That's what my dog gets and I'm almost out of them. I'll take them.' And that would be that. Okay?"

"And what's in the bottle besides vitamins, Nystrom?"

His little eyes were watching me closely, still suspicious.

I shrugged. "That's none of my business, friend. I know how it's packed and how I'm supposed to carry it and where I'm supposed to turn it over to somebody else, but what it is, I don't know and don't want to know. Of course, you've just told me it's a magic key of some kind, but I'm going to forget that as fast as I can. The less I know, the fewer people shoot at me, I hope. I've been target once too often on this trip already."

Again I'd disappointed him by making the right response. I held out my hand. After a moment's pause, he shrugged, gave me the bottle, turned and started for the door.

As the door closed behind him, I looked toward Libby Meredith and started to speak, but she shook her head quickly and put her finger to her lips. With the same finger, she then pointed to the little table by the door. Stottman's hat lay there: one of the oldest tricks in the world.

I grinned, stuck the vitamin bottle into my pocket, stepped forward, and took the woman into my arms, doing what seemed indicated. She did not resist or protest; in fact she seemed to feel it was an interesting project, worthy of her cooperation. We were both convincingly flushed and disheveled, both breathing hard, when the door burst open. We jumped apart in a suitably startled and embarrassed manner.

"Really, Mr. Stottman!" Libby said indignantly.

"I'm sorry. I forgot my hat." Stottman looked at us bleakly for a moment. What he'd hoped to catch us doing, instead of what we'd been doing, I couldn't imagine and probably he couldn't either. He'd just felt obliged to give it a try. Behind him, in the hallway, I saw the brown-faced man called Pete. "My apologies," Stottman said, backing out of the room once more.

After he'd gone, I checked the door to make sure that, this time, the lock was set and the latch had caught. I turned to face Libby Meredith.

"Now what?" I asked.

Then I saw that she was calmly unbuttoning her blouse. She looked amused at my expression. "It's what

they expect, isn't it?" she murmured. "We wouldn't want to disappoint them, would we?"

We didn't.

10 *I AWOKE TO FIND MYSELF LYING* in a big motel bed without any clothes on, with a naked woman for company. Morally speaking, it was no doubt very shocking, but we don't do much moral speaking in this line of work. I was more concerned with the professional aspects of the situation.

Ungrateful and unappreciative though it might seem, after the pleasant night we'd just spent together, I couldn't help wondering just what the glamorous Miss Meredith really wanted from me. I mean, it hadn't been essential for her to go to bed with me as part of the act—in fact it hadn't been necessary at all—and I've long since given up the notion that I'm so irresistible that any woman who meets me just naturally grabs at any excuse to get out of her clothes and into my arms. I've found it much safer to assume that ladies who act in this uninhibited manner probably have nasty, ulterior motives for their behavior.

"What's your name, darling?" Libby Meredith's voice interrupted my wandering, early-morning thoughts. "And I don't mean Grant Nystrom."

I turned my head to look at her. She was being very casual about security. I certainly don't make a fetish of it myself, but I am aware that there are such things as electronic eavesdropping gadgets that can easily be installed in motel rooms. She read my thoughts and laughed at me.

"Relax, darling. I'm a very important person in the organization. They still trust me implicitly; they don't suspect a thing. I'm sure they wouldn't bother to put a microphone in my room."

It was a naive little speech for anyone as deeply involved with a lot of unpleasant people as she seemed to be.

I said, "If by organization you mean this Russian west coast espionage outfit we're trying to trip up, this is the first I've heard of any Communist group having implicit faith in any of its members, particularly amateur help playing at intrigue just for kicks."

I was trying it for size. Apparently it fit well enough, or she wanted me to think it did, because she didn't get very mad. A truly dedicated idealist, whether radical or reactionary, will blow his stack violently if you accuse him of being a thrill-seeking political amateur. Miss Meredith merely narrowed her eyes slightly.

"Don't be obnoxious, darling. I helped you out of a lot of trouble last night. You might at least be grateful enough to be polite."

"Sorry, ma'am," I said. "I always take off my manners with my pants. And I'm grateful enough for the trouble you helped me out of, but that doesn't keep me from wondering about the trouble you're helping me into." I reached out thoughtfully and drew a finger across her breast, incompletely covered by the sheet. "I mean, Miss Meredith, it was a lovely evening. Now what am I expected to do to pay for it?"

Her eyes remained narrow a moment longer; then she laughed softly. "I think I'm going to like you," she murmured. "Grant was sweet but he wasn't very bright. A woman gets bored with a man who has implicit faith in her. Poor Grant."

"Sure," I said. "Poor Grant. Did you get bored enough with him to set him up for murder?"

Still she didn't get mad. "No," she said quietly, "no, just bored enough to con him into betraying his country. I mean——" She hesitated, and made a wry little face. "——I mean, when you get a man like that trailing you around with big sheepy eyes and offering to do anything in the world for you, the temptation to take him at his word is hard to resist. But I didn't know I was putting his life in danger. In fact, they promised me that, as a courier, he'd be running no real risk except, of course, of going to jail. And there wasn't even much chance of that, they said, if he used his head."

"And you believed them?"

"Why not? The whole business had turned out to be pretty much a drag, as far as I was concerned. I mean, I'd gone into it for excitement, mostly, but all it was was a bunch of mousy little men and drab little women making a big deal of sneaking around snapping pictures of dull documents snitched from dusty files. No sex, no shooting, no nothing. I was about to ditch them and take up shoplifting or something for real kicks when . . . when Grant disappeared. And then a couple of government men were waiting for me, a day or two later, and they took me to see the poor damn guy and his poor damn dog. . . ." She stopped. After a little, she said, "They just looked so damn *dead!* Do you know what I mean?"

"I know," I said. "So you decided to change sides and give the government boys a hand, by way of atonement."

"Atonement, hell!" she said. "Those lousy red bastards promised me he would be safe, didn't they? I'm going to wreck their lousy red spy ring, every crummy cell of it, clear up to Point Barrow, Alaska. Well, Anchorage. I don't think they've got anybody much north of there, this particular gang anyway. And I'm going to take care of anybody else who had anything to do with Grant's death! You still haven't told me your name."

The sudden change of subject caught me off balance. I stalled by asking, "Didn't they tell you in San Francisco?"

"Those government boy scouts? Everything was a big secret to them. All they'd say was that they'd picked somebody to take Grant's place, and that this somebody needed all the information about Grant and his route and his instructions that I could supply." She paused. "Oh, they did show me your picture after you'd had your hair bleached. They asked what I thought of the resemblance. I had to tell them I didn't think it was very close."

I grinned. "Well, that figures. They wouldn't tell me much about you, either. What little I got, I got the hard way, and it's a good thing I did. They've got a serious epidemic of professional lockjaw in that department."

"It isn't your department?"

"No, thank God," I said. "I'm just kind of out on loan to them temporarily."

"But you are a government man, too?"

"That's right."

She smiled. "This is a hell of a place for a public servant, darling, in bed with a female subversive—even if she's a reformed female subversive."

"Maybe I'm a hell of a public servant," I said. "And my name is Matthew Helm. Now you know it, you'd better forget it."

"I will, but thanks for trusting me with it. I get a little tired of everything being so goddamned classified." She hesitated. "If they hadn't told you I was helping them, why did you risk coming here with Stottman? How did you know I wouldn't reveal you as a phony the minute you put your face on the door?"

"I didn't," I said. "I was bluffing. Stottman suspected me. I had to back him down, somehow. I was hoping that, by the time we got here, you'd have taken off for parts unknown. Or fallen out a window, headfirst, onto a concrete sidewalk. Which brings up the point: why are you here in Seattle, anyway? Those omniscient lads in San Francisco told me I didn't have to know anything about you because there wasn't a chance of my running into you up here."

"I don't take orders from them," she said. "They may think I do, but they're wrong. How about a drink?"

I shuddered and glanced at my watch. "At seven-thirty in the morning? What are you, a dipso or something?"

"Right now I'm a girl who wants a drink at seven-thirty in the morning."

She got out of bed, quite unconcerned about her nakedness. Her figure was as trim and attractive without clothes as it had been with them, which isn't often the case except among the very young. She kicked around among the garments strewn about the carpet—hers and mine—to find the pants she'd discarded the evening before, and pulled them on without benefit of underwear. Then she unearthed her blouse from the same heap, made a face at its wilted appearance, and struggled into it. Wearing it open, like a thin, loose, ruffled jacket, she moved, still barefoot, to the dresser, where she peeled the paper sock off a motel glass and poured herself a healthy slug from a

bottle standing nearby, tempering it with barely a splash of water from a pitcher.

"You're sure you won't have some?"

"Positive," I said. "I've got a long way to drive today, if I'm to make contact up in British Columbia tomorrow like I'm supposed to."

I got out of bed and started dressing. I probably didn't carry it off quite as well as she had. Not that I was actively embarrassed, but we hadn't really been acquainted very long and I felt more comfortable after I'd got a few clothes on. When, after zipping up my pants, I glanced her way again, she was sprawled in the big chair in the corner, grinning at me.

"Skinny, aren't you?" she murmured.

"No skinnier than some others you've known. At least one other."

Her grin vanished. "Why bring that up?"

"Because it's the central fact of our existence, sweetheart—or should I say of our coexistence. At least I'm here because I'm supposed to look somewhat like a tall skinny guy you used to know pretty well. I was kind of assuming you were here for the same reason."

"Well, I came here to back up your impersonation of him, if that's what you mean."

"I wasn't told I'd be having any help from you. Quite the contrary."

She laughed. "Neither was, I, darling. In fact, I was told I was staying in San Francisco on pain of drastic penalties, I forget just what they were. Probably a whole gaggle of government pretty-boys is searching for me right now, to lock me up for getting independent. But I could see this impersonation deal just wasn't going to go over, the way they had it rigged. Sooner or later, somebody was going to get suspicious of you, probably sooner . . ."

"Somebody did. Stottman."

"Yes," she said, "and if you hadn't had a member of the lodge in good standing to vouch for you, your act would have been finished right there, wouldn't it? And so would you. That's why I managed to get myself sent up this way without letting those government jerks know about it, so I'd be handy if you needed me."

"Your efforts are appreciated. Can I expect more assistance farther up the line, if required?"

"I'll do the best I can. After all, I've done some good work for this creepy spy outfit; I've earned a certain amount of latitude. And Grant and I are—were—known to be pretty close. I don't think anybody will suspect anything if I continue to dream up excuses to be near him—you."

I said, "Just the same it could be risky."

"I told you, I got in this mainly for kicks. I don't mind a few risks." Her lips tightened. "I'm going to smash this whole lousy apparatus, no matter what it costs. At least I'm going to louse up this operation for them so they'll never put it back together—and you know how Moscow deals with failures!" After a moment, she asked in a totally different tone of voice: "What do you know about these other people, the ones who tried to have you killed so they could bring in their own imitation Nystrom?"

"Very little, so far," I said, tucking my shirt into my pants. "I've seen three of them, but there may be more. There's a blond girl in jeans. There's the guy you saw in the vet's office, call him Nystrom. And there was a juvenile gun expert with moustache and sideburns, but he's dead."

"You don't know what they're after?"

"Well, that's fairly obvious, but I don't really know why they're after it," I said. "It seems pretty clear that they're trying to do the same thing we are: hijack the information Stottman and his friends—your ex-friends—have collected on NCS, whatever that may be."

Libby glanced at me sharply, surprised. "You mean, you haven't even been told *that?* The government sure makes you boys work blindfolded! NCS stands for Northwest Coastal System, darling. Everybody knows that."

"Sure," I said. "Everybody."

"Well, almost everybody. Of course, only a few people know what it actually is; in that respect, security is very tight. But it's something very fancy being tested here in the Northwest, a defensive system of some kind, we hear, but that could mean anything. Nobody, but nobody, builds aggressive systems these days, or admits it if they

do. Anyway, Moscow is very eager to learn all about NCS. And obviously somebody else is, too."

"Maybe Peking," I said.

Libby gave me another of her sharp, surprised looks. "Why do you say that? Were any of those interfering brats Oriental?"

"No," I said, "but they could have been hired, couldn't they? Or persuaded by the customary, cockeyed ideological arguments? And if something interesting is being developed on this shore of the Pacific, the people on the other shore would seem like logical customers for the information. And I had a case over in Hawaii not too long ago where young people were being pumped full of highfalutin notions and used as suckers by shrewd professionals. That one was run from Moscow, but some Chinese agents were involved, too. Maybe they're not too proud to borrow a good idea from their fellow Marxists."

She shrugged. "You're just guessing."

I said, "Sure. But I don't think Bellman and Company dreamed up an operation like this on their own. . . ."

"Bellman?"

"That's the girl's name. Pat Bellman."

"Is she pretty?"

"Don't be corny," I said. "The kid's not bad. Not a sexpot like you, but not bad. Incidentally, if you were to button that damn blouse, I could keep my mind on our conversation without the distraction of wondering if I'm being seduced all over again and why."

She made no move to comply with the suggestion, smiling up at me in a provocative way. Trousered women don't do much for me as a rule, but this one managed to overcome the handicap nicely. Lounging there half-naked, glass in hand, in somewhat bedraggled remnants of yesterday's elaborate fancy-pants costume, she was a wanton challenge to the whole male sex.

The catch, as far as my libido was concerned, was that my mind really did want to know why. She was putting on a fine, tarty act for me—had been, ever since we met— but my instincts warned me it was just that: an act. Not that she was necessarily an unspoiled and innocent child at heart, but neither was she, I thought, just a sexy slob

who normally drank whiskey at the crack of dawn. Last night, after a long hard day, when she'd had plenty of reason to relax with a couple of stiff ones, there had been no liquor on her breath. To the best of my knowledge, there are very few morning drinkers who don't lap it up at night as well. So why was the lady deliberately making herself look cheap and dissipated for my benefit?

I looked down at her bleakly for a moment longer. When she didn't speak, I said, "Honest, it's a great routine, Libby. But what does it mean?"

Her eyes narrowed. After a moment, she rose and drew the blouse closed over her breasts, buttoned it up, and stuffed it into her pants. Then she looked up at me and, after a little pause, laughed softly.

"I keep thinking you're really Grant, I guess," she murmured. "He was kind of a coward where women were concerned. You had to make things easy for him. I mean, when we first met, I gave him the glamour treatment for weeks and nothing happened. Finally, I realized he was actually scared of touching the shining lady in her expensive clothes. I mean, he wanted to, God how he wanted to, but he was afraid he'd make me mad by mussing my dress or wrecking my hairdo or something. I had to let him catch me cleaning house with my hair tied up and some old rag on, drinking beer. . . . Ugh, how I hate beer! As the man said, they ought to pour it back into the horse. But it's a nice, lower-class, down-to-earth drink, and we got lit on the nasty stuff, and it did the job. In a faded old dress with dirt on my nose and a skinful of beer, I was human enough that he dared grab me and maul me the way he'd wanted to for weeks." She grimaced. "That sounds pretty snide, doesn't it? I didn't mean it to. Actually, he was a sweet, shy guy without too much between the ears. Whereas you're a smart, cold, calculating bastard who knows everything about women. Aren't you?"

"Sure," I said. "Everything except why this particular woman gives a damn whether I go for her or not."

She said, smiling again, "I guess I underestimated you. I thought you'd just put it down to your personal magnetism. Most men would."

"In my line of work," I said, "those who overestimate their personal magnetism tend to die very young. Come on, Libby, give. You want something, and it isn't me. What is it?"

"Oh, I don't mind you," she murmured. "In fact, I rather like you."

"Thanks."

She hesitated. "Tell me something. That young punk with the gun, the one you shot—that would probably be the one who killed Grant, wouldn't it?"

"Probably," I said. "Why?"

She reached out and took me by the arms, drawing me closer, so close that our bodies touched here and there. The contact obviously wasn't accidental; very little about this girl was accidental, I warned myself. She looked up at me searchingly for a moment.

She said, "Because I want you to get the rest of them, too."

I was just as conscious of the fact that there was nothing but Libby under the thin pants and blouse as she wanted me to be; but this was beside the point.

"Sure," I said. "Will just the scalps do, or do you want the ears, too? Or should I bring you the heads in a basket, individually wrapped like fancy oranges?"

"Don't be funny," she said quietly. "I'm not joking. I want you to get the remaining two we know about—the girl and the tall man with the dog—and any others that may be working with them; I want them all. Dead." Her eyes were steady on my face. When I didn't speak, she went on: "I just paid you, last night, for the one you've already taken care of. Please don't think I fall into bed with *every* man I meet. I owed you a debt, and I paid it. Do you understand?"

I said, "Libby, I'm afraid you're a screwball. I don't like working with screwballs."

"That's too bad," she said calmly, "that's too bad, because you're stuck with me just as I'm stuck with you. And I'm telling you that for every additional one you get, you can collect the same fee. Me." She waited again for me to speak. When I didn't, she continued in the same

cold, steady voice: "Of course, if you'd rather have money, I've got that, too. Name your price. But get them for me. Kill them for me. All of them."

11 HANK WAS SO GLAD TO SEE ME

that he tongue-washed my face all over before darting off to take care of his business in the bushes. He was really a pretty good pup. In spite of having been locked up all night, he'd made no mess in the camper. He hadn't chewed up anything, either, although there was plenty of gear in there for him to exercise his teeth on if he got the notion.

I should have played with him a bit—at least tossed him something to retrieve as a reward for good behavior—but at the moment human considerations took precedence in my mind over matters canine. I whistled him back, therefore, as soon as he'd concluded his rendezvous with nature, locked him up again, got into the cab of the truck, and hesitated, feeling for the bottle of vitamins in my pocket.

It was still there, and whatever it contained besides dog pills was presumably intact since I was in a good position to swear that Libby Meredith had had no chance to get at it and, in spite of distractions, I was fairly sure nobody else had entered the room all night. I don't sleep that soundly, particularly when I'm not alone in bed. There were certain things I was supposed to do now to make Mr. Smith happy, but they didn't weigh on me very heavily. I had other things on my mind; I could play secret agent later.

I started the truck and drove out of there fast, heading north. What I really wanted was a telephone, but I didn't want to be seen using one, since I preferred not to be asked, later, whom I'd been calling. Of course I'd used one in Pasco, but then I'd been following Mr. Smith's childish instructions to the letter, since there had seemed to be no good reason not to. Now the situation had

changed rather spectacularly, and I figured I'd better be a little more careful until I'd heard Mac's ideas on the new developments.

All the way up through Seattle, the freeway traffic was too heavy for me to determine whether or not I was being tailed. Even after I'd left the city limits behind, I still had enough company to make it look as if half the population of the state of Washington had decided to move up to British Columbia, but apparently most of these north-bound emigrants were making for Vancouver, on the coast. When I turned off the big coastal highway and headed slantingly inland on a smaller road that crossed the Canadian border near a little town called Sumas, I had more privacy, but I decided to wait a little longer to be quite sure I was safe from observation.

The border ritual was no trouble at all. I told the man I had a sporting rifle and shotgun, and he said fine, just keep the weapons unloaded and cased while in Canada. He didn't even ask me about sidearms as they generally do, so I didn't have to lie about Grant Nystrom's .357 which was chafing my hipbone. He just checked on Hank's rabies inoculation and waved me on.

Pretty soon I was rolling eastward along a four-lane highway more or less paralleling the border. The day was bright and warm and windless, and the truck ran straight and true down the smooth pavement, like a locomotive on tracks. It's one of the mysteries of the automotive business, how few people really appreciate the virtues of the ordinary American half-ton truck. On the highway it'll keep up with the fastest traffic, and off the road it'll go just about anywhere you'd care to take a jeep. Please understand, I'm talking about the real truck now, not about all the dressed-up little bastard delivery vans that are sold under sporty names to people too proud to be seen in an honest, work-horse commercial vehicle with the engine out front.

The vehicle Nystrom had bequeathed me was a fast, powerful, and rugged machine. I wouldn't have matched it against a Ferrari on a twisty road-race circuit, but I thought it would probably run down any ordinary car on any ordinary back-country road, particularly one that was

paved badly or not at all. For the sparsely populated areas of the continent toward which my mission was leading me, I couldn't have asked for better transportation.

Since angling was still part of my act, I stopped to buy a fishing license at a tourist-bureau office set up along the highway to make such purchases convenient for visitors to the province. Afterwards, I turned north again, according to instructions, on a two-lane blacktop road leading up the Frazer River—a historic waterway, I'd been told: the ancient gateway to the interior. No single car had made the whole route behind me. Of course, somebody could have assigned me a surveillance team, two or three different cars taking turns, and probably Mr. Smith's people were using just this technique to watch over me, since I'd detected no signs of them. As for the opposition, the people in whom we were interested, if they were going to that much trouble it meant that my cover was blown anyway and a phone call more or less wouldn't make much difference.

I wasn't really worrying about the whole west coast Communist spy *apparat* ganging up on me. What concerned me was the possibility that a single gent with a suspicious nature—say a guy named Stottman—might be running an unofficial check on my activities in the hope of catching me doing something Grant Nystrom wouldn't, like telephoning Washington, D.C.

By now I'd taken as many precautions as the possibility would seem to merit, but just to be on the safe side, rather than be seen standing in a roadside booth, I stopped for lunch at a small-town restaurant that boasted an inside pay phone. As a final precaution, I made my report to Mac by way of our relay man in Vancouver, insuring that there'd be no incriminating record of a long-distance call across the border.

"Indeed," Mac said when I'd finished. "Very intriguing. What do you make of the lady, Eric?"

I said, "I know what she'd like me to make of her, sir. A crackpot nymphomaniac with alcoholic tendencies complicated by an obsessive guilt complex—that's the picture she was painting for me, stroke by careful stroke. She wants me to believe that deep down in her subconscious

she knows it was she who got Grant Nystrom killed by roping him into this courier job in the first place. I'm supposed to think that her mind rejects this knowledge and instead, in self defense, blames everybody else for her lover's death; her Communist pals—or ex-pals—and this gang of youthful interlopers that did the actual shooting. To keep from admitting her own guilt, she's embarked on a career of vengeance against everyone else involved. At least that's the theory I'm supposed to buy."

"But you don't?"

I said, "Hell, that isn't a picture, sir, it's a psychiatric caricature. She's just making it up as she goes along. This girl is as phony as a ten-dollar pawnshop Stradivarius. I don't know who she is, but I do know what she isn't, and that's a rich, dipso, nympho society woman who went Communist for kicks, talked her boyfriend into joining up with her, and is now overwhelmed with remorse because he wound up getting shot as a result."

Mac said dryly, "You seem to have an attraction for interesting young women who aren't what they seem. Don't forget, whoever and whatever she is, this one did save your mission, and probably your life."

"Yes, sir," I said. "I'm keeping it in mind. Question, sir."

"What is it?"

"She couldn't be one of ours, could she?"

Apparently the question took Mac by surprise, because there was a rather lengthy pause. When he spoke, his voice had a stiff and offended note: "If we'd had any agents on the job who might possibly be of assistance to you, I would certainly have let you know when I briefed you, Eric."

This, of course, meant nothing at all. If the girl was working for us, and there were good reasons for her to keep her mouth shut even with me, they were still good. And if those reasons had caused Mac to refrain from mentioning her earlier, he'd certainly lie about her now. In other words, asking the question had been just a gesture on my part; a way of establishing for future reference—if my suspicions proved correct—that I wasn't quite as easy to fool as people seemed to think.

"Yes, sir." I drew a long breath. "Well, what do I do about the instructions I received from the lady?"

"Instructions?"

"I mean, should I or should I not go out and earn myself some wonderful nights with Miss Meredith?" When Mac didn't speak at once, I said irritably: "For God's sake, sir! Do I kill them or don't I?"

"Oh," he said, "I see what you mean. The answer is fairly obvious, is it not? As long as they're alive, these people are a constant threat to you. Not only are they interfering with your mission, but also, if captured by the opposition, they will undoubtedly reveal that Grant Nystrom—the real Nystrom—is dead because they shot him, and that you are therefore an impostor just as this fellow Stottman suspects."

I said, "I thought we wanted them to suspect me. I thought, since Holz is riding shotgun on this espionage operation, we were trying to give him a motive for descending on me, breathing fire and destruction."

"That was what we'd hoped to do, certainly," Mac admitted. "But I think you can see that the plan must be revised in the light of your recent experiences. Apparently we can't count on Holz coming to you. You must therefore be prepared to go to him, by continuing as Grant Nystrom. It follows that you cannot afford to have your cover compromised by anybody, and that, whatever Miss Meredith's motives may be, her suggestion is quite sound."

"Yes, sir," I said. "Sound. What about the authorities? Dead bodies tend to attract attention, and I'm told the Mounties always get their man. It would be awkward if I were the man."

"Arrangements have been made. The Canadians have a large stake in your mission. You have nothing to fear if you are reasonably discreet. Is there anything else?"

"No, sir," I said. "Not a thing. Eric, signing off."

Hanging up, I made a face at something on the wall of the booth, or maybe it was just in my mind. I tried to tell myself firmly that the fact that she knew how to swing a fishing rod and talk about dogs didn't really say much about a girl's character, and that Pat Bellman was noth-

ing to me but a female fink who'd tried to set me up for murder. This was perfectly true, but I found that I wasn't particularly eager to shoot, or otherwise dispose of, any female finks.

Thinking this, I came out into the warm sunshine after lunch to see a small car—a battered red Opel two-door—carrying two men in front and a rear seat full of luggage, being driven slowly through the parking lot. It seemed about to pause behind my camper rig; then the driver spotted me emerging from the restaurant and put on speed again, swinging back onto the highway. He was a tall man I'd seen once before, leading a black dog into an animal clinic south of the border; he was Pat Bellman's entry in the great Nystrom sweepstakes.

There was no sign of the dog among all the luggage, which was all right with me. I'd been given no instructions to destroy the poor beast, but Mac might insist on a clean sweep if he was in a bloodthirsty mood and I was fool enough to ask.

12 I'D BEEN PLANNING TO DRIVE straight through to the next rendezvous, on a body of water up north called Francois Lake. My intention had been to get up there early enough, by staying on the road all night, so I'd have plenty of time to look the situation over ahead of the contact, which was set for six-thirty the next evening. However, with Nystrom Number Three and his friend hanging around, it seemed advisable to take things a little more easily and maybe get some idea what the boys—not to mention the girl—had in mind.

I thought I knew what it was. The last time I'd seen the tall man, he'd had a black dog like mine conspicuously in tow. I couldn't be absolutely sure there wasn't an animal hidden in the rear of the Opel, but the man had also, undoubtedly, waiting somewhere, a Chevy-based camper rig similar to the one I was driving. At the scene of Nystrom's murder, Mr. Smith's eager operative had inter-

fered before the murderer could dispose of Nystrom's body and appropriate his truck, but Chevy pickups, and pickup campers, aren't hard to come by. Bellman and Company wouldn't have tried the impersonation without a suitable vehicle. But Nystrom Three wasn't driving it now, even though it would have been faster and more comfortable than his present transportation.

The implication was that he'd given up his Nystrom act. That left only one Nystrom in the running: Nystrom Number Two—me. But apparently I wasn't to be allowed to garner the fruits of victory undisturbed.

Pat Bellman hadn't looked like a girl who gave up easily, and she was bright enough to see the obvious. If her Nystrom couldn't get the stuff—and he'd been pretty well disqualified in Pasco—she still had a chance, if she let somebody else's Nystrom get it for her, and then moved in and took it away from him. At least I figured that was the way her mind worked. If I was right, I was in no immediate danger. She wouldn't act until I'd picked up all the material she wanted. But I could count on having plenty of company on my journey northward.

After giving Hank another run, I put the rig back on the road again, watching the big truck-type rearview mirrors. Sure enough, after a few miles, the battered little Opel appeared behind me. It wasn't much of a car— General Motors' uninspired answer to the Volkswagen— and with over two hundred horses under the hood I could have run away and hid from it, but that wasn't the idea. Besides, while international arrangements seemed to have been made to let me commit murder with impunity, I might not be able to get away with speeding.

I poked along deliberately, therefore, up through the spectacular canyon of the Frazer, and north across the rolling country beyond. Once out of the canyon, I didn't find it particularly interesting driving. The scenic mountain ranges pretty well hug the coast in that part of the world. Inland it's just forests and fields, lakes and rivers and more forests. After a few hours, one evergreen begins to look pretty much like another.

Nystrom Three kept up pretty well, considering his limited mechanical resources. It occurred to me that if he

continued to come along like a good boy to a suitably lonely place—discreet, was the word Mac had used—I could get started on the secondary phase of my assignment and, incidentally, promote myself a couple of nights of bliss with Libby Meredith, one for each man in the car behind. It seemed like earning your sex the hard way. Maybe I should have checked to find out just what she was willing to pay in cash.

How the Opel had managed to pick me up was, of course, no real mystery. After all, these interlopers, whoever they might be, had managed to learn about the last rendezvous somehow. Presumably they'd found out about the next one the same way. I considered the possibility that the real Nystrom might have talked a little more than was good for him, but the precise source of the information didn't concern me greatly. Obviously there had been a leak in Communist security somewhere, but it wasn't my problem, at least not at the moment.

Knowing I was heading for Francois Lake, the boys in the Opel would only have had to start early, get up here in B.C. ahead of me, and pick a suitable spot to wait for me to go by. There weren't enough good roads this far north to make my route even slightly unpredictable.

It occurred to me that others might be using the same leapfrog system for keeping tabs on me. Pat Bellman, for instance, could have buzzed up here in her little maroon pseudo-sports car and stationed herself somewhere along the road ahead to tag me if I should elude or outrun this pair. She might even have other reinforcements spotted around: a real dragnet.

And the fact that I'd seen nothing of Stottman and his Indian-faced partner didn't necessarily mean I was through with them for good. They could also have gambled on my running a predictable course, like a circling rabbit, and headed up here to cut me off. I sincerely hoped they hadn't. I hoped the pudgy man had given up trying to prove I was an impostor and returned to his own stamping grounds farther south. He was a pro, and I preferred not to tangle with him unless I had to.

Judging by their performance so far, the rest of them—all the bright young interlopers, alive and dead—were

strictly amateurs and nothing to worry about. If I had needed evidence on this point, the clumsy tailing job being done by the characters in the Opel would have set my mind at rest. There are circumstances under which a clever agent will deliberately let a man know he's under surveillance, but instinct and experience told me these people weren't that clever. They were doing their best to be inconspicuous, but they hadn't had much practice at it, and it wasn't very good.

We passed through small communities with names like Seventy-Mile House and Hundred-Mile House, reminders of the days when every mile up this pioneering road, away from civilization, had represented a real achievement. Farther on, we came to a good-sized lake with a sandy beach, and I pulled up to the office of a motel in the nearby village and rented a large and pleasant unit complete with bath and kitchenette for six dollars, which didn't seem exorbitant.

With Hank romping outside, happy to be free after the long ride, I carried the essential luggage, and groceries enough for breakfast, into my room. Then I whistled in the pup, closed the door, drew the blinds, and took off his collar. It was time for me to make like a real secret agent once more; I'd stalled long enough. I got the bottle of dog-vitamins Stottman had given up so reluctantly. With the point of my knife, designed for more lethal purposes, I pried the waxed cardboard liner out of the metal cap. Underneath was a small round wafer of tinfoil about the size of a dime—to be exact, two thicknesses of foil with something sealed between them, perhaps a little disk of film, perhaps not.

I was tempted to separate the layers of foil and do some snooping. What stopped me wasn't my orders from Mr. Smith to leave everything in this line to his boys, but the possibility that the communication I held might be rigged to destroy itself somehow—perhaps by exposure to light or air—if not handled in a specified way. Besides, I'd never be able to reseal the wafer properly, and I probably couldn't make much sense of what was inside, anyway. Weapons are our specialty; microdots and ciphers and such are out of our line.

I followed instructions, therefore, and used the knifepoint to pry one of the big metal studs from Hank's collar the way I'd been shown. I fitted the wafer inside, and refastened the shiny stud to the black leather collar. There were five flat studs in all, alternating with five smaller and more pointed metal decorations, perhaps designed to keep hostile dogs from chewing on Hank's neck. If everything went according to plan—which would be a welcome change—I'd fill another receptacle tomorrow evening, leaving three to go. By this manner of reckoning, the job was barely started. It was a discouraging thought.

In the morning, I rose early, cooked myself some breakfast—I'm no great chef, but I can manage bacon and eggs—and hit the road well before daylight. No headlights followed me away from Lac La Hache, as the place was called, but by the time the sun had come up and burned the mists out of the hollows where it lay like cotton, the beat-up red car had taken up its station behind me once more. You had to say this for the boys: they might not be expert but they were persistent.

Later, I stopped for a cup of coffee and a doughnut in the good-sized town of Prince George. The road forked here, the right-hand branch leading inland to Dawson Creek and the Alaska Highway proper, while the left-hand branch led to the coast and the town of Prince Rupert, the southern terminal of the Alaska Ferry system. By taking the ferry, the less rugged traveler could bypass all but a few hundred miles of that he-man highway in smooth comfort.

I didn't think comfort was the reason Grant Nystrom's Communist superiors had chosen to send him by the latter route. The Alaska Highway, built in wartime, had been routed through the remote interior where it would be reasonably safe from hostile action by sea. The ferry, on the other hand, went up the coast; and the coast presumably was where most information on the Northwest Coastal System was to be found.

I reached Francois Lake in the afternoon with plenty of time to spare, and found the lodge at which I was supposed to stay without any difficulty. It was some miles off the main highway on a small dirt road, but there were

plenty of signs to point the way. The place, when I got there, consisted of a good-sized main building, half a dozen log cabins overlooking the outlet of the lake, and a dock with some boats. I checked in, rented one of the boats, and went fishing.

There was just one hitch, when Hank refused to enter the boat. Apparently, he'd never ridden in one, and none of Mr. Smith's canine experts had taken the trouble to check this aspect of his education. But he was a good dog, and I managed to coax him aboard, hoping that nobody was watching the performance, at least nobody who counted, like Stottman or the local contact I was to meet. Grant Nystrom's rig sported a trailer hitch, and I'd been told that he'd used it for towing some kind of fishing boat, but that we didn't have to worry about it since he hadn't brought it along on this jaunt. But if Nystrom had owned a boat, his dog had probably been a seasoned sailor. My dog was making it quite clear that he wasn't.

He stood on the middle seat, very tense, ready to unload in a hurry if this crazy, unstable, waterborne vehicle should sink or explode. I talked to him reassuringly while I shoved off and got the motor started. He almost went over the side when the outboard fired; but gradually, as we swung out of the river and into the lake, he relaxed a bit and sat down to enjoy—or at least endure—the ride. I snapped some kind of a flashy lure to the end of my line, tossed it overboard, and settled down to tow it around the lake in a slow and purposeful manner, as if I really expected it to catch a fish.

I trolled down the shore away from the lodge for half an hour, then cut across to the south side of the lake and came back, passing opposite the outlet and the lodge. I continued in that direction for another half hour, and turned back again, having seen no fish and very few fishermen. Reaching the spot opposite the lodge once more, I glanced at my watch and found that the time was a few minutes before six. I'd hit it about right, just a little early.

I reeled in my well-traveled lure, exchanged it for a gaudy red-and-white spoon, and made a show of casting for a while. No fish were intrigued by this performance,

either, which was just as well, since I wouldn't have had time, now, to mess with one if I had managed to hook him. At a quarter past six, I cranked in my line once more, started up the motor, and headed straight across the lake toward the lodge I could see on the distant shore.

It was a big lake. East and west it ran, according to my road map, for better than fifty miles; but even its narrow north-and-south dimension was impressive to a landlubber brought up in the relatively waterless areas of south-western U.S.A. I was glad that the day was clear and calm, and that the rented motor was running strongly. I wouldn't have wanted to have weather trouble on a body of water that size, or engine trouble either.

"You and me both, pup," I said, as Hank shifted position nervously. "Take it easy. We'll be back on terra firma pretty soon."

I saw my contact coming. Another boat was approaching from the left—excuse me, from port—running down the lake on a course that would intersect mine about a quarter of a mile ahead. It was another open fishing boat, pretty much like my rental job, but slightly larger and with a somewhat bigger kicker hung on the stern. When we were within about thirty yards of each other, the other man cut his motor and I did the same. The boats ran on silently, losing speed until they lay still in the water, almost side by side.

I saw that my contact was a big, red-faced, city-fisherman type with sunglasses. He was wearing a straw hat that had a number of glittering lures hooked to the band. A fancy tackle box was open on the seat beside him. I was aware of his eyes studying me and my dog appraisingly from behind the dark lenses. The way the luck had been running on this job, I reflected grimly, it wouldn't surprise me a bit to discover that this man had gone to high school with the real Nystrom, or raised the real Prince Hannibal from a pup.

But if he had any doubts about our authenticity, he didn't show it. He just went smoothly into the act that had been prepared for us.

"Any luck?" he called.

"Not even a strike," I said, reading off the lines I had memorized in San Francisco. "How about you?"

He shook his head. "I guess they're just not biting." He plunged into the identification routine: "Isn't that a Labrador retriever? He's a beauty. What's his name?"

"Yes, he's a Lab," I said. "His name is Hank."

"No, I mean his full name. He's pedigreed, isn't he?"

These were the exact words Stottman should have used to me in the pet clinic in Pasco, only he hadn't got a chance to. They were almost the words Pat Bellman had used to me earlier the same day. I wondered if, knowing the required gibberish, she had perhaps paraphrased it deliberately to confuse me. But anyway, it was nice to have a contact proceed strictly according to plan, for a change.

I said, "His registered name is Avon's Prince Hannibal of Holgate." That took care of the identification part of the dialogue, and I went on casually, "Say, you don't happen to have a jug of water or something. I forgot to bring anything to drink and I'm parched."

"I've got some beer," he said. "Here, have one. . . . No, no, it's all right, I've got plenty more in the cooler. Well, I'm going to try that cove over there. Good luck."

"Same to you," I said. "Thanks for the beer."

The red-faced man yanked his motor into life once more. I pulled the cap off the beer bottle, and raised the bottle in a salute, which he answered with a wave of his hand. I drank deeply, watching him draw away, riding out of my life, I hoped, as rapidly as he'd come into it. What happened to him next was none of my concern. Mr. Smith's boys would presumably put a tail on him, hoping he'd lead them to other members of the local cell. Or maybe the Canadian authorities would take over. In any case, like Stottman and his partner, this man would be rounded up later, after we'd spotted the rest of Nystrom's contacts.

I wondered what the Canadians had worth spying on in this remote part of the north woods, but it wasn't really any of my business. I drank some beer and it was flat. Well, that figured. You can't keep capping and recapping a bottle without losing some of the fizz. I set the bottle

on the seat, pried the cork liner out of the cap, took out a little tinfoil wafer similar to the one I'd obtained from Stottman, and hid it in the second stud of Hank's collar. Then I carefully stuck the cork back into the cap, dropped the cap overboard, and watched it sink out of sight to where nobody would ever see that it had been tampered with. The beer I drank, flat or not, and the empty bottle I left in the bilge for the benefit of anybody who might have been watching through binoculars, from the shore.

When I reached the dock, it was just about dark. The proprietor and his wife were climbing into a big outboard runabout. They said they were heading up the lake to have dinner with some friends, and asked if I minded holding the fort alone. I said I didn't, and watched them disappear around the point. I whistled for Hank, and started for the cabin, and told him to shut up when he growled softly as we approached the door.

It was nice of him to warn me, but I'd set a few indicators about the door before I left, and I already knew somebody had been inside and very likely still was.

13 *I TOOK A CHANCE AND LET THEM* catch me by surprise. I mean, having no inkling of their presence—well, admitting none—I walked right into the trap, just like any of those handsome, brave, bone-headed movie operatives who are forever strolling casually into dark rooms and getting clobbered by sinister gents hiding behind doors.

This was another of the housekeeping cabins popular up here, and the room into which I sauntered innocently, dog at heel, was actually the kitchen. To my relief, the guy who stepped out behind me didn't actually clobber me. Maybe he was afraid of what the dog would do if he used open violence, or maybe he just didn't like hitting people over the head unnecessarily. Anyway, he merely told me to set down the fishing tackle I was carrying, very carefully, and put my hands up, which I did.

Then he hit a switch and the lights came on, dispelling the twilight gloom of the place. Nystrom Three appeared in the bedroom doorway, holding a familiar-looking .357 revolver—a mate to the one I was carrying—in a gingerly sort of way.

"Close the door quick!" he snapped at the man behind me. "Don't let the dog out!"

I heard the door being shut, but I didn't move or turn my head. There are advantages to dealing with amateurs, but there are disadvantages, too: they're much more likely than pros to blow your head off accidentally. You don't want to do anything to startle them as long as they're pointing firearms in your direction, since as a rule they've never bothered to learn how much trigger pressure—or how little—it takes to make their guns go boom.

I stood very still, therefore, while the man behind me reached around to get my .357 from its trick holster. Hank was sitting beside me, looking up and whining softly. He knew something was wrong, but he was a hunting dog. Just as the technical aspects of espionage were out of my line, so the K-9 routines were out of his. Pheasants he could handle, ducks were his meat, but these oddly behaving human beings baffled him. Instinct told him he should be doing something about them, but he'd had no training to tell him what.

Nystrom Three had stepped into the little kitchen. As his former role required—the role he seemed to have abandoned now—he was a tall, skinny character with whitish hair, probably bleached for the part just like mine. For two men who were supposed to look like the same man, we didn't look much like each other. At least I hoped I didn't have that nervous, shifty-eyed, slack-lipped look.

"Careful!" he snapped, as the other man moved behind me, doing something I couldn't see. "Don't take your eye off this guy! Don't forget, he's the bastard who stalked Mike Bird and killed him in cold blood: one shot from that hand-cannon at a hundred and fifty yards."

That eighty-yard shot was getting longer every day, I reflected wryly; but the attitude of the two men, particularly the one I could see, bothered me. I mean, I had

been operating on the assumption that they couldn't intend anything very drastic here, since I had collected only two of the five little tinfoil wafers Pat Bellman presumably had her eye on. Figuring that they needed me to get the other three, and knew it, I'd let myself be captured to see what kind of deal or arrangement they had in mind. Besides, I had plans for them, too, and this was the kind of discreet, off-the-road place I thought Mac would approve of. But there was a tenseness in the room that didn't bear out my reassuring theories.

The man behind me said, "Hell, if you're scared of the guy, let's finish him off now and get out of here with what we came for, before somebody comes."

I drew a long, cautious breath. Scratch another bright idea. Obviously there was something very wrong with my elaborate reasoning. The boys were playing for keeps.

"There won't be anybody," Nystrom Three said. "The other cabins are empty, and the people running the lodge have gone out for the evening. I heard them talking. And we're supposed to make this character tell us who he represents and what he's up to before we get rid of him. But first let's make sure he's got the stuff we want. Get the collar off the dog."

The man behind me laughed shortly. "That's sixty-seventy pounds of solid black pooch, and it's got big white teeth. You're supposed to be our dog expert; you get the collar off."

"Don't be a fool," the tall man said irritably. "It's a Labrador; it won't hurt you. They're very friendly dogs."

"Swell, you prove it. Show me how friendly it is. Take the collar off it."

"All right," Nystrom Three said contemptuously, "all right, if you're afraid, you watch the man. I'll handle the dog."

He stepped forward quickly and grabbed for Hank's collar. It was no way to approach a strange dog, gentle or not, particularly one that was already suspicious. The pup dodged, jumping back and to the side; and crouched there warily. The muscular tail slashed from side to side in a very unfriendly fashion. I was a little startled, myself, to see my happy young retriever pup suddenly transformed

into a reasonable facsimile of a junior-grade black panther about to spring.

"Friendly, is he?" the man behind me said softly. "With friends like that, who needs enemies?"

"Come here, you dumb mutt!" Nystrom Three was getting mad. He made another grab for the pup and got another lightninglike sideways jump for his pains. He took another step forward. Hank, trapped in a corner, showed his teeth in a snarl that, for his age, was really quite impressive. All along his back, the black hair stood on end; and when the tall man reached for him once more, he gave a sharp, savage little bark, and snapped at the outstretched hand warningly, indicating clearly that the next time he wouldn't miss.

Nystrom Three jumped back and yanked out the revolver he had put away.

The man behind me said quickly, "If you shoot, we'll have to get out of here fast. I thought you wanted to ask this guy some questions."

"All right, what's your suggestion?"

The unseen man nudged me with his gun. "It's his dog; let him take the collar off it. . . . Go on, friend. You see how it is. Either you take it off your live dog, or we'll take it off your dead dog. Make up your mind."

I made a show of hesitating, and shrugged resignedly. "All right, all right, don't hurt the pup. And go easy with that gunbarrel; you're bruising my kidneys. And I'm going to have to get down on my knees. Your animal-loving friend has got him all worked up. I've got to get down to his level to win back his confidence. Okay?"

"Okay, but don't try anything."

I knelt on the floor. "Hank," I said, holding out my hand, "Hank, come! Come on, there's a good dog. *Come!*"

The pup didn't like it. At the moment, the human race held no attraction for him, any part of it. Things were all wrong in this room and he knew it. Even I might have gone wrong while he wasn't looking. However, in the past week or so, he'd got into the habit of obeying me, and he'd had good training before that. He came.

When he reached me, I scratched his ears for a mo-

ment, speaking to him soothingly and telling him what a good dog he was. Then I unbuckled the black leather collar with the shiny studs. I held it for a moment, then abruptly flicked it across the room, sliding it along the linoleum right through the space between the tall man's feet.

"Hank!" I snapped.

Other hunting dogs may go on the command "fetch," but a retriever goes on his name. The pup went charging across the room after the collar, a black missile aimed straight at Nystrom Three.

Another characteristic of amateurs, and one I was counting on, is that while they're likely to shoot when they shouldn't, they almost never shoot when they should. The tall man didn't fire in the second during which he could have stopped the pup. The man behind me didn't fire either, in the fraction of a second it took me to pivot and cut his legs from under him. Then I had the little knife out of my pocket. I flipped it open one-handed and drove it home, once to disable and a second time to kill.

Across the room, there was a lot of scratching and several human gasps of fright. When I looked, Nystrom Three was on the floor, apparently sitting on top of the dog collar. He obviously thought he was being torn to shreds, and maybe he was, a little, but all the pup really wanted was the object he'd been sent after. In spite of earlier disagreements, he had nothing personal against the man, but he was a retriever and he'd been ordered to retrieve. Anybody who got in his way would just have to suffer the consequences.

He seemed to be trying to dig the collar out from under the fallen man, who seemed to be trying to get away from him, but they were working at cross purposes and neither of them was gaining. I suppose it was funny, but I wasn't laughing. For one thing, I had blood on my knuckles, and for another, the tall man was still waving the revolver around wildly, and there was no telling when it would go off and hurt somebody.

I started forward, but the mess untangled itself before I could get there. The pup got his collar and came trotting toward me proudly, and Nystrom Three sat up and

aimed the Colt .357 at me with the obvious intention of, at long last, using it for the purpose for which it was designed. I figured my chances, and they were pretty good. If he'd ever fired the gun before, the tremendous recoil of the Magnum cartridge had probably scared him into a permanent flinch that would keep him from hitting anything; and if he hadn't, well, it takes a good man, in a time of crisis, to make good his first shot from a totally unfamiliar weapon. I didn't have him figured for a good man, with a gun or anything else.

Still, nobody likes to be shot at. As I decided that a dive to the left, toward the bedroom door, was a slightly better gamble than a dive to the right and the kitchen sink, I felt the familiar, sweaty sensation of fear. After all, experienced agents *had* met their deaths at the hands of clumsy amateurs. It could happen to me. I braced myself to move as the gun lined up, waiting for the last possible moment, so that he'd miss his first shot and, I hoped, not recover from the outsize kick in time for a second.

But before I got to carry out this strategy the kitchen window broke with a dramatic crash. Amateur to the last, Nystrom Three stopped aiming at me and swung that way. I mean, a pro would first have shot the man under the gun and then turned to look.

I didn't look. Whoever had smashed the window could wait. Before the tall blond man in front of me could look back in my direction, I had him. I had his gun clamped firmly in my left hand; and I held it away from me while my right hand did the work with the little knife. I made quite sure of him, before looking toward the broken window.

Stottman's face, and his .25 caliber automatic, were watching me from the opening. The pudgy man and I stared at each other for a moment, while I caught my breath.

"You're pretty handy with that sticker," Stottman said calmly. "You're pretty handy with lots of things, for a mere courier. And it's funny that your dog doesn't know boats, isn't it? And that your girlfriend has been driving her yellow Caddy almost eight months, but you didn't recognize it. Don't you think that's funny, Mr. Nystrom?"

It was obvious that he'd found the answers for which he had been searching. He had enough to go on now, and he'd never give up until he'd demonstrated to his superiors that I was not the man they'd sent on this mission. There was nothing else to do, so I shot him through the head with the dead man's gun, left-handed, before he could pull the trigger of his little pocket pistol.

14 WHEN THINGS HAD SETTLED

down a bit—in my mind, at least—I became aware of something nudging me in the side as I crouched against the wall, watching the door and windows and listening intently, knowing I wasn't out of trouble yet. After all, Stottman had had a partner, and until I learned what Pete-the-Indian was up to, I couldn't afford to relax.

The bump in my side came again. I looked and saw the black pup with the collar still in his mouth. He was sitting beside me, trying to deliver it stylishly to hand as he'd been taught, instead of just dropping it at my feet. His expression said what the hell, I'd sent him for this lousy strap, wasn't I ever going to take it from him?

I drew a long breath, took the collar, and buckled it around his neck. It was very quiet in the cabin after the deafening report of the .357 Magnum. At least I thought it was quiet, but I realized that if there were any significant noises, hostile or otherwise, I probably couldn't hear them, the way my ears were ringing. It's a bad enough gun to fire outdoors; indoors it's just too damn loud. I patted the pup and looked him over for damage.

"Everything okay, Prince Hannibal?" I asked.

He grinned at me and swung his big tail back and forth cheerfully by way of answer. As far as he was concerned, everything was fine. Something had been badly wrong here, but it had got fixed. Well, I couldn't argue with that. It had got fixed, all right.

I rose and looked grimly down at Nystrom Three for a moment. Then I walked over and looked at the other

man, for whom I'd never even concocted a name. I raised him gently with my foot so I could see his face. It seemed too bad to knife a man to death and walk off without ever really seeing what he looked like.

His face was just the face of a dead man. I got my revolver from his jacket pocket. The pup wanted to sniff the blood and was offended when I called him off sharply; he couldn't see that he'd done anything to get mad about.

I went to the door and listened some more, doing a better job of it as my hearing returned to normal. I still couldn't hear anything except the splashing of little waves down at the boat docks. Of course, dealing with an Indian, I most likely wouldn't hear him until he was on top of me, if he came. But the pup, whose senses were a lot sharper than mine, didn't seem to detect anything out in the dark worth warning me about.

I took the chance, and slipped out the door, accompanied by my black, four-legged shadow. I made a swing around the premises, finding nobody. It was a quiet night, with only a light breeze blowing, but if the shot had been heard at any of the other resorts along the lake, it hadn't aroused enough curiosity to lead to action. Well, that's often the case with a single shot, particularly one muffled inside four walls. People outside aren't quite sure they heard it in the first place, so they just listen briefly and, if the sound is not repeated, forget about it.

At last I went over to look at Stottman where he lay outside the kitchen window, still clutching his toy pistol. It wasn't as bad as I'd anticipated. Sometimes, with a head shot, those souped-up Magnum loads will blow a man's brains right out the back of his skull, but this bullet had simply done its work without any spectacular frills. Since there was no mess to amount to anything, it was feasible for me to consider changing the overall picture—retouching it judiciously, so to speak—in the interest of international diplomacy.

But first I regarded the plump man for a moment, with a vague sense of embarrassment. I mean, I hadn't dealt quite fairly with him. I'd taken advantage of him. I'd known that he'd hesitate before shooting me because there were so many things about me that he still wanted to find

out; while there had been nothing about him that I really needed to learn. Well, fairness is not a principle that rates very highly in our profession.

I picked him up, after putting his little pistol back into his pocket, and carried him inside. Dragging him would have been easier, but I didn't want to plow up the ground unnecessarily. I arranged him artistically on the kitchen linoleum and placed my bloody knife in his hand. I hated to leave it—it had been given to me by a woman, now dead, who'd once meant a good deal to me—but this was no time for sentimentality. The .357 revolver with one fired cartridge in the cylinder, belonging to Nystrom Three, I wiped clean of my fingerprints and put into the hand of its owner, who had a holster to match.

The idea I was trying to convey, of course, was that Stottman had knifed the other two men in the room, but one had managed to shoot him before dying. It wasn't watertight by any means. A paraffin test, for instance, would probably show that Nystrom Three hadn't been shooting any guns lately. There was a broken window to explain, and perhaps some blood spots on the ground outside. By the time the bodies were discovered and the proprietors were questioned there would also be, I hoped, a mystery man who couldn't be found; a totally vanished tall character with a dog, who'd rented the cabin for the night and then driven off in the camper rig leaving carnage behind him.

Any good cop who wanted the right answer could find it if he looked, but that wasn't the point. I was arranging a nice, safe, discreet answer for a cop under orders not to look.

I went into the bedroom to get my belongings. Since I hadn't unpacked, except to dig out some fishing gear, it didn't take long. I was just starting for the kitchen, bag in hand, when the pup growled softly, the hackles rising along his back. I set down my duffel bag with extreme care, and drew the short-barreled Colt revolver from under my waistband.

I heard the outside door swing open slowly. Then I heard a startled and quite audible feminine gasp of shock and dismay.

When I stepped into the doorway between the two rooms, Pat Bellman was standing just inside the other door. She was wearing the same or another pair of faded jeans, a short cowboy jacket of the same durable material, and some kind of a checked cotton shirt, red and white. She was standing there as if she'd been suddenly struck by paralysis, very pale, with a look of horror on her face as she stared at the small, crowded, bloody battlefield before her.

"That's my girl," I said. She didn't even look up at the sound of my voice; she just kept on staring. I went on: "Stay just like that. Don't move a muscle, or the body-count will rise to four practically instantaneously."

She didn't move. I went over and checked her for weapons. There weren't any, or, if there were, they were small and well hidden. When I stopped in front of her, she raised her eyes slowly to my face, and licked her colorless lips.

"You . . . you killed them!"

"Don't say that," I protested, hurt. "Here I've just gone to a lot of trouble to make it look as if they killed each other. . . ."

"You *killed* them!" she whispered, unheeding. "All of them! Just like you killed Mike Bird. What kind of a murdering monster are you?" Her voice rose in a shrill, hysterical way on the last words.

I looked down at her for a moment. I'd been kind of taken with her for a while, I remembered, but it seemed a long time ago. Now I was, to say the least, disenchanted with her; and I guess a reaction of sorts was setting in. Even in my line of work, three dead men in less than a minute is a shade over the quota. Anyway, I obviously had to do something fast to keep her from throwing a noisy wingding in here. I'll admit I welcomed the excuse.

I changed my revolver from my right hand to my left, drew back the hand thus freed, and slapped her face, once, just about as hard as I could without breaking my hand or her neck. She staggered aside and almost fell over the nameless man lying face down nearby. She caught herself, gagged, and moved away from the corpse, putting a belated hand to her cheek.

"You hypocritical little phony!" I was surprised to hear that my own voice was noticeably shaky. Like I say, reaction. I went on harshly: "First you smiled at me and sent me out to where your sniper was waiting to shoot me down! When that failed, you dispatched a couple of other boys to take care of me. . . . Oh, yes, they made it quite clear what their orders were! And then, for God's sake, *then*, after trying twice to have me killed, you have the unmitigated, gold-plated gall to come in here and complain because all your inefficient assassins bungled their jobs and got themselves dead! Just what kind of monster are *you*, Skinny?"

She licked her pale lips once more, not looking at me directly. "I never thought . . . we never expected . . ."

"What? That somebody might object to being murdered for your convenience?"

"It was . . . it was such a lot of money." Her voice was almost inaudible. "*Such* a lot of money. Fifty thousand dollars. And we thought it would be . . . would be kind of fun. Exciting."

It wasn't the same old grim racket anymore, I reflected sourly. All kinds of people were taking it up for kicks. Or pretending to.

I asked. "Who was going to pay you all this money?"

She didn't seem to hear me. She said in a choked voice: "Fun! Oh, my God! They're dead! They're all *dead*, and it was all my idea. But I never dreamed . . . "

Her face changed abruptly. She gulped, and turned toward the door in sudden distress. Her problem was obvious, and I stepped aside and let her stumble out into the dark. The sounds she made out there were quite convincing, so I took advantage of her momentary helplessness to retrieve my bag, tackle box, and fishing rod. I made sure I'd left nothing behind that I didn't want to leave, turned out the lights, and locked the door. When I came to Pat Bellman, she was still doubled up with cramps, but they weren't producing much anymore. I waited for her to recover. At last she fumbled in her pants pocket for a Kleenex and wiped her mouth and turned to face me.

"Damn you," she said shakily. "Damn you, you didn't have to stand there watching!"

I said, "Skinny, cut it out. Of course I had to stand there watching. And you'll lay off the proud-lady routine or I'll smack your face again."

She licked her lips, "What do you mean?"

"I mean, you'd better get things perfectly clear, Miss Bellman. You're not a fine lady who can demand respect and consideration from the gentlemen around her. You're not a nice girl who can expect the nice boys to look the other way politely while she upchucks her dinner. You're a murdering bitch who's been caught in the act, and I'm the guy you tried to murder—or have murdered. Remember that, and conduct yourself accordingly, and maybe we'll get along without any more slugging or shooting. Where's your car?"

She hesitated, apparently considering some kind of argument or protest, but she decided against it. "Back along the dirt road about a mile and a half. I ran it off into the woods where it couldn't be seen."

"Let's hope you did a good job, so it'll still be here when you come back for it. If you come back."

"What . . . what are you going to do with me?"

I said, "Whatever's necessary to make you tell me about fifty grand, and the people who were willing to pay it, and what they thought they were buying for it." She started to speak, and I interrupted her: "But not here."

I led her to the truck. Thirty minutes later we were on the main highway heading west toward Prince Rupert and the coast.

15 *THE PHONE BOOTH WAS PRETTY* exposed, standing near the highway in the bare dirt parking area serving a small roadside restaurant, now closed for the night. However, I didn't have much choice. I wanted to get a warning message through as soon as possible, now that we were a reasonable distance from the

scene of my latest crimes, and this was the only facility we'd encountered in over an hour. Up ahead, according to my information, were some sixty miles of construction work, where the highway through the coastal mountains, formerly a gravel road, was being rebuilt and paved.

My chances of finding any kind of a suitable communications center along the torn-up stretch didn't seem promising; and while Mr. Smith's fine young men were supposed to be keeping a cautious watch over me and reporting my progress and my problems, I never like to count on other outfits to do things right if I can get our own people on the job. After everything that had happened tonight, if I loused up the mission, it didn't seem likely that it would be on account of a mere phone call.

I drove into the lot, therefore, and jockeyed the rig around until I could more or less cover both cab doors from the booth. The girl beside me stirred uneasily.

"What are you doing?" she asked.

"Just making sure I can nail you if you make a break while I'm on the phone." I looked at her and put a mean grin on my face. "You remember that guy back there with the hole in his head? I hope you appreciate that I made that shot left-handed—and while he had the drop on me, or thought he had. I'm even better with my right hand. Give it a try if you like. I'll bet you don't make ten yards, measuring from the sill of the car door to the nearest point of your body, wherever it falls."

I waited, but she made no response, and I went over to the booth and called our relay man in Vancouver, keeping an eye on the truck and the highway at the same time, as best I could.

When Vancouver answered I said, "Eric here. Three packages, perishable. Francois Lake. McAllister Lodge, Cabin Number One. Got it?"

"Got it. Sounds like you've been a busy little man. What do you want, a pickup-and-disposal squad?"

"Not if it can be avoided. If they just disappear, people will ask questions I'd rather not have to answer. How much international pressure can we apply through channels? It would be very nice if the local authorities could give out that the boys obviously killed each other off, for

reasons unknown. I've got it set up to look that way, more or less. A mystery man who rented the cabin is being sought for questioning, but not very hard, since it's all cut and dried. Can do?"

"I'll forward your recommendation. It's supposed to be a hands-across-the-border job, so maybe we can swing it for you. Anything else?"

"Yes. What the hell is NCS?"

The man in Vancouver laughed. "If I knew that, I certainly wouldn't blab it over the phone. The Northwest Coastal System is one of the biggest secrets on this continent since the Manhattan project."

"Sure," I said. "A secret everybody knows except the poor suckers trying to protect it, like us."

"Not me, friend," said the man in Vancouver. "And not you. Protecting systems is other people's work. We're protecting a man, remember?"

"Keep talking."

"Never mind NCS. We want the Woodman, and we want him dead; dead enough so that he can't fire his little rifle a few months from now at a very well-known gent— exact identity not yet determined—about to assume a very important office. It's been a rough summer and we'd hate to see a worse autumn. This country just can't take any more snipers mowing down any more popular citizens. If it happens while election hysteria is still upon us, indications are that the lid will blow off. Our job—your job—is to head the Woodman off at the pass, and to hell with NCS. You don't have to announce this to Mr. Smith and his merry men, but on the other hand, you don't want to forget it for a moment. Message received?"

"Received and understood," I said. I'd been about to ask a silly question about the mysterious Woodman to whom he'd referred, but when he'd repeated the nickname I'd caught on: it was just one of the in-jokes that circulate through an organization like ours, easy enough to dig if you remembered that wood translates to *Holz* in German. I just said, to put it on the official record: "In other words, I have now been instructed that chopping the Woodman down to size takes priority over dealing with secret information no matter how priceless and irreplaceable."

"You have been so instructed. Sleep well."

"And pleasant dreams to you," I said. "Eric out."

I hung up. No cars had passed on the highway, and Pat Bellman hadn't moved. I got back on the seat beside her and drove off, keeping an eye on the big, truck-type mirror on my left, the one outside the cab she couldn't see me watching. No lights appeared in the glass, but I kept catching ghostly hints of movement far back on the road behind us. Well, that figured.

I mean, the girl beside me had seemed like a very competent person when I'd first met her in Pasco. She'd set me up for murder with cold-blooded efficiency. Yet tonight she'd treated me to a brainless-ingenue performance that would have shamed a high-school melodrama. She'd walked in on me too carelessly, acted too shocked and stunned by the gory scene in the cottage, and lost her dinner too dramatically.

Lots of girls in the business can blush and weep and faint on demand. A determined young lady, trying to create an impression of total helplessness, might even manage to puke as required. I hadn't believed her act even before I'd spotted a car running dark behind us. Now the question was: just what did she and her accomplice have in mind for me, and where did they intend to try it? It occurred to me that there was no reason for me to await their pleasure.

I put my foot on the brake as a roadside sign flashed into the headlights, advising of a campground ahead. Pat Bellman glanced at me quickly but did not speak.

"Chow time," I said. "Your friends kind of interfered with my dinner and I'm getting hungry."

The camp turned out to be located on a fair-sized stream. I swung in, found a suitable parking space along the bank, and placed the rig so it was reasonably level. There were no other truck-type campers here, and no trailers or tents, either. We had the place to ourselves.

I escorted Pat to the rear of the camper, hitched the pup to a chain outside, and ushered the girl into the little cabin. There was a dinette forward that converted to a double bed, if you needed a double bed. Aft, stove and refrigerator faced sink and clothes closet across a narrow

aisle. A space heater, and various racks and lockers, were ingeniously fitted into the remaining space.

Pat made her way forward and sat down on one of the dinette seats, shrugging off her denim jacket. I sat down to light the stove. Nystrom's choice of camper was decidedly limited in headroom, perhaps on the theory that a man six-four is bound to bump his head, anyway, so he might as well get a low unit, easy to drive, and learn to do his indoors chores sitting down. After a little, as I juggled pots and pans and groceries, the girl on the other side of the booth looked up.

"You're going to kill me, too, aren't you?" she said dully. "Just as you killed all the others. My God, they're all dead, all of them! I'm the only one left. . . . "

Outside, as if to call her a liar, Hank hit the end of his chain suddenly, shaking the camper. I looked around, putting a frown on my face. At the edge of my vision, I was aware of Pat Bellman grasping the edge of the dinette table tightly, starting to push herself up. She was obviously trying to think of some way of keeping me from going out there, or looking out. Then she forced herself to relax, with an obvious effort.

I rose deliberately and went to the door, crouching to avoid the low ceiling. I looked out at the black pup, almost invisible at the end of his shiny, galvanized chain.

"What's the matter, Hank?" I called loudly. "You got nightmares or something? Lie down and go to sleep."

I saw that he was eating something. As I watched, he licked up some invisible scraps from the ground in front of him. Considering the contents of the collar he was wearing, it was the obvious play, but that didn't make it any easier to take. I realized that I'd become quite fond of the mutt in the week or so we'd been together. I reminded myself that it was always a mistake to get sentimentally involved with your partner in a mission; and that applied whether your partner was human or animal.

"You be quiet out there, hear?" I said, deliberately turning my back on the pup and his unauthorized midnight snack, not to mention the stuff he had around his neck. The priorities had been assigned. We were protecting a man, not a system—and not a dog, either.

I saw Pat Bellman's face go smooth with relief as I pulled the door shut behind me. I stopped to fiddle with the stove, to give her time to get her expressions sorted out, before I returned to my seat facing her. Outside, the pup jangled his chain once more, either picking up a new tidbit or cleaning up the final scraps of the one he'd just swallowed. I looked at the girl across the table; the girl who'd claimed to be a dog-lover, who'd already had one good Labrador shot, along with his master.

"Hi, Skinny," I said. "Under other circumstances, this would be nice and cozy, don't you think?"

She didn't smile. "What's your name?" she asked. "What's your real name? I think I'm entitled to know that before you kill me. And who you're working for."

"The name is Nystrom," I said. "Until the job is finished, that's my real name. And I work for a man in Washington whose name wouldn't mean anything to you."

"Are you trying to make me think you're employed by the U.S. government? A killer like you? I don't believe it!"

"That's your privilege," I said. "How do you like your eggs?"

"What?"

"Eggs."

"Oh, I couldn't. . . . Well, all right. Sunny-side up. Two. And three strips of that bacon. And black coffee, lots of black coffee. And some toast if you've got it. Lots of toast." Apparently she felt the need to explain her sudden hunger, because she laughed brightly. "You've kept me so busy chasing you that I've hardly had time to eat. I guess my last real meal was the one you bought me in Pasco. I really shouldn't have let you pick up that check, should I? After all, it was my invitation."

From not talking at all, she was now beginning to talk too much. I saw her steal a glance at her wristwatch and look up quickly, clearly hoping I hadn't caught her at it.

"If I were to try to talk you into sparing my life," she said, "If I were to try, where should I start?"

"I told you where. I'd like to know who's offered you fifty grand for what." I glanced at my own watch as I

turned toward the stove. The time was a few minutes after ten, if it mattered, and apparently it did. I went on, "Oh, and there's another question I'd like an answer to. Why did you send your boys after me tonight?"

"What do you mean?"

"Don't act stupid, Skinny. You know I've made only two of my scheduled five contacts. Yet you sent a couple of fumble-fingered goons to grab the dog collar tonight instead of waiting until it held all the information you wanted. They were going to grab it, they were going to question me, and then they were going to dispose of me. It seems like a pretty shortsighted performance. Who was going to get the rest of the stuff for you if you had me killed?"

"But I wasn't really . . ." She stopped. "I mean, I didn't really . . ."

"You didn't really what?"

"They weren't *really* trying to kill you."

I said, "I was there. I heard what they said."

"They were just supposed to *talk* as if they were going to kill you. To scare you. And then I'd have come in and stopped them and you'd have been grateful and . . ." She grimaced. "All right, maybe it was silly. But that's the way I was told to do it. You're not the only one operating under orders, Mr. Nystrom, or whatever your real name is."

"I see," I said. "So you'd been instructed to grab the available stuff now, and then try to get me to cooperate gratefully to bring you the rest, because you'd saved me from your terrible thugs." I laughed. "Whose brainwave was that?"

"I can't tell you."

"Sure you can."

"He . . . he'll kill me if I talk."

I put a plate down in front of her. "I'm right here, sweetheart, dangerous old me. Where's this other guy? What can he do to you that I can't?" I set my own plate on the table, dumped a fistful of implements between us, and sat down. "Dig in," I said.

She took a bite, and started to speak, and stopped. We ate in silence. Not until she had cleaned off her plate

thoroughly did she look up and say. "He was Chinese. A Chinaman named Soo."

I regarded her small tomboy face across the table. She was telling the truth now, and I thought I knew why. She was telling the truth because for some reason she had to keep me talking in here for a certain length of time, and if I caught her in a lie I might get annoyed enough to break off the conversation. What she'd said was highly interesting. I guess I should have felt kind of vindicated and triumphant. After all, I'd suggested the possibility of Chinese involvement to Libby Meredith, who hadn't seemed very impressed by my logic. But the fact that my guess had proved correct didn't intrigue me as much, at the moment, as the name that had been mentioned.

"Soo?" I said. "Kind of a stout Charlie Chan type with a precise way of speaking English?"

"Yes, do you know him?"

"We met over in Hawaii a year or so back. If it's the same Soo. Did he by any chance tell you that his name wasn't really Soo, but it would do for purposes of reference?"

"Why . . .why, yes, that's exactly what he said! It must be the same man. What was he doing in Hawaii?"

"Just about the same as he seems to have been doing in San Francisco or wherever you met him: making trouble for decadent capitalist nations like the U. S. of A. for the benefit of a certain People's Republic of the Orient." I grinned. "I saved his life out there, in a manner of speaking, but I don't suppose the debt really weighs on him. Well, well. Good old Peking Soo. With fifty grand to shell out for what?"

"For information on the Northwest Coastal System, naturally."

"How did you happen to meet him?"

"He looked me up. He'd heard of me from some characters I'd met, political types."

"I don't suppose I have to ask what brand of politics."

She shrugged. "There's no bore as deadly as a Marxist bore. We didn't have any more to do with them than we could help. But they sicked Mr. Soo on us."

"We?" I said. "Us?"

She hesitated. "At the University, I'd got to know some pretty bright people, several of whom later wound up working in some pretty hush installations. In fact, there was a kind of group of us that used to get together and experiment with . . . well, never mind that. It was just experimental. We weren't hooked or anything, but you like to try anything once. Anyway, even after we all graduated, we'd still meet from time to time, those of us who could make it."

"Did Mr. Soo use your experiments for blackmail?"

"Oh, no. Nothing like that. He just laughed his slick laugh and said he enjoyed meeting young people with inquiring minds. And then he started dropping hints . . ." She moved her shoulders awkwardly once more. "Of course, some of the characters I'm talking about, the bright people, turned out to be totally square about things like security and loyalty and patriotism, real conformist jerks. I was kind of surprised. I mean, you know a guy for years and you still don't know how he's going to react to . . ."

"To treason?" I said.

She made a sharp little gesture. "Why make with the loaded words? Anyway, the rest of us . . . well, as far as we're concerned, that kind of stuff is strictly for laughs these days. What's to betray, what's to be loyal to, Nystrom? You start getting an attack of ideals about something, peace for instance, and a cop comes and beats you over the head with a club, right? And these were pretty bright people, too bright to go around demonstrating in the streets and getting their brains knocked out. Even if you take your ideals that seriously, why buck city hall when you can dig the foundations right out from under it and get paid for doing it?"

I said, "Did you work this out in advance, or did it take Mr. Soo to help you see the light?"

She said sharply, "We didn't need any help to see that things were all wrong and getting worse! It's fairly obvious, isn't it, that the older people who've been running things have made a mess of them and just won't admit it . . . "

I said, "Personally, I don't trust anybody under thirty. But then, I don't trust anybody over thirty, either."

"Funny!" she said bitterly. "That's all people like you can do when challenged: make jokes!"

I caught that quick sneaky glance at the watch once more as I refilled the coffee cups. It would have been nice to know how much time we had to kill and what was supposed to happen when it was up. Obviously she was stalling desperately, trotting out all the youth-versus-age and world-we-never-made clichés and rationalizations; as well as all the excuses and justifications they always have, young or old, for selling out.

I'm not saying that some of her points weren't valid. I'm just saying that it gets kind of monotonous, to a man in my line of work, the way they've always got it worked out so neatly, all the clever folk, when they hand the stuff over to the enemy—whatever it may be and whoever he may be—and walk off with the cash.

Somehow, they're always saving the world by betraying a piece of it. I bet myself that in a minute this girl would come up with some ingenious twist that would clinch the argument, proving that actually she and her friends had been working in behalf of the human race as a whole, and that the fifty grand was just incidental to the whole shining scheme of world improvement.

But she fooled me. She said, "We don't make jokes. We don't think it's funny, Nystrom. We think it's a dirty, fouled-up mess that's been left us, and there just isn't a damn thing that can be done about it now. It's too late now, so we might as well make a little money any way we can and have a few kicks while we can, before the whole thing blows up with us . . . "

Well, you can take a few more yards of that and cut it to fit. It was too bad in a way. I have some sympathy for the misguided young coffee-shop intellectuals, but they don't really tug at my heartstrings. But I couldn't help remembering this girl at the river with a fishing rod in her hand. Whether or not it had been an act for my benefit that particular morning, at some time she must have been truly fond of the outdoors to have learned the techniques so well. She undoubtedly had other talents and virtues;

she might be straightened out if somebody wanted to take the time and trouble—and could talk the California police into overlooking an accessory-to-murder charge. Neither was likely. She might be worth saving, but nobody was going to bother. Certainly I wasn't. Saving young doomsday cynics from themselves wasn't what I'd been sent up here for. Quite the contrary.

I caught a glimpse of my watch as I reached for the coffeepot once more. I was surprised to see that it read well past eleven. We'd been playing her delaying game for more than an hour. It should be enough, I decided. Anyway, I'd learned what I wanted to know, as much of it as I could expect to get from her, and I was tired of games. I didn't particularly want to see her go into the sexy Mata Hari act I figured had to come next because it practically always does.

I refilled our cups once more, put the pot back on the stove, and said, "Actually, I may not have to murder anybody else tonight, if I can persuade you to show some sense for a change."

Her eyes widened slightly. "What do you mean?"

"Bellman, I'm a pro," I said. "Three of your friends have already died trying to take me. They haven't even come close." This wasn't quite true—it had been close enough in that cabin before Stottman took a hand—but we weren't dealing with truth here. I went on harshly: "Why don't you get smart before it happens to you?"

She licked her lips. "I . . . I don't understand. . . ."

"Sure you do. You know exactly what I'm talking about. Now listen closely. I've got orders concerning you, but I'm allowed some discretion. Suppose you give me your word that you'll beat it out of here and go straight home without talking to anybody, taking your friend outside with you . . ."

She was pretty good. She didn't really start; she just sat very, very still for a moment, holding in the start that wanted to betray her. After a brief delay, she managed to put a puzzled frown on her face.

"My friend? I don't know what you mean!"

I went on as if she hadn't spoken. "Of course, the whole deal depends on what he fed my dog. I suppose that's why

you've been stalling, to give it time to take effect. If it was something like strychnine, to hell with both of you. But if it was just a harmless knockout drug to let him get that collar, we can work it out. Signal your boy to come in here unarmed, with his hands up, bringing the collar with him. Promise you won't talk, and tell me what the pup got and what the antidote is. I'm kind of fond of him; besides, I'm going to need him for identification again, farther up the line. You do that, and I'll forget my orders and turn you both loose." I looked at her across the table. "Well, what do you say?"

She was back in control once more. She gave me the straight, level, clear-eyed look of the accomplished liar. "Honest, I don't know what you're talking about! There were only the four of us, and three are dead. I'm right here. Who's left to be prowling around outside? You're just imagining things."

It was what I'd expected, of course, but it was still too bad. If she'd accepted the deal, I'd have been stuck with it. Maybe I'd even wanted to be stuck with it, a little.

"Sure," I said. I rose and pulled out the short-barreled Colt revolver. "Sure. So let's go out there and look. If I'm wrong, we'll find nothing but an empty campground and a sleeping pup. . . . After you, Miss Bellman."

I gestured with the gun. With her eyes on the weapon, not speaking, she rose stiffly and moved to the door and looked back. I nodded for her to open it, and she did.

16 THE NIGHT WAS CLEAR AND CALM

and moonless. The stars were bright enough up there, but they didn't give much light down here. I let the girl stand in the illuminated doorway for a moment, and showed myself close behind her, to make the situation clear to anyone outside. Then I switched out the camper lights.

Pat Bellman started to look around. I said, a little more loudly than would have been necessary if I'd been speaking to her alone, which I wasn't: "Eyes front, doll!

103

straight ahead now and no tricks. The first twig that snaps, the first shadow that moves, and this .357 blows a hole right through you, back to front."

In ordinary circumstances, against professional opposition, this would have been a waste of good menace. All pros are expendable, and a gun in the back of one means nothing to another with a job to do. But I was gambling that I still had one more amateur to deal with, confused by unprofessional notions of comradeship and loyalty.

If I was wrong—if, for instance, Mr. Soo had decided to come up here and intervene personally—I was apt to be shot very dead very soon. That I'd probably take the girl with me would be of no consequence to Mr. Soo; he could spare an occidental female or two. But in my favor was the fact that any operative of Mr. Soo's caliber, having got what he came for, as by this time he should have, wouldn't hang around to perform a sentimental rescue of an irrelevant blonde.

The girl in front of me stepped to the ground and wriggled uncomfortably against the pressure of the gun barrel as I stayed right with her.

"Really, you're being unnecessarily melodramatic."

"Hank," I called, ignoring her. "Wake up, pup. Hank!"

There was no response. Pat Bellman said, "Maybe he slipped his collar and ran off."

"Sure," I said. "Like your imaginary bitch opened her kennel door. He slipped his collar, all right, or it was slipped. But I don't think he ran off. Go straight ahead along the chain now. . . . "

The galvanized chain was a pale streak along the ground. I couldn't see anything at the end of it, but a black dog is hard to see against a dark background on a dark night. Then the chain ended.

"Stop right there," I said, bending down cautiously to examine the empty snaphook. I dropped it, and straightened up. I said harshly, "You've got one more chance. Call in your boy, fast!"

"I told you, there's nobody. . . . Wait a minute, there's your dog! On the ground way over there. At least there's something black. . . . Oh!"

Moving off, she stumbled over something on the ground:

the black pup, not off where she'd pointed, but right near the end of the chain where he'd logically be and where, I had no doubt, she had seen him plainly. But it gave her an excuse to lose her balance and fall, or pretend to fall. Actually, it was a little more than a fall, it was a kind of tumbling somersault, as she went diving over the shadowy form on the ground headfirst, lit on one shoulder, and kept rolling.

It was prettily done. It showed some nice gymnastic training. There were only two or three different split seconds in which I could have drilled her. However, she wasn't the one I wanted at the moment. She had no gun; she'd keep. And I didn't want to produce any bright Magnum muzzle-flashes for her associate to zero in on.

She was calling as she rolled: "All right, Wally! Now!"

The gun opened up from the bushes to the left, near the creek, but I've had a little training, too, and I was already flat on the ground, with my face well down, so there was nothing but shadows for Wally to shoot at. His bullets—small ones, perhaps .22s—pecked at the dirt off to one side. An occasional slug found a pebble to glance off and went screaming away into the distance. Meanwhile I was aware that Pat Bellman had found her feet and was sprinting in the direction of the highway.

Without raising my head and displaying my white face for a target, I got Wally located by the fireworks he kept setting off. I could make out his white face through the bushes. He seemed to be wearing a white shirt as well. Anyone who goes out to commit murder at night wearing white, must leave half his marbles at home.

He tried still another couple of shots, no closer. Then I heard him changing clips over there and jacking home a cartridge. I suppose I could have tried for him while he was momentarily out of action, but shooting through brush is chancy business with any gun, even a .357. I just lay there and waited him out. A little distance away, I heard a car door open.

"Come on, Wally! That's enough. Bring the keys!" Pat Bellman called.

Wally waited a little longer. Then he started to crawl away. Done right, belly-crawling is no fun. Pretty soon

he was up on hands and knees, which is easier and faster but still hard work and painful. Having covered a total of about ten yards, roughly what I'd figured him good for, he gave up the struggle and got up to run, giving me the broad, white, clear target for which I'd been waiting.

I shot once and went over and took the dog collar and a bunch of keys out of his pocket. I stood up again, brushed the dust and pine needles off my clothes, and walked toward the parked car gleaming dully near the campground entrance. As I came closer, I saw it was the little fastback Ford I'd seen before. Pat Bellman had the hood up. She was groping for something in the engine compartment, presumably a spare key.

"Try these," I said, tossing her the bunch I'd taken from Wally.

She whirled to face me, missing the catch. As a matter of fact, she didn't even make an effort. The keys hit the fender of the Mustang with a clanking sound, and fell to the ground, jingling softly.

"Pick them up," I said. She didn't move. I said, "Be your age, Bellman. If I shoot you, will it hurt any more bending over than standing up straight?"

"You killed him!" she breathed. "You killed him, too! You shot him in the *back!*"

I said, "Oh, for Christ's sake! I didn't notice him being particular about which way I was turned when he opened up on me."

"You . . . you *assassin!*"

"That's just about enough of that," I said. "I'm getting a wee bit tired of having you call me names every damn time you set me up for murder and I shoot my way clear."

"He wasn't trying to kill you! We've got orders not to kill you, don't you understand? He was just covering for me, so I could get away!"

It wasn't a very plausible story, but for various reasons I was inclined to believe her. Not that it mattered, as far as my conscience was concerned. There are too many people in the world who really deserve my sympathy for me to waste any of it on characters who get cute with firearms.

I said, "So next time let me in on the gag, and maybe nobody'll get hurt. When I'm shot at, I shoot back. I gave you a chance to stop it—several chances—but you had to play it your way. Now pick up those keys. Fine. Put them in your pocket. Now come over here and carry the pup into the camper for me. Never mind *him!* He's dead; I checked. You can't do anything for him." She hesitated by the dim black shape of the dog. "Gently now," I said. "Pick him up. You had him poisoned. The least you can do is carry him."

Inside the trailer, I had her put the pup on one of the dinette seats. She was breathing deeply when she turned back to look at me. Even a young Labrador is a hefty load for a girl. I saw that Hank was breathing, too, not deeply, not well, but enough to show that the systems were still functioning and might be persuaded to continue to do so. On the whole, I reflected, it had been a successful operation. I had used the pup and the collar for bait, and I'd caught my fish and got my bait back.

I was aware that the girl was watching me steadily. I met her eyes. After a moment, the defiance seemed to go out of her all at once, leaving her looking pale and tired and defeated.

"You'd better give me something to cover him with," she said. "He should be kept warm."

"Sure." I dragged some bedding out of a locker and gave it to her. She put it over the unconscious pup. I heard her laugh oddly and I asked, "What's funny?"

"Making this fuss over a dog, when there's a man lying dead outside."

"To hell with that," I said. "This pup's a lot better at his specialty than your man was at what he was trying to do."

"And you're the real expert, aren't you?" Some of the old resentment was back in her voice.

"Yes, ma'am," I said. "It happens to be my profession."

"I'd be ashamed to admit it!"

"Cut it out, Bellman," I said. "You've been trying hard enough to horn in on my racket. You're just knocking it

because you flopped. Now tell me what the pup's got in him, and how much."

She hesitated, as if she wanted to continue the argument; then she shrugged and said, "It isn't poison. If it were strychnine or arsenic, you'd have heard him, wouldn't you? They're painful. You should know that much, an expert like you."

"There's always cyanide," I said. "And all kinds of quick and fancy death drugs. Mr. Soo would have a good supply."

"Mr. Soo wasn't handy," she said. "Mr. Soo was at the other end of a telephone wire. We just used what we had. Sleeping pills. Nembutal, to be specific, about twelve grains, one grain for each five pounds of body weight. It's slow, over an hour, even on a young dog. That's why . . . why I had to keep prattling away in here like a damn fool."

I said, "Twelve grains; eight yellow-jackets. That's quite a dose. Will he live?"

"If there's nothing organically wrong with him otherwise. But it might be better if you got him to a vet and had him given an analeptic, a respiratory stimulant."

"The nearest vet's probably in Prince Rupert, on the coast. You seem to know a lot about veterinary medicine yourself."

"I told you, I have a lot of bright friends. When I knew I was going to have to do this, I called one who's a practicing DVM nowadays. The stuff you want is called Mikedimide. It should bring him around."

"Sure."

She drew herself up, as well as she could inside the camper. "And now . . . and now you'd better finish your assignment, hadn't you? Now you'll have got us all, just like you were ordered, all five of us, as soon as you kill me."

I regarded her for a moment. People give a lot of importance to things like political opinions and moral attitudes and actions good and bad, and no matter which of these you used for a standard, this girl was a total loss. I mean, she just wasn't worth preserving by any rational scale of values. She'd even tried to have me killed, at least

once and maybe three times. I should have been able to wipe her out without a qualm.

I said, "You know you're a patsy, don't you, Skinny?"

A little frowning crease showed between her eyes. "What do you mean?"

"He set you up for this. Soo. He knows me. He knows perfectly well no bunch of inexperienced juvenile operators is going to survive going up against a guy who's been in the business as long as I have—certainly not if they're handicapped by instructions not to kill. When did he give you those intructions? That first guy, the one on the hill with the rifle, he wasn't up there just to scare me."

"No. Mike Bird was supposed to . . . to shoot straight. But then the instructions were changed, over the phone. But why would Mr. Soo want us killed? It doesn't make sense!"

I said, "I don't know. Think about it. If you figure something out, drop me a line. Now beat it."

She licked her lips. "What?"

I looked at her bleakly. I had no business doing what I was doing, and most probably it would have serious consequences, all bad. Sentimentality usually does. But there's a little gauge in the mind that says "go" or "no go," and it was no go here, if only because there had been enough knives and guns for one night. I drew a long breath.

"I said beat it! Your car's out there. The keys are in your pocket. *Vamos,* as we say down along the border; the other border."

"You . . . you're letting me go?"

"Yes, and I'll catch hell for it. But I'm damned if I'll do any more of Soo's dirty work for him. If he wants you dead, as he apparently does, he can shoot you himself. Go on. Get out of my hair, Bellman. You've got four people killed so far, five counting Nystrom. And one dog. Now see if you can keep yourself alive, just for a change of pace."

She hesitated, watching me. When she spoke, her voice had changed. "Thank you," she said quietly. "I . . . I promise I won't tell anybody. Anything."

"Like hell you won't," I said sourly. "If these espionage characters we're dealing with get you and question you,

you'll spill your guts just like anybody else. That's the chance I'm taking."

"What about . . . what about Wally?"

"I'll have Wally taken care of. Just beat it. Here. Don't forget your jacket."

She took it and slipped past me in the narrow space, pausing at the door. "I really did have a Lab named Maudie once," she said.

"I figured you had," I said. "That's another reason I'm letting you go. That and because you swing a mean fish-pole. And I'll pay hell trying to explain *that* to my chief."

She paused, as if she had more to say, but she didn't say it, which was just as well. She went out, and a moment later I heard the Mustang start up and drive off, heading back inland, to the east. I looked at the pup on the seat, frowned, and moved him carefully to the floor where he couldn't fall, remembering that I still had sixty miles of road construction between me and the coast.

17 IT WASN'T A FANCY KNIFE. IT HAD

plain wooden grips, brass caps, and a single heavy blade about four inches long, which is a little longer than I like for everyday pocket wear, although not as long as the scimitars the armaments experts in Washington would like us to lug around. It was a folding hunting knife of a well-known U.S. make, and it hadn't been used much, so that it was stiff and very hard to open. My old knife, the one I'd left a couple of hundred miles back along the road, you could flick open with a snap of the wrist.

"It is a very good knife, an American Buck knife," the storekeeper said hopefully. "I bought it from a boy just off the ferry who'd spent all his money up north and needed gasoline to get back to the States. I will let you have it for twelve dollars."

I bought it, and some supplies I needed, and went out into the sunshine and looked around at the town of Prince Rupert, B.C. It wasn't much to look at. I don't mean it

was a bad little town; that was just the trouble, from the standpoint of a romantic tourist like me. A bad little town, a very bad little town, was what one expected and kind of hoped for up here in the big woods at the end of the pavement: something wicked and picturesque to bring home the fact that between this end of the Alaska Ferry system and the other, some four hundred miles to the north, civilization was represented only by a few scattered coastal communities that could be reached only by boat or plane. But instead of a ripsnorting frontier hell-hole, there was just a rather ordinary small town complete with motels and filling stations.

I went over to the truck, parked at the curb. Nobody in Prince Rupert seemed to be paying it any attention. Campers from the States, waiting to take the ferry up the coast, are a dime a dozen in that place.

I looked in on Hank, in back. He raised his head and thumped his tail on the floor when the door opened. He was going to be all right, but it had been a long night, first locating and awakening a local vet to give the appropriate shot, and then keeping the pup awake for several hours. A sixty-pound Labrador that wants to go to sleep on you gets pretty heavy toward morning. He looked kind of naked without his collar and I reached into my pocket, but took my hand out empty. Dopey as he still was, he might get hung up on something and be unable to get free; besides, in his present condition he couldn't be counted on to defend it properly.

"Okay, Stupid," I said. "That'll teach you to go taking handouts from strangers."

He grinned at me woozily, unimpressed. I closed the door, got into the cab, and drove over to the bus station and general transportation center that also, I'd been informed, sold ferry tickets. When I came out, I was in lawful possession of a one-way fare to Haines, Alaska. The sun was still shining, the weather still seemed too warm for that far north, and the town was still, at first glance, totally uninterested in me and my vehicle, but there was a difference.

On hazardous duty—and this job seemed well qualified for the title—I generally set a few telltales when I leave

111

my transportation, to make sure there has been no tampering in my absence. Now I saw that those on the hood were undisturbed; the cab remained securely locked; but somebody had entered, or at least looked into, the camper. I drew a long breath. It had been quite a night and I wasn't really in the mood for monkey business.

I was tempted to simply yank open the door and see what, if anything, I had acquired back there. Whatever it was, it had to get along with a black dog, which made it either a man who was very good with dogs or one who'd made friends with this particular dog earlier. The only gents who qualified in the latter respect, who'd be likely to be up here in British Columbia, belonged to Mr. Smith— and why Mr. Smith's people would be jeopardizing my cover by hiding in my camper this morning, when I had a contact scheduled with them this afternoon, I couldn't guess. Well, the way to find out was obvious, but the middle of Prince Rupert wasn't the place to do it.

I got behind the wheel. Nothing showed in the rearview mirror, although the back window of the cab corresponded with a forward window in the camper that gave me a partial view of the interior. Whoever was back there, if anybody was, was keeping low. I started the truck and drove out of town the way I'd come, found a dirt road leading back into the woods, and took this to a clearing out of sight of the highway where I could get the long-wheelbase job turned around facing out.

I cut the switch, set the brake, walked back, and opened the camper door. A young man sitting in the dinette pointed a sawed-off revolver at me.

"Come in, Mr. Helm," he said. "I was sent to get the dog's collar, but he isn't wearing it. Where is it?"

I looked at him for a moment. The face and the voice were both familiar. The voice I'd heard most recently over the telephone in Pasco, complaining about grasshoppers. The face I'd seen the previous week down in San Francisco, one among many eager young faces I'd met there, all owning allegiance to Mr. Smith. I looked at the gun.

"Hank," I said. The pup was lying docilely on the floor, obviously feeling himself among friends. He looked

at me questioningly. I snapped my fingers. "Hank, get out of here."

"Mr. Helm——"

I said, "On the double, pup! Easy now, watch that step, you stumblebum. Okay, go do your stuff, but stick around." Still watching the gun, I spoke to the man holding it. "We have a date this afternoon," I said. "Why not wait and get your collar then?"

"We want it now, Mr. Helm," he said.

I said, "That firearm. Put it away."

"The collar, Mr. Helm."

"Put it away," I said.

He shook his head, and gestured with the revolver. "Come inside. I have my instructions. . . ."

I'd had enough of amateurs. I was sick of amateurs. I said, "To hell with your instructions. You have about five seconds to put that thing away. After that, you eat it."

"Mr. Helm, I am only carrying out my orders. . . ."

"Not around here, you're not." I drew a long breath. "Pee or get off the pot, Sonny, because here I come."

"But . . ."

He was still saying something by way of protest as I stepped up into the camper, bending to clear the low doorway. I saw his eyes waver as I approached, and I knew I'd judged him correctly. No matter what kind of fancy training he'd had, he was still an amateur at heart and would always remain one. Training means nothing when applied to a certain kind of mentality. He was one of the new ones, brought up on togetherness and TV. He was one of the innocents who'd never learned, and probably would never learn, that the only thing you can do with a gun is shoot it.

He didn't shoot his, of course. He never really considered it. He probably wasn't even authorized to shoot me, when you came right down to it. He'd just been told to wave his magic .38 caliber wand at me, if necessary, and I would be his helpless slave. He was still talking, breathlessly and indignantly, when I took the weapon away from him.

I held it for a moment, almost angry enough to ram it

down his throat as I'd promised—as if I hadn't had enough firearms pointed my way during the last few days, without having my own people, such as they were on this lousy job, getting into the act! I seriously considered pistol-whipping him a bit, just as an object lesson, or maybe breaking an arm or two so he couldn't wave any more guns around, at least for a little. Then I sighed, backed off, pressed the latch, swung out the cylinder of the revolver, and shook out the loads. I tossed the empty gun out the open door, and heaved the cartridges after it. It's only in the movies that you toss loaded guns around like beanbags.

The embryo secret-agent type was glaring at me, full of resentment and injured pride. I could see what was going through his mind: I had humiliated him and he ought to redeem himself somehow. It was typical of his training. They'd taught him how to use judo and invisible ink, but they hadn't bothered to teach him to think like a pro. Nobody'd hammered into the space between his ears the primary fact of undercover life, to wit, that his damn little personal feelings were, or should be, of no concern to anyone, not even to him.

I said, "If you jump me, Sonny, I'll stomp you. I swear I will. I'll mash you right into the ground. There won't be anything left but a bloody spot the dog will be glad to lick up for me."

He didn't speak. I reached into a cabinet for an oil can and put it on the dinette table. I took from my pocket the Buck knife I'd just acquired, sat down on the empty seat, put a drop of oil on the hinge of the knife, and began working the blade back and forth to free it. The white hope of the undercover services watched me warily. I guess he thought I was threatening him, or something. Maybe I was.

"What's your name?" I asked.

"That's none of your business."

I said, "What's your name, Sonny? I won't ask you again." He was silent. I said warily, "Look, I'm pretty tired. I've been up all night with a sick canine friend. All I was planning to do today was sleep until our afternoon rendezvous, and then sleep some more until ferry time

tomorrow morning. But if you think I can't find reserves of strength somewhere, enough to get a few answers out of you, you are sadly mistaken. Now answer the question."

"My name . . . my name is Smith."

"Fine," I said. "I don't insist on the truth. Use your imagination if you like. Just so I get some answer." I looked at him hard. "Smith, eh? Would you be any relation to Mr. Washington Smith, whom I met very briefly a week or so back?" He was silent. I said, "Never mind. You don't have to answer that. But there is kind of a family resemblance. The same long, pointed, snoopy nose, the same humorless, fanatic eyes . . . "

"Damn you, you can't talk that way about my——!"

He stopped abruptly. I grinned at him. "Okay, Junior Smith. Now tell me what this is all about. You boys hauled me off my other duties to do some work for you. You spent a lot of time and effort briefing me about a character I was supposed to resemble slightly, whom you wanted me to impersonate. It was a vitally important mission, you told me. The exact details were shrouded in security, but the fate of the nation, if not the world, depended on my playing this part for you. And now, suddenly, now that I'm on my way and doing fine, you march in with a gun, taking a big risk of blowing my cover and wrecking the whole operation—if only by making me so mad I'll throw your lousy job in your faces. Just what the hell are you people pulling on me, Junior Smith? Or trying to pull, to be more precise."

Young Smith locked his lips. "You can't throw the lousy job, as you call it, in our faces, Helm. You haven't got a job. You're through!"

"Says who?"

"Says my . . . I mean, the orders were issued in Washington right after the gist of your last phone call was received there, the one you made early this morning, reporting another dead body. You're finished, Helm. You're out. You're to turn over to me what's in the dog collar, and then you're to have nothing further to do with this mission, nothing whatever."

Still working the knifeblade back and forth, I frowned at him thoughtfully across the table. "And just what was

115

there about these orders that made it necessary for them to be delivered over a .38 Special?"

"Well," said Junior Smith, a little embarrassed, "well, the way you've been acting, we didn't know . . . I mean, we weren't quite sure how you'd take . . . anyway, I was supposed to take no chances with you."

I nodded. "I see. Pointing a loaded firearm at a guy in my line of work comes under the heading of taking no chances. It would be interesting to know just what you folks consider really risky." I reached for the oil can once more. The knife was loosening a bit, but it still had a long way to go before I could count on getting it into action in a hurry. "And just how have I been acting, Junior?"

"Well . . . well, you know," he said. "You know what you've done!"

I said, "Frankly, I thought I'd done pretty well. I was told to get through, come hell or high water, and I'm through, this far, anyway. I was given a schedule to keep and I'm right on time. There were a few obstructions to overcome, but I dealt with them without letting them delay me significantly. So what's the gripe?"

"A few obstructions!" he said sharply. "You've killed five people getting here, Helm! The Canadians are complaining bitterly about the one-man crime wave we've turned loose on them. You've left a trail of blood across the whole Northwest! Did you really expect us to sit by and *approve* what you've been doing in our name?"

I regarded him with a certain amazement. The idea that anybody would draft an experienced agent—a specialist in homicide, no less—for a dangerous mission, tell him that the fate of humanity depended on his carrying it out, and then complain about the breakage, was so childish that for a moment I couldn't believe he was serious.

I said, "I see. You people want the lawn mowed, but you don't want to hurt a single dear little blade of grass doing it, is that it?"

"Well," he said defensively, "well, I suppose there are times when an agent has to kill in self-defense, but . . . "

"And what am I supposed to have been doing, shooting and knifing people for the pure sadistic fun of it?"

"The man in Pasco was shot in the back, Helm. In the back! And so was the one at the campground just east of here. How can you possibly call that self-defense?"

I studied him carefully. He was human, all right. At least he had a nose, a mouth, and two eyes. There was presumably a brain somewhere behind the eyes, but it had never been given a chance. It had early been washed clean of all practical and sensible and logical thought processes and supplied with a bunch of automatic TV cliché reactions to take their place.

It occurred to me that if I'd had any matchmaking ambitions, I would have made a great effort to get this specimen together with Pat Bellman. They were obviously made for each other. She, too, had been firmly convinced that, homicide-wise, there was a great moral distinction to be made between an eastbound victim and one heading west.

I said, "I will correct my statement. The man in Pasco was shot, not in defense of me, but in defense of my dog. I was told that the animal was intrinsically valuable, wasn't I? And that the whole mission depended upon my having him constantly available for identification? Besides, he's a pretty nice pup. Fuzzy-face was going to shoot him, so I shot Fuzzy-face. I apologize for not asking the gentleman to rise and turn around before I fired, but it didn't seem advisable at the time. Okay? As for the other guy, he had the collar in his pocket, and I didn't think he should be allowed to reach his car with it. Again, rotating him so the bullet hole would be in front wasn't exactly feasible, or didn't seem so to me. I wasn't aware that it was a detail of earthshaking importance."

"You don't think killing a man is important?"

He was deliberately misinterpreting my words, but I said patiently, "I think killing a man is important. But I assumed the job was more important. Most jobs I'm given are. At least that's the theory on which we operate, rightly or wrongly. And if I'm going to kill a man, I don't think it matters a good goddamn, either to me or to him, which way he's facing when it happens. This is not a sport with me, Junior. I'm not supposed to fight fair, win or lose. I'm not sent out to lose. I don't lose. At least I haven't yet."

117

"That's where you're mistaken!" Junior said in the same sharp voice. "You've lost this time. At least you've lost your job. We don't want the responsibility of sponsoring a cold-blooded killer."

"I see," I said. "Do I gather this job isn't really important after all? Or is it that the welfare of the world, or the U.S.A., can go hang, just so you people keep your reputations as fair-minded ladies and gentlemen with clean, bloodless hands?"

He said, "Never mind the rationalizations, Helm. Just give me the collar."

I nodded, surprising him. I said, "Okay, I'll give you the collar, since you're here. And you'll give it back this afternoon, exactly the way we planned." I looked at him hard. "Make any changes you care to, but don't even think about not returning it in good shape, Junior. Because if you give me any trouble at all, I just won't bother to give you a look at the rest of the stuff I pick up along the route. And there are three pickups left, remember?"

He licked his lips. "I told you! The orders from Washington are that you're to have nothing more to do with the operation!"

"Did Washington tell you how to stop me? Of course, you can shoot me. I mean, if you ever find your gun again. Otherwise, there isn't much you can do about it, is there?"

"You mean . . . you mean you're going right ahead and——"

"That's right," I said. "And if you boys behave yourselves, I'll let you play your little juggling tricks with any material I get, just the way we had it worked out in San Francisco. But if I get any more static from you, I'll just go it alone. You can blame yourself if the stuff gets delivered in Anchorage unaltered."

"You . . . you'd turn over the information intact? You'd betray your country's secrets. . . . "

"You know how to prevent it from happening. All you have to do is carry through just the way we planned."

He frowned at me suspiciously. In a perverse way, I was happy to see that he was at least smart enough to spot the logical fallacy behind my position. I'd hate to think

the next generation of agents is going to grow up totally brainless.

"But why?" he asked. "What reason have you for wanting to go on independently? You said you had other work to do. We're releasing you from this operation; why don't you just go back and do it?"

I said, "Oh. Now you're releasing me. A minute ago it sounded very much like you were kicking me out for behavior unbecoming an officer and a gentleman." He flushed and didn't answer. While I had the advantage, I went on quickly, "I make a habit of finishing my missions, Junior. I wouldn't want to get in the habit of copping out every time the going got tough, even when it's my own people who make it tough. It's a psychological thing. You can always find some excuse for quitting a job if you look hard enough. I just don't want to get started looking."

This was nonsense, of course, but it was, I hoped, the kind of inspirational psychological hogwash he was used to hearing. Anyway, it silenced him, and saved me from having to tell him that I was actually sticking with the crummy, cockeyed little job assigned me by his Mr. Smith only because it happened to be part of a much more important mission assigned me by somebody else. To keep him from asking any more embarrassing questions, I reached into my pocket.

"Here's Hank's collar," I said. "Where's the temporary replacement?"

Junior hesitated; then he brought out a second collar, identical to the one I was holding except that it was just a little blacker, shinier, and new-looking. We made the trade.

"I . . . I'll have to confer with Washington," he said.

"You do that," I said. "But at four o'clock this afternoon, I'll be at the field at the edge of town specified in the original instructions. I'll heave a training dummy out into the brush in the place I was told, the place somebody's supposed to be hiding. I'll send the dog after it, with this phony collar on him. And if he doesn't come back wearing the right one, the one you're holding now, with the contents looking just as they should, that's the last

contact I'll make with you people. Tell Mr. Washington Smith I said so." I stood up. "Okay, you go find your gun while I call in the pup. You'd better ride back here again. I'll tap the horn when it's safe for you to unload. Where do you want me to let you off?"

"My partner is waiting in the lab truck. It's parked just around the corner from the transportation building or whatever they call it. . . . "

After dumping him in the proper area, I drove down to the waterfront, cooked and ate a rudimentary lunch, and slept until three-thirty. Then I went through the contact routine as specified. I could only guess at Mr. Smith's reaction to my ultimatum—he didn't look like a man who'd approve of backtalk from the hired help—but the collar I got was the right one with the right stuff in it. At least it looked right to me, and would to anyone who didn't examine it too closely, which was all that mattered.

I had dinner at a motel restaurant, fed the pup, and caught up on some more sleep, parking out by the ferry terminal this time, a mile or so out of town. Well before dawn, cars started lining up at the entrance to the boarding area. I got dressed and drove over, putting my rig in line behind a Volkswagen bus loaded with kids and camping gear. Then I went in back and cooked some breakfast, sticking my head out frequently to see what progress was being made. I could have saved myself the trouble. The ferry was three hours late, delayed by fog up the coast.

After it arrived it had to unload, so the morning was more than half gone before we were permitted aboard, first doing the customs-and-immigration bit once more since the next stop was U.S. territory. Because I was riding almost to the end of the line, I was shunted to the farthest depths of the car deck, a cavernous space that looked very much like the flight deck of a small aircraft carrier roofed over, except that the island was in the center of the ship rather than at the side.

It was a tricky piece of driving—they were packing us in like sardines—and I had no opportunity to study the cars around me until I finally got the truck parked to the satisfaction of a man in a nautical cap who undoubtedly

did jigsaw puzzles in his spare time. He left me barely room enough to open the left-hand cab door and the door to the camper. The right-hand door to the cab, he said, I wouldn't be needing anyway.

I'd wiggled out into the tiny space between the truck and the car alongside and had started making my way toward a marked stairway when I saw a yellow Cadillac convertible with a dark-haired woman at the wheel being guided into a slot three cars back.

18 THE MOTOR VESSEL MATANUSKA

was a good-sized ship. Above the car deck was a deck of staterooms for those who wanted privacy on the two-day voyage up the coast and were willing to pay for it. The purser seemed to be doing a good business in accommodations; however, I got the impression that most of the passengers were planning to divide their time between their cars below, and the numerous upholstered chairs and airplane-type seats up above.

Over the stateroom deck was the observation and nourishment deck, with glassed-in lounge, snack bar, restaurant, and a cocktail bar called the Totem Room, not open at this hour of the morning. I made a special note of its location, since that was where I was to make my next pickup at five o'clock that afternoon.

Outside, a promenade deck for fresh-air lovers ran clear around the ship. It was out here, after doing enough exploring to get my bearings, that I stopped to await developments while watching the last cars driving aboard. Developments weren't long in coming. Almost immediately a feminine voice spoke softly in my ear.

"You're a hard man to catch."

"I didn't know if I was supposed to be caught," I said without turning my head. "If I was, I figured you were just the girl to do it."

Libby Meredith laughed. "Well, now that I've found you, you'd better kiss me, darling," she murmured. "Do a

good job. I know it's rough but it's in the line of duty. You're supposed to be Grant Nystrom and mad about me, remember?"

"How could I forget?"

I turned to face her. She was wearing another smartly cut pantsuit, yellow-brown corduroy this time, with a rather long tailored jacket buttoned over a brown turtleneck sweater. Pants or no pants, the outfit looked too fashionable, and her short dark hair was too smooth and her makeup too perfect, for a lady about to plunge into the great northern wilderness. One was tempted to muss her a little so she'd fit the rugged scenery to come. Maybe that was the idea. Unlike Pat Bellman, I reminded myself, this was a girl who'd been around long enough to know all about temptation.

"Libby, darling!" I said, putting amazement and delight into my voice. "What a wonderful surprise!"

I took her by the shoulders, pulled her close, and kissed her hard, to the amusement of the camera-toting passengers on both sides of us.

"Grant, please!" She made a pretense of flustered embarrassment as she freed herself. "Not among all these people, dear!" Then she relented and patted my cheek affectionately, smiling. "But I'm glad you're glad to see me."

"Come on, let's get out of here," I said. "I've seen a boat leave a dock, haven't you?"

I led her away, with my arm around her waist. Corduroy isn't my favorite material by a long shot—I'm an oldfashioned silk-satin-and-lace man at heart—but somehow she managed to make me very much aware of the woman under the ribbed, velvety cloth.

"Have you got a stateroom?" I asked.

"Yes, why?"

"Because you owe me three nights of bliss, sweetheart."

I felt her hesitate, and keep on walking. "That many? You've been a busy little man."

"Somebody else said that. Is it supposed to be funny?"

"Did you get the girl?"

"I had her," I said, "but I let her go."

This time, Libby stopped abruptly and swung to face

me. We were on the other side of the ship now, away from the shore, and we had it pretty much to ourselves.

"You let her go!" Libby's voice was incredulous. "But *why*?"

"Maybe I just didn't want to seem greedy." I said. "Or maybe I figured that after three wonderful nights together we'd probably be getting on each other's nerves anyway."

She said stiffly, "I don't think that's very amusing!"

I went on, "Or maybe I just figured I'd left enough dead people around for the cooperative authorities of a friendly foreign nation to dispose of. In that, I seem to have been right. The Canadians aren't a bit happy with me, I'm told, and neither are the boyscouts I'm supposed to be working with, or for."

Libby was studying my face carefully. "Of course, the fact that the child is fairly good looking had nothing to do with your decision."

"Child, hell," I said. "She could wring you out and hang you up to dry."

"I didn't say she wasn't a tall child, or a strong child, or a smart one. A very smart one, apparently."

"Sure," I said. "But say she twisted me around her little pink finger and made a fool of me, so what? Are you going back on your bargain, Libby? Or changing the rules of the game after the starting whistle? The original deal, as I understood it, was that any dead body would count for points, as long as it had, alive, had something to do with the outfit that murdered your backward lover. Well, these were all members of the same gang, there's no doubt about it. But now you're acting as if I had to produce one particular female cadaver to qualify——"

"Don't!"

"Don't what?" I asked innocently.

"I . . . I didn't realize . . . " She stopped and her throat worked. "Anyway, don't talk about it like that. So . . . so cold-blooded!"

I had been pushing hard for a reaction. Now that I'd got it, I had to decide whether it was genuine or phony. I made a sound of disgust.

"I might have expected it!" I said bitterly. "I've never yet known a woman to arrange for a killing that she didn't

get squeamish when the job was done and the payoff was due. Very damn convenient, I must say!"

"Oh, stop it!" she snapped. "I'm not backing out of any deals. I just don't want to talk about . . . about the gory details, or hear you talk about them, that's all!"

We faced each other for a moment longer, and I still had no clear sign to tell me whether or not she was really the rich bitch on a vengeance kick she'd claimed to be, now a little subdued by the actual fact of homicide. I had to admit to myself, however, that I wasn't quite as sure she was faking as I'd been when I talked with Mac two days before.

Abruptly, Libby shrugged, dismissing the subject. "If you know the coordinates of the dining room on this bucket and are willing to guide me there, I'll let you buy me some breakfast. I thought we'd be under way hours ago, so I came down to the dock without anything to eat. Now I'm starving."

"Sure."

As we went inside, the big ferry began backing out of its slip; by the time we'd settled at a table in the dining room, it was moving forward and the spruce-clad shores were slipping by the windows at a respectable rate of speed. It was a relief, I found, to be under way. I hadn't been quite sure that I wouldn't be yanked off the boat by the Canadian police, perhaps egged on by an offended Smith or two.

Now I had a contact to make on board today; and then, tomorrow, there was the island town of Sitka coming up, and another pickup. That was as far ahead as I let myself think; the business up north on the mainland could wait. I glanced at my watch.

"What's the matter, am I boring you?" Libby asked sharply.

"Go to hell," I said. "I'm a working man; I've got a schedule to keep. I'm not supposed to be wasting time on stray brunettes."

"Oh, that's right. You're to contact somebody right here on shipboard, aren't you?"

She still had no more notion of security, it seemed, than a gabby parakeet. Furthermore, Mac has a thing about

people who use "contact" that way, and it seems to have rubbed off on me. Or maybe I just found her irritating today, on general principles.

I said sourly, "Wait a minute and I'll have the head waiter arrange for a P.A. system so you can tell the whole ship all about it."

"Don't be so stuffy. Nobody's listening to us. Matt?"

"Call me Grant, just for practice."

"All right, *Grant*." She wasn't very fond of me, either, at the moment. "I don't want to run the subject into the ground, *Grant*, but aren't you afraid that little girl you let go is going to louse up the whole mission. If she talks . . . "

I said, "Look, you play your hunches and I'll play mine. My hunch said it was time to stop killing people and turn one loose alive. Maybe I was right and maybe I was wrong, but that's the way it stands. And at the moment I'm not half as worried about the girl I let go as about the girl I can't seem to get rid of. Just what are you supposed to be doing here, Libby?"

She looked surprised. "Last time we talked, you were very anxious to know I'd be around if you needed me."

"Sure, and it's great as far as I'm concerned, but how did you wangle it without arousing suspicion elsewhere?"

"It's all right," she said confidently. "It's been cleared with everybody who counts, all the way to Moscow. Well, almost. As a matter of fact, you're looking at a competitor in the Communist-courier business. I'm running a special message up to Anchorage for them. I asked if it would be all right if I arranged to make the ferry ride with you. Permission was granted with an indulgent laugh and a crude joke or two."

I said, "Let's hope they really bought your act, and aren't just being tricky. Did they mention Stottman at all? Or his partner, an Indian named Pete?"

"Stottman, yes. They asked if he'd bothered me, and I told them about our little scene in Seattle, and they said to forget it, Stottman and his paranoid suspicions had caused trouble before."

"That's reassuring, if true," I said.

"You think they could be setting a trap for me . . . us?"

"It's always a possibility."

"They didn't mention any Indian. What kind of an Indian? An American Indian or an Indian Indian?"

"American, but don't ask me what kind. I'm not up on the west coast tribes. He was in the hall outside your room when Stottman came barging back in that night. Didn't you see him?"

"No, I wasn't looking out in the hall. Why is he important?"

"Because Stottman is dead, and Pete seemed the kind of stubborn guy who could conduct a vendetta that would make a Mafia enforcer look like a schoolboy mildly annoyed because somebody stepped on his toe." I became aware that Libby was staring at me, and said, "What's the matter?"

"So Stottman is dead, too?" She whistled softly. "You really have been a busy little man, haven't you?"

I couldn't see that a response was required. Besides, a waiter was approaching to take our orders. Having eaten in the camper, I settled for coffee. Libby's big talk about breakfast and starvation turned out to be mostly bluff: coffee, juice, and toast was all the nourishment she'd take. It was nice that she was looking after her figure so well, but I couldn't help remembering another female who, despite some screwy ideas, had been a lot more fun to feed.

Afterwards we parted company, and I headed down to the car deck to carry out phase one of the day's contact operation, which consisted of turning the pup loose to run and giving him a little retrieving drill in an open area beyond the cars up forward. As I tossed the training dummy—actually a canvas boat fender—and sent him scampering after it, I was aware of various people stopping to watch, among them a smallish rather good-looking young blond woman with a nicely rounded figure, the effect of which, for me, was pretty well spoiled by the fact that she was wearing one of those ridiculous garments that seem to be nice enough short dresses at first glance, but turn out, when the wearer moves, to have a lot of stuff between the legs, the purpose of which I haven't got quite clear. I mean, in these days of miniskirts, no woman can

really kid herself that men are all that interested in what she's got to hide. Or can she?

It was hard to say whether the ultra-modest young lady caught my attention because she watched our little training game more intently than the others, or just because she was the best-looking female who happened to come by. I must admit I can't trust myself to be totally objective in such matters; besides, I was supposed to be concentrating on the pup.

I took the dummy from him and tossed it once more and sent him after it. When I glanced toward the stairs again, the girl was gone—but six hours later, when I came into the cocktail lounge right on schedule for phase two, she was sitting at the bar, still in her neat, safe little pale blue romper suit. At close range like this, I noticed the odd thing about her: her hair was very fine and blond, apparently genuine, but her eyes were brown. It was quite a striking effect. You don't meet many brown-eyed blondes who didn't get their hair-color from a bottle.

When I sat down a couple of stools away, she looked my way and said, "I saw you playing with your dog downstairs. Isn't that a Labrador retriever? He's a beauty. What's his name?"

19 I'D ARRANGED TO MEET LIBBY

afterwards and take her to dinner. We'd set our date for six, to leave as much time for the contact as the instructions allowed—if nobody'd appeared by six, I had an alternate time and place set for later. As it turned out, my business was concluded shortly after five, but Libby didn't make her entrance until six-twenty. After making sure that I was alone with my martini, she sat down beside me at the bar and asked, "How did you make out with the baby-faced blonde in the chastity-dress?"

"Well, I think I got what I came for," I said.

"That's all you'll ever get from that one," Libby said.

Then she laughed. "Don't mind me, darling. There's something about prissy little blondes that brings out the feline in me. What routine did she have worked out for slipping you the coin? I didn't stick around to watch the whole show."

"She asked me to get her some cigarettes from the machine. I offered to pay for them, of course, but she insisted on giving me the change. I palmed the Canadian quarter she gave me and substituted another I had handy, according to instructions. Any more questions, Nosy?"

She said, a bit defensively, "You wouldn't know anything about Grant's instructions if it wasn't for me! Don't I have the right to ask how they worked out?" When I didn't answer, she sighed. "You really are in a lousy mood, aren't you? I can see it's going to be a wonderful voyage. Well, maybe the scenery will be pretty."

"Maybe," I said, "but you won't get to see much of it unless the fog lifts."

"Fog?"

"When I stepped out on deck for a breath of air a little while back, you could hardly see the water. I hope the captain knows where he's steering this tub. The Canadians put one of theirs on the rocks in a fog not so long ago." I heard a voice in the dining room calling for a Mr. Nystrom, and remembered that was me. I said, "If you want a drink, get it quick and bring it along, before the headwaiter gives our table to somebody else."

It wasn't much of a dinner. That is, the food and the service were both satisfactory—a pleasant change from the backwoods hash joints I'd been patronizing along the road —but the conversation left a great deal to be desired. We simply didn't seem to have much to say to each other. After we'd eaten, we had a couple of brandies in the bar. Then we took a turn around the deck, but it was cold and damp and windy out there and a little unnerving, the ship charging recklessly, or so it seemed, through fog and darkness. We ducked back inside.

I said, "To hell with Alaska. I liked working in Hawaii better."

Libby was patting her windblown hair back into place. She glanced at the watch on her wrist. "It's a little early,"

she said in an expressionless voice, "but it's been a long day. Give me fifteen minutes. You know the stateroom number by this time, I suppose."

"I know it."

"That's the advantage of dealing with a real secret agent. He doesn't have to be told things." She faced me in the passageway. Her voice remained cool and impersonal. "Fifteen minutes. Don't keep me waiting, darling."

I watched her walk away, a slim, very feminine figure despite the mannish corduroy suit. I checked the time, went down two flights of stairs, squeezed between the cars to the camper, got in and said hello to the pup, and took his collar off, and gave him his dinner. Then I dug the quarter I'd palmed out of the pocket into which I'd dropped it; also my stiff new knife—still so stiff that I had to use the coin to pry it open far enough so my fingers could get a good grip on the blade. It wasn't really what you'd call an instant-defense weapon yet, I reflected wryly. I used the knife to separate the two halves of the coin. . . .

That is, I tried to use the knife to separate them, but I could find no crack into which to insert the edge. Well, it was a heavy blade. I got a smaller knife with a finer edge from a drawer, and tried again, without success. Then I got a ten-power magnifier and studied the coin carefully. I tossed it on the table and listened to the sound it made.

I sat there for a while. The pup, who'd finished eating, came up and licked my hand in a worried way, sensing trouble. I scratched his ears, and buckled the collar back around his neck.

I said, "Hank, old pal, this is getting strictly ridiculous. Three contacts so far, and only one has gone the way it was supposed to—and some guys were waiting for me with guns when I came back from that one. Well, I've got to see a customer about some homicides she ordered and I delivered. Be good."

I took the stairs to the deck above, and walked forward to where the super-deluxe staterooms were, the ones whose occupants didn't have to go down the hall to use the plumbing. I knocked on the door that had the right number on it. Libby's voice told me to come in. When I

entered, she was sitting in front of a mirror, brushing her hair. She didn't turn her head.

"You're late," she said.

"Go to hell," I said. "I waited twenty minutes for you this evening; you can wait three minutes for me." I looked around. "The trouble with love on shipboard is those damn berths. You have the choice of falling out of the upper or cracking your head in the lower."

The cabin wasn't much bigger than the camper I'd just left, but the ceiling was higher and the arrangements were different. The furnishings consisted mainly of the stacked berths and a built-in dresser with a little stool, upon which Libby sat. She was wearing a scrap of ruffled black lace—a little more than a chemise, a little less than a nightie—just enough to decorate the property without spoiling the view. There was a half-full glass at her elbow. She took a drink from it, and went on brushing her hair, which didn't seem long enough or tangled enough to require so much attention.

"Well, take off your shoes or something," she said, still without looking at me. "Don't just stand there."

I said, "You make everything so romantic, sweetheart. There was something said about cash, as an alternative. Under the circumstances, I think the subject is worthy of consideration. What are you offering?"

The hairbrush stopped moving. Deep in the ship below us, powerful machinery vibrated steadily. After a very long moment of silence Libby said very quietly: "You can't do that to me, darling. Not now."

"Cut it out," I said. "Let's skip the clichés. You're not a nymphomaniac. You're not hurting for a man; obviously not for this one. You're not going to go into a frenzy of frustration if nothing happens between us tonight. So let's talk business. I don't know the going rate, but I think three grand a head should be about right. That's nine thousand you owe me. Cash. No checks. You can make the financial arrangements in Anchorage, I'm sure. When we get there. I'll trust you that far."

She swung around on the stool to look at me. "You bastard," she said softly.

I shrugged. "That's between mom and pop, and they're not here."

"What are you trying to prove? Was I rude to you, is that it? Didn't I receive you properly? Did I hurt your damn little feelings? What did you expect, throbbing love and panting passion?" After a moment, she said, "You didn't find me repulsive in Seattle, darling."

"Maybe that's because you weren't repulsive in Seattle."

"But I am here?"

"Let's just say I'm not in the mood, and you don't seem to be, either. Anyway, I don't really like playing dirty games with sex; and the way we've been tonight, it's not worth nine grand of my money. For that I can get a willing woman and have change left over."

"*Your* money!"

"It's mine. I earned it. And don't you forget it."

"Get out of here!" she breathed. "Get out of here before I kill you!"

"Nine grand," I said. "In Anchorage. Cash."

I got out of there, checked my watch again as a matter of habit, and went upstairs to the snack bar and got two cups of black coffee from the vending machine that dispensed all the requisite beverages: coffee without, coffee with, coffee with double, hot chocolate. I carried my purchases below and managed to avoid the pup's eager greeting long enough to set the cups safely on the dinette table.

"Sorry, Prince Hannibal," I said. "You're going to have to sleep up forward tonight and leave the camper for us humans."

I arranged his pad on the floor of the cab and made sure he was curled up on it comfortably before I closed the door. Sixty-odd pounds of Labrador with insomnia, I'd learned, can make a half-ton truck sway on its heavy-duty springs like a small boat on a high sea. I got back into the camper and sat down to wait. It didn't take long. Thirteen and a half minutes from the time I'd left her stateroom, Libby was knocking on the camper door, asking to be let in. I took the .357 Magnum out of my belt and opened the door.

"What's that for?" she asked, acting shocked by the sight of the weapon.

"Just a precaution. Come inside and close the door behind you," I said, keeping her covered. I looked at her closely when she'd obeyed. She was wearing a belted trench coat, the kind without which no TV spy, male or female, could stay in business. Her feet were stuck into the same low yellow-brown suede shoes she'd been wearing all day. "Take it off," I said, gesturing toward the coat.

She hesitated, and shrugged. "Why not?"

"And pass it over carefully."

"Yes, Mr. Nystrom, sir."

Underneath the coat, she was dressed—if you want to take liberties with the word—as I'd seen her last, in a brief cascade of black lace ruffles suspended from two black satin ribbons over the shoulders. I checked the coat and found nothing.

"Lift it," I said.

"Yes, sir." She grasped the lacy hem of her garment daintily and raised it a few inches.

"All the way."

After a moment, she shrugged and obeyed, revealing nothing—that is, no weapons, in the strictest sense of the term. Letting the black stuff fall once more, she said, "Now what's this all about, darling?"

I said. "You have a short memory. Your last words upstairs concerned killing me."

She laughed again. "You weren't supposed to take me seriously!"

"Killing is something I always take seriously," I said. "If you didn't come to murder me, why are you here?"

"Silly," she said. "I came to apologize. I acted like a snotty bitch, Matt. I'm sorry. Can we ... can we start over and try it again?"

I grinned and drew a long breath and put the gun away. "All right, sweetheart," I said. "That's what I wanted to hear. Now sit down and drink your coffee before it gets cold and tell me who you really are."

20 *WE FACED EACH OTHER ACROSS*
the little formica-covered dinette table. Libby started to
raise her paper cup to her lips, checked herself, and
looked down at it, frowning. She turned her gaze on me.

"You *knew* I'd come?"

"Two chances out of three; enough to gamble a cup of
coffee on." I grinned. "Strictly a grandstand play, of
course."

She didn't smile, but watched me steadily. "How did
you figure it, Matt?"

"Say you were exactly what you'd been claiming to be:
Miss Elizabeth Richbitch Meredith, a spoiled, willful society lady who got involved with some nasty commies for
kicks, but later saw the light for one reason or another and
changed sides to join us good guys. In that case, what
would you do if an unappreciative jerk refused to accept
your priceless favors as sufficient reward for his services
and asked for cold cash instead? Well, there was a chance
that you'd just scratch the cad off your social list; but
there was also a chance, considering your parting words,
that you'd come after him with a gun."

"That's one chance out of two that I'd come," she said.
"What's the third possibility?"

"That you weren't the thrill-seeking Miss Richbitch at
all; that you were a simple working girl with instructions
to keep the guy under close—not to say intimate—
surveillance for purposes still to be determined. In that
case, of course, no personal considerations like wounded
pride would apply. You'd realize at once that you'd made
a strategic error in letting the bastard walk out on you,
regardless of insults, and that the only way you could
repair your mistake was to grit your teeth, go straight to
the crummy slob, and apologize as humbly and seductive-
ly as possible. Which was exactly what you did."

There was a little silence, broken only by the steady
rumble of the ship's powerplant—louder down here on the

car deck—echoed by minor rattles and vibrations in the camper. At last Libby laughed shortly.

"All right," she said. "All right. It's nice to deal with a bright man, I guess, even if it's a little hard on the ego. But if I'm not Miss Richbitch Meredith, darling, who am I?"

I said, "That's *my* question; I asked it first."

She hesitated and looked down at her coffee cup, frowning again. She spoke without looking up. "Does King's Mountain mean anything to you, darling?"

I let my breath go out in kind of a sigh. I said, "Well, it's a place where people got killed, like Bull Run."

She looked up and smiled. "So now you know."

But of course I didn't. What had just passed between us was the current identification signal—a Revolutionary War battlefield answered by a Civil War battlefield— applicable to all undercover agencies of the U.S. government. To an old cloak-and-dagger type like me, it didn't mean very much. I've been around too long to trust a password known to that many people, some of whom are bound to let it slip, intentionally or accidentally.

Still, it was an indication of something I'd already considered as a possibility. I said, "Assuming that you came by that I.D. routine legitimately, how does it happen that a bright girl like you is working for a stupid gent like Smith?"

"What makes you think I'm working for Mr. Smith?"

I shrugged. "Well, you're not one of ours or you'd have used a different call sign; besides, my chief has assured me we have nobody else on this job. And I hope to God there are no other U.S. spook shops mixed up in this operation. Two are enough, or one too many."

She laughed. "Assuming I am working for the man you call Smith, and have been right along, what makes you think he's stupid, Matt? Don't tell me a smart agent like you was fooled by his pompous act and the boyscouts he employs as a cover!"

"Go on," I said.

"You ought to know that in this business the cleverest thing you can do is act very dumb and make it stick. Mr. Smith, as you call him, puts on a deliberate show of

running something closely related to the YMCA, full of bright, earnest, high-minded young people. However, the real work is done by nasty, immoral characters like me, reporting through totally different channels. That way, nobody worries much about Mr. Smith and his apparently ineffectual activities, which is just the way he likes it. Okay?"

"It seems complicated, but okay. Do the boyscouts know about you?"

"As far as they're concerned, I'm a genuine double agent, discovered, recruited, and briefed by them. They're very proud of me; I'm their prize exhibit. The fact that I was planted on the Communists in the first place by the very man who gives them their orders would disillusion them terribly if they found it out."

"Sure."

She went on: "Of course, if you ask Mr. Smith, he'll say that he never heard of me except as an ex-commie agent who was persuaded to change her mind, and that what I've just told you about his setup is a figment of my imagination."

"Naturally," I said.

She laughed. "But that really makes no difference to our relationship, does it, Matt? Because you have no intention of trusting me, anyway, no matter how many signs or countersigns I produce, or how many important people vouch for me—or don't vouch for me."

"No intention whatever," I said. "I'm a suspicious bastard, particularly when it comes to lovely ladies who invade my quarters in black lace lingerie."

She glanced down at her brief garment. "It *is* pretty tarty, isn't it?" she murmured. "I ought to be ashamed of myself, oughtn't I?"

"You most certainly ought," I said. "But I find it all very sad. I don't suppose you really have nine grand to give me. And now that it's been more or less established that we're professional colleagues, our relationship will have to be strictly business, won't it? I mean, except when people are looking, of course."

She hesitated, then spoke without expression. "As a matter of professional technique, Mr. Helm, I have always

felt that when I'm assigned to play a role—like pretending to be madly in love with a man—I can do a much more convincing job if I play it all the way, whether people are looking or not."

I regarded her across the table. She had, I noticed, very nice shoulders, pleasantly white against the black ribbons and ruffles of her scanty, sex-doll garment. Her face was very nice, too. In fact, she was damn near beautiful, or perhaps it was the intimate circumstances that made her seem so.

I said, also poker-faced: "We certainly wouldn't want to handicap you in carrying out your assignment, Miss Meredith." I looked at her for a moment longer, and decided we'd been subtle and clever enough for one night. I said, "Look, doll, you don't have to, you know."

"What do you mean?"

"I mean we had a good time in Seattle and I'd be happy to repeat it, but if you're just under orders to sleep with me for reasons of strategy or something, hell, I'll move up front with the pup. In the morning, I'll give you a notarized certificate of copulation you can show your boss if he asks. Say the word."

Something changed in her eyes. She said, "You're really a pretty good guy, aren't you?"

I grimaced. "Go to hell. I just like my victims tender and willing, that's all."

"I know I don't have to," she said quietly. "And I don't have any such orders, Matt." She hesitated and looked down and, so help me, actually blushed a little. Her voice was almost inaudible when she spoke again: "I'm acting strictly . . . strictly on my own initiative."

"Well, in that case . . . " For some reason, I found it necessary to stop and clear my throat. "In that case, suppose you go stand over by the door for a moment, while I transform this eating-booth into a more useful and comfortable piece of furniture . . . ."

uneasy knowledge that there was something I was supposed to be doing instead of lying in a warm bed with an attractive woman in my arms. After a moment, I remembered what it was. I glanced at my watch, holding it up into the shaft of illumination cast by one of the lights of the ship's hold shining through a crack between the window curtains of the camper. I saw with relief that the time was barely midnight. Love or no love, sex or no sex, the mental alarm clock was still on the job.

"Where are you going?" Libby asked sleepily as I got out of bed.

"Sorry, I just remembered that I've got a date with a blonde," I said.

"Well, this is a hell of a time to——!" She stopped, and laughed at her own quick, jealous indignation. She said, "Oh, *that* blonde. But you told me your meeting in the cocktail lounge went off according to plan."

"I said I thought I got what I went for. I didn't. The girl slipped me a real, honest-to-God Canadian quarter instead of the trick coin she was supposed to pass. Probably because you spooked her by snooping around."

Libby sighed in the darkness behind me. "I knew it was all going to turn out to be my fault, somehow."

I grinned, pulling on my pants. "Well, she was apparently spooked by something, since she didn't complete the transfer. So now I've got to try the alternate drop. And this time, stay out of it. Stay put. I'll tell you all about it when I get back."

The steady vibration of the ship's machinery seemed more noticeable outside the camper. The poorly illuminated deck was a jungle of tightly packed vehicles. I saw people stirring around the cars up forward near one of the big landing doors. They were presumably getting ready to disembark at our next port of call, a small town called Petersburg. We should have docked there around nine,

but we'd started late from Prince Rupert and been slowed down still further by the fog: the official ETA was now one A.M.

The Communist agent who'd made up Grant Nystrom's itinerary had apparently been aware that the ferry often ran hours behind schedule, because he'd set no fixed time for the contact. Instead, I was to present myself in the snack bar forty-five minutes before the predicted moment of arrival in Petersburg, as chalked on the purser's blackboard, which I'd checked on my way to Libby's stateroom earlier in the evening.

It was exactly twelve-fifteen when I entered the snack bar, a rather long, narrow, well-lighted room with a newsstand at one end and a hamburger kitchen at the other, both closed for the night. In between was a battery of vending machines, one of which I'd already patronized for coffee, and half a dozen good-sized tables. One table was occupied by a bunch of sleepy-looking, aggressively ragged, grubby, long-haired kids, male and female; the rest were empty.

I stopped by the beverage dispenser, fished out some change, and, deciding that I'd drunk enough coffee, punched the hot-chocolate button. The machine gave birth to a paper cup which it proceeded to fill.

"Hit it again for me, please," said a feminine voice behind me. "Here's the money ... Oh, it's the man with the nice doggie!"

She was just as cute and brown-eyed and blond as she had been earlier, and she was still in the short blue linen dress with the trickily pleated modesty-insurance between the legs, but the basic pants-structure of the garment was more obvious now that it had got a bit rumpled from some hours of being slept in, I judged, on a car seat or in one of the ship's chairs. I took the quarter the girl held out, palmed it, and stuck one of my own into the vending machine.

"Thanks," said my contact when I handed her the cup. She glanced at the small watch on her wrist. "I'm supposed to get off at Petersburg, but I guess I've got time to drink this ... No, let's sit over here, away from the hippies." She gave the long-haired contingent a disapproving

look designed, I figured, to go with her rather prissy appearance. She went on, still in character: "I just don't see how people can bear to show themselves in public like that, all hairy and dirty and disgusting!"

"They're rebelling," I said.

"That doesn't really prevent them from getting a bath and a haircut occasionally, does it?"

"Of course it does," I said. "You just don't understand what they're rebelling against. Pay no attention to the guff they spout. They're not really fighting society, or the establishment, or war, or the draft. Not primarily. Their big fight is with all the television commercials commanding them to be clean and smell sweet and have soft shiny hair and bright white teeth and no sweat under the armpits. They're showing the world that they'll sweat if they damn well want to, and that no damn TV announcer is going to tell *them* what to do."

She laughed. "Well, that's a new slant. I hadn't thought of it exactly that way."

"I hadn't either, until a minute ago," I said, grinning.

"What's your name?" she asked. "I can't keep calling you The-Man-With-The-Dog."

"Nystrom," I said. "Grant Nystrom."

"I'm Ellen Blish," she said, and held out her hand. "It really is Blish. Honest. There is such a name, even though people don't seem to want to believe it. Hi, Grant. . . ."

I didn't pay much attention to what her mouth was saying, because her small fingers were talking a different language. For the second time that night I was having an identification routine thrown at me; this time the old fraternity grip of my own—well, Mac's—peculiar organization. It was a sign that meant somewhat more to me than the one I'd got from Libby, because it's known to relatively few people, all carefully selected and highly trained.

Perversely, it made me want to burst out laughing. Signs and countersigns are corny enough at any time; this one made me wonder just how many Communists were actually involved in the nebulous Red spy ring with which I was supposed to be dealing. It had apparently been infiltrated by just about everybody, like some of those

legendary subversive groups in which the FBI men finally outnumbered the genuine Marxists.

I made the proper response, searching the pretty little face of Ellen Blish, or whatever her true name might be, for signs of the toughness she'd have to have to be one of ours. But it doesn't always show. I remembered another small, rather delicate-looking blonde of ours—the more common blue-eyed variety—who'd come out of the jungles of southeast Asia and died in my arms beside a back road in southern France . . .

But it was no time to be thinking of blondes I'd loved and lost, or brunettes or redheads either. "Hi, Ellen," I said, retrieving my hand.

"You're Eric," she said. Her rather high-pitched, sweet-young-thing voice had changed to something lower and more businesslike. "You made a telephone call two days ago to a certain number in Washington," she went on and gave the number. "That's in case you don't have any more faith in fancy recognition signals than I do."

"If I'm Eric," I asked, "who are you?"

"Just Ellen," she said.

"And what do you have for me, Justellen?"

"Information. A warning. It looks as if you may be met at the dock."

"Any particular dock?"

"We haven't been able to determine that. It could happen at Haines, where you get off, or at Juneau, Sitka, or maybe right here in Petersburg. Do you know a brown-faced, black-haired gent, stocky, about two hundred pounds."

"I know him. His name's Pete. What about him?"

"He was seen making contact with Holz. We don't know what was said, but they left Anchorage by plane, heading south, this way. I was told to alert you."

I grinned. "We're always alert, we never-sleeping guardians of democracy. You know that."

"Never-sleeping, hell," said Ellen Blish crudely. "Just what do you claim to have been doing this evening? Well, I guess it wasn't exactly *sleeping*, at that."

"You are a disgusting little snoop," I said severely. "And why is it that a man's going to bed with one girl—it

was strictly in the line of duty, of course—invariably gets all other females in the neighborhood all worked up, even if they have no designs on the guy themselves? Or have you?" When she didn't speak, I went on: "Incidentally, you can tell our friend in Washington that I'm kind of allergic to creeping security. He told me quite definitely that if we had any agents up this way who might possibly be of use to me, I would certainly have been informed at the start. What was the point of his lying about it when we were going to meet anyway? That's the kind of compulsive secrecy that makes me want to lose my lunch."

Ellen said, "It wasn't known when you talked with him that we were going to meet, or that I'd be in a position to be useful to you. I've been working way inland on a problem that seemed to have very little connection with your job, but at the last moment the people I was working with—the group I'd infiltrated, to use the jargon—picked me to make this delivery on the coast. I couldn't very well refuse. It was an honor, I was told, a mark of trust and confidence. Well, maybe. Anyway, I had to scramble like hell to catch this ferry. Do I hear apologies?"

"Sure," I said, "if you want to hear them. And I do have a question. If there's somebody close enough to Holz to watch him, why doesn't the guy just pull the trigger and get the job done?"

"Because that's not his job. He's a watcher, not a trigger-puller; he's not up to tackling the Woodman. You're the specialist in triggers, my friend."

I nodded and studied her for a moment, knowing that we were far enough north now that there was nothing much inland of us but wilderness, clear across the North American continent. It didn't seem like the place for a fragile little blonde in a pale blue linen playsuit.

"You'd better watch yourself when you go back to whatever it is you're doing," I said. "I figure I'm under suspicion—if nothing else, the fact that Holz is heading this way proves that. If your Communist associates suddenly and unexpectedly picked you to make contact with me, that could mean their top brass has its eye on you, too, and brought us together for some tricky reasons of their own."

She moved her shoulders briefly. "It's occurred to me, but there isn't much I can do about it."

"Why didn't you identify yourself when we met in the bar?"

"Your brunette sexpot was sneaking around. I didn't want her to get any ideas . . . " Ellen steadied her cup as a series of mild jolts went through the ship; then she drank the last of her chocolate and stood up. "I guess that means we're docking. I'd better get down to the car deck. Good luck, Eric."

"The same," I said.

She was laughing gaily as she left the table, as if we'd just shared a final joke. "Tell that pretty black doggie goodnight for me," she called in a high sweet voice and was gone.

I waited awhile; then I went out on deck. Visibility was poor, so I can't say much about the town of Petersburg, only about the dock, and it looked pretty much like any ferry slip in a fog at night. I stood on deck watching the cars drive ashore without knowing which one was being driven by the girl who'd called herself Blish. Checking up on my Communist contact, even to the extent of identifying her transportation, would have been contrary to my orders. Well, Grant Nystrom's orders.

Then I watched the cars come on board. It should have been an equally profitless occupation since, from my observation post high above the loading ramp, I couldn't see anything of the drivers. Luck was in my favor, however, if it was luck. Presently a white station wagon nosed its way down to the hole in the ship's side and out of sight; an elderly Plymouth built back in the days when that particular company was conducting some unique experiments with tortured sheet metal. I knew the car. I'd sat in it once with a gun at my head, far to the south in a town on the banks of the Columbia River.

I drew a long breath and made my way below. I went straight to my truck, resisting the temptation to do a little scouting among the newly loaded cars up forward. We were pulling away from the dock, and barring accidents, murders, or helicopters, whoever had driven the Plymouth aboard would still be on the ship in the morning.

I checked the camper door. My faithful telltales indicated that my guest had either been very clever or had stayed put as I'd told her to. There was no indication that she'd been away from the truck. I stepped inside and turned on the light. Libby sat up in bed abruptly, as if startled out of a sound sleep. Her short, dark hair was tousled and she was wearing a wristwatch and nothing else. She ran her fingers through the hair and glanced at the watch.

"My God, I must have fallen asleep again," she said, yawning. "What took you so long?"

"Blondie said she was leaving the ship here. I wanted to make sure she did."

"Did she give you the right coin this time?"

"I hope so. I haven't had a chance to check it out."

"Are you going to let me see it?" she asked, swinging her legs out of bed.

"Sure," I said. "We're colleagues, aren't we; fellow soldiers in the secret war against international evil?"

Libby laughed. "You don't sound as if you trust me very much, darling."

I grinned and picked up a handful of lacy black stuff that had somehow found its way to the floor and tossed it at her.

"You'd better put this on, for what it's worth," I said, "so I can keep my mind on numismatics."

Actually, sexy as she looked sitting there naked, she wasn't distracting me at all. I opened the phony quarter and found the tinfoil disk that was supposed to be there, but my mind wasn't on coins, either, no matter what interesting material they might contain. I was thinking very hard about an Indian called Pete and a car I knew that he knew damn well I knew. Say he'd come this far up the coast on an earlier ferry, which was quite possible. Say he'd left his station wagon in Petersburg, flown north to Anchorage, and returned in time to meet my ship with his rather distinctive old vehicle, the question was why.

It looked as if I was being presented with something clever in the way of decoys, meant to attract my attention to one man while I was being stalked by another.

22 *SITKA LOOKED LIKE A CITY STILL*

under construction, which seemed odd considering that it was supposed to be one of the oldest communities on the coast, dating from the days when this far northwestern territory was claimed and governed by Russians. I decided that the unfinished effect was mostly due to the fact that the city fathers had apparently just discovered sidewalks and, mad about their new and unique invention, were laying concrete all over town.

It was raining steadily but not very energetically as the taxi carried me toward a display of totem poles that, I'd been told, was one of the main attractions of the place. This was not, however, my primary reason for going there. I was involved in another of the complicated contact routines some deskbound Communist genius had devised for the benefit of a courier named Nystrom.

After the ship had docked and the first rush of shoregoing passengers had subsided, I'd taken Hank for a walk so that he wouldn't forget what dry land looked like—not that any part of this drizzling region could really be called dry. At least the pup's welfare was the ostensible object of the expedition. Actually, I figured, I was displaying myself on shore with dog and whistle so somebody could get a good look at me for purposes of later recognition.

Hank had been deliriously happy at encountering grass and rocks and trees again after twenty-four hours of doing his stuff on greasy metal. I'd let him enjoy himself for ten minutes by the clock, after which I'd taken him back on board and stuck him into the camper to wake up Libby, figuring it was about time the girl got out of bed.

When I strolled off the landing ramp a second time, dogless, a taxi drove up right on schedule. Transporting me through the muddy little town, the cabby gave me a lengthy tourist spiel, telling me all about a pre-Communist Russian gent named Baranov who'd once been uncrowned king of the area; about a fine old Russian church that had

burned down; and about the great Good Friday earthquake of a few years back that actually hadn't affected Sitka much although it had played hell elsewhere along this coast.

His chatter made me uneasy at first, but I came to the conclusion that it held no coded messages to which I was supposed to respond in kind. The guy was just talking because he was nervous, and because he always talked this way to tourists off the boat and wanted our relationship to look perfectly normal.

He let me out by a grove of totem poles standing in front of a neat, park-service-type building, inside which, I was sure, I could learn all about them if I had the time and the desire. The poles themselves were quite impressive: tall, slender timbers, carved and painted, reaching up into the gray sky. The masklike wooden faces were much less garish than I'd been led to expect by photographs I'd seen, and the muted colors went well with the misty day.

But I hadn't come here to study primitive art, and I went on into the building and made a pretense of taking in the exhibits before wandering into the little movie theater off the lobby. It was dark inside. On the screen, a copper-faced gent was showing the steps involved in totem-pole construction. He reminded me a little of Pete, although Pete was probably not a member of the totem-carving Tlingit tribe.

I found an aisle seat near the rear, as instructed, and settled down to watch. Some time passed, which I spent wondering just what the real Pete was up to and what Hans Holz had in mind for me. Well, there wasn't much doubt about his basic intention, but I could speculate on whether he'd had himself smuggled aboard the ship to do the job or was waiting for me further up the line.

I became aware that someone had entered the theater by the door I had used, letting in a moment of daylight. A small, slight man paused at my row, murmured an excuse, and made his way past me with some difficulty, since theater seats are seldom spaced adequately for legs as long as mine. After the man had settled down somewhere off to my right, I felt under the seat-arm he'd used to steady himself briefly. I found a small container about the size

and shape of a bottle cap stuck there with some kind of tough rubbery contact adhesive.

I pried it loose, and pickup number four was completed, but I felt a little deprived at not having got a chance to use the identification spiel that I could now rattle off quite glibly.

After watching the educational film a little longer, I glanced at my watch like a man afraid of missing his boat and hurried out, leaving my latest contact sitting there in the dark. I'd never got a good look at his face, but Mr. Smith's boys would have him spotted if they were on the job as they should be—another fish for the dragnet, to be hauled in later, with friends if possible.

The waiting taxi driver returned me to the dock, still spouting his mechanical spiel. I wondered if he'd stop talking when they took him off to jail. When I reached the camper, a little piece of unraveled screen wire that had been caught in the crack of the door a certain way—one of my telltales—was no longer visible.

I hesitated. It could have been done by Libby leaving, of course, or even returning to learn if my mission on shore had been successfully completed. And even if someone else had entered the camper, the chances were slight that they'd planted a bomb, or were waiting inside with gun or knife. Like me, Holz would undoubtedly have orders emphasizing discretion. He would wish to perform a neat and quiet operation that would not reflect discredit on, or draw attention to, his current associates. Alone on the promenade deck at night, I'd be taking a chance, but on this crowded car deck I was reasonably safe.

I opened the door deliberately. Libby was no longer there, but a familiar, stocky, Indian-faced gent was sitting in the dinette. He didn't really look much like the Tlingit carver in the movie. My fine, big watchdog had his head on the intruder's knee and was letting his ears be scratched, with a blissful expression on his silly black face.

"Nice dog," Pete said, glancing at me as casually as if we'd arranged this meeting in advance. "I always like dogs. Can't say as much for people."

"Sure," I said. "I saw you drive aboard last night. Figured you'd be around to see me sooner or later. How

about a beer?" I pulled the camper door shut behind me, and turned to the refrigerator. "Tough about Stottman," I said.

Without looking, I was aware that Pete's fingers had paused very briefly before continuing their skillful scratching. "What do you know about it?" Pete asked.

I said, "Hell, I found them, man. I'd been out on that Lake—Francois Lake—making contact as ordered. When I came back to the cabin, there they were on the kitchen floor, all three of them. God, what a mess! I just grabbed my stuff and lit out fast, before the cops caught me there knee deep in blood and dead bodies. Do you want a glass?"

"What?"

"A glass? For the beer?"

"No, the can's okay." Pete took the beer I gave him, swallowed deeply, and passed the back of his hand across his mouth. "That's your story," he said.

I sat down facing him. "That's my story," I said, drinking from my own can.

"Mr. Stottman didn't like you much." Pete's voice was flat and expressionless. His dark eyes watched me steadily.

"I didn't like Mr. Stottman much," I said. "Come to that, I don't like you much. So what?"

"You didn't report. Some people higher up are annoyed. They had to read it in the Canadian papers."

"Stiffs aren't my business, friend. I'm not required to report anything to anybody. I just carry the mail."

"Mr. Stottman had a funny idea you aren't exactly what you pretend."

"I know Mr. Stottman's funny idea," I said. "He made it pretty clear. Frankly, I think your Mr. Stottman was a paranoid crackpot who should have been put away in a room with upholstered walls."

Pete drank more beer and studied the can thoughtfully. "Paranoid," he said softly. "Hell, I'm just an ignorant redskin, Nystrom. Don't waste those big words on me."

I grinned. "Sure, you're stupid like Hiawatha."

"That imaginary, romanticized creep!"

"Sitting Bull, then. Mangas Colorada. Chief Joseph of

the Nez Percé." He remained silent, and I went on. "Okay, for the sake of your limited intelligence, which I don't believe in for a moment, let's just say that friend Stottman was the kind of sick guy who sees enemies and traitors where there aren't any. I took time out to drive clear to Seattle just to humor him. I got myself a copper-riveted, brass-bound identification to make him happy, and he still wouldn't drop his crazy suspicions. So they got him killed, and we're sorry about that, but—"

"How do you figure?" Pete's voice was sharp.

"If he'd minded his own business," I said, "he'd still be alive down in the state of Washington where he belonged, wouldn't he? He wouldn't have got himself shot, carelessly walking in on a couple of guys laying for me."

"Mr. Stottman didn't walk into places carelessly. And he never used a knife. Those other two guys were killed with a knife, it said in the paper. He didn't even carry a knife, Nystrom. I did the knifework for both of us when it had to be done."

"So he took a knife from one of them. They weren't very bright, judging by their clumsy tailing techniques—they'd been following me a whole day. It wouldn't take a genius to disarm one of them. Only Stottman wasn't quite fast enough with the blade when he did get it, and the other got off a shot."

"You didn't say anything about hearing a shot."

I said, "With an outboard motor running, how much could I hear, a mile out on the lake?"

"You've got answers for everything, don't you? But if it happened like you say, and the punks were laying for you, Mr. Stottman saved your life."

"Who asked him to? I handled the creep with the rifle in Pasco, didn't I? I could have taken care of those two. Hell, I knew they were around, I was just waiting for the right time to ditch them or deal with them when your friend blundered into the line of fire and got himself massacred."

"Pretty cocky, aren't you? For a mere courier who never killed a man in his life before this week. Where's *your* knife, Nystrom? Could it be in the hands of the cops, labeled exhibit A?"

I hesitated, shrugged, took out the Buck knife, and slid it across the dinette table. Pete looked down at it and up at me. He picked up the knife, opened it, ran his thumb along the edge approvingly, and tried to close it.

"Press the back of the handle near the end, there," I said. "The blade locks. Keeps it from shutting on your fingers when you're skinning out your elk." I reached out and reclaimed my knife. "Just what the hell is your theory, Pete? That I mowed them down, all three of them? That makes me pretty good, doesn't it? Thanks for the compliment."

"You're pretty good, all right," Pete said. "Whoever you are. The question is, are you good enough? Thanks for the beer."

He gave the pup a casual pat, pushed him aside, and went to the door and stopped, looking back. I met his look. It was a moment of understanding. Regardless of what had been said he knew quite well that I'd killed Stottman somehow, and I knew that he was going to make me pay for it somehow, if he could. He was announcing the fact quite openly.

Of course, he wasn't being completely frank. He wasn't telling me that he was delivering his flamboyant challenge, threat, or whatever it was, in order to keep my attention firmly fixed on him while another man sneaked up for the actual kill.

23 *AFTER LEAVING SITKA, WE SPENT* the rest of the day cruising along sheltered passages between large, spectacularly mountainous islands—well, spectacular when the fog let us see them—with thickly wooded shores. At least the forests were thick where the lumbermen hadn't been at them, but in many places it looked as if a mad barber with giant clippers had been at work, leaving the dirty bare skull of the earth shockingly naked.

"What's the matter, darling?" Libby asked, coming up

beside me where I leaned against the rail. "You look like another kid ran off with your ice cream cone."

I gestured toward the denuded shoreline we were passing. "I thought they only hacked them down like that back in the days of the bad old lumber barons who never heard of conservation."

Libby laughed. "You worry about the damndest things, Matt. I mean, Grant. You worry about that dumb mutt you've got to drag along for identification—and I don't thank you for turning him in with me this morning when I was sleeping soundly—and now you're worrying about trees, for God's sake! The Japs need the lumber and somebody wants their money, so what's the problem? After killing four men in less than a week, are you going to weep over a pine tree?"

I didn't think the stuff was pine, but in other respects she was perfectly right, of course. However, as usual, her sense of security was microscopic. I glanced around casually. A stocky male figure in jeans and a heavy, hip-length jacket was hunched over the rail up forward.

"Raise your voice a little," I said. "Pete didn't hear you the first time."

Libby followed my glance, but ignored my sarcasm. "That's the man who visited your truck this morning after I'd left? Stottman's assistant?"

"That's the man. Now he seems to have appointed himself my shadow. It's an old psychological device: keep haunting the evildoer and eventually he'll get nervous and betray his guilt, you hope." I grimaced. "Pete would just love to hear you confirm that I killed his plump sidekick, not to mention those other characters. He's pretty sure already, but not quite sure enough to get mad enough to act."

She made a face at me. "Let's go inside and discuss it over a drink. It's cold out here!"

"I've got to go feed that dumb mutt, as you call him," I said. "I'll meet you in the bar in half an hour."

She frowned, clearly annoyed in her feminine way that I'd prefer a dog's company to hers, even briefly. She turned without speaking, marched away to the nearest door, and paused a moment to look at herself in the glass,

tidying her windblown hair. She disappeared into the cabin.

I grinned; then I shivered as the raw wind bit through the ski parka I'd inherited from Grant Nystrom. It seemed a long time ago since I'd been warm enough to welcome a swim, down in British Columbia. I went down to the car deck, said hello to the pup, checked my watch, and at five o'clock sharp turned him loose to run while I stirred up his meal—five cups of dry dog food, water, and half a can of horsemeat, if you're interested in the dietary details. He wasn't what you'd call a dainty eater.

Then I glanced at my watch once more. I waited until exactly ten minutes had passed, then leaned out the camper door and blew the come-here whistle softly. It took Hank a minute or two to respond, and when he came romping up between the cars, I could see that the collar he was wearing was just a little newer and blacker than the one he'd had on when I turned him loose.

I carefully didn't look toward the aft end of the hold where, jammed in among a bunch of passenger cars, stood a vehicle that looked like a boxy Ford delivery van converted for camping—a vehicle I'd first seen in Prince Rupert when I'd delivered Smith, Junior, to what he'd called his lab truck. Even without looking, I was aware that a bearded young man I didn't recognize was leaning casually against a door of the truck.

That would be the partner young Smith had referred to, ostensibly drinking a Coca-Cola, actually standing watch while the youthful pride of the undercover services, inside, checked the material I'd gathered from the last two drops and altered or replaced it judiciously so Hank's collar would do the nation's interests no harm, and maybe even a little good, when I finally delivered it in Anchorage.

It was the kind of tricky secret-agent stuff that always makes me kind of embarrassed; it seemed like a kid's game a grown man wouldn't want to be caught playing. On the other hand, I was relieved to have the latest information in the pup's collar defanged and defused, so to speak; and even more relieved to realize that four of my five contacts were now history. Only one act of my super-spy drama remained to be played—Nystrom in the North-

west, or the Courageous Courier—well, two, if you counted the delivery in Anchorage, assuming that Holz let me get that far.

After the pup had finished eating, I turned him loose once more while I busied myself cleaning house after a fashion. When ten minutes had passed again, I called him in with the whistle; and he had his old collar back. It was a cute routine. I didn't know if it had actually fooled anybody, but I was sure it had made the boys in the lab truck feel clever and useful.

Hank was licking his chops happily, savoring the aftertaste of whatever tidbit they'd used to lure him in. I regarded him sternly.

"Some one-man dog you are, Prince Hannibal," I said, "making up to anybody who scratches your ears or offers you a handout! Now try to be good and stay off the furniture."

When I came into the cocktail lounge and looked around for Libby, I couldn't spot her at once. Then a woman lounging at the bar shifted position and smiled at me, and I realized that it was my attractive colleague, self-styled. I'd got so used to seeing her in pants that I hadn't recognized her in a dress. It wasn't much of a dress; at least there wasn't much of it. The main impression she gave, sitting there, was of slim, endless legs in figured black stockings. Above was something brief, black, and sleeveless.

I gave the exposed limbs, as the Victorians used to call them, the amount of attention they deserved by whistling softly.

"Where's the party?" I asked. "Should I break out a tux or am I all right in slacks and a wool shirt?"

Libby laughed. "It's our last night on board, darling. According to the purser's blackboard, we'll be landing in Haines, Alaska, around six A.M. After that, I understand, we cross the border under our own power, and the going through Canada can get pretty rugged. I . . . I just thought we ought to celebrate a little while we have the chance."

We did.

bathroom of the stateroom we'd finally put to use, I shaved, after a fashion, with a dainty, pink lady-type machine supplied by Libby. I'm not partial to those power mowers, even the gentleman-type ones, but it did a half-way decent job, and I didn't figure folks up there on the last frontier would be too critical of a few remaining whiskers. As I was finishing, several shocks ran through the ship.

"You'd better hurry," Libby called from the other room. "We seem to be docking."

I came out of the cubbyhole to find her fully clad, packing her suitcase. I got my shirt buttoned up and tucked in while she was completing the task; then I picked up the single item of luggage and followed her out into the corridor and down the stairs, which were crowded with people hurrying to their cars. When we reached the deck below, one of the big landing doors was open, and the ramp was being lowered into place.

Libby made her way to the yellow Cadillac, unlocked the trunk, waited for me to place the suitcase inside, and slammed the lid. She was back in her mannish corduroy pantsuit, but it still didn't make her look noticeably like a man. Her short, dark hair was a little tousled—we'd slept too late for her to take much time with it—and her face looked pink and young and sleepy.

"Wait for me at the border," I said. "Or I'll wait for you. They don't open it until eight anyway, I heard somebody say. There'll be time for me to stir us up something to eat in the camper before they let us through."

"I'm not hungry," she said and hesitated. When she spoke again, her voice was soft. "Matt."

"Yes?"

"It was nice," she said. "Whatever happens, last night was nice."

I looked at her for a moment. She wasn't the sweetest,

153

gentlest woman I'd ever met, or even the most beautiful. I still wasn't quite sure of her motives and loyalties. Nevertheless, we'd managed to share something special for a few hours—something a little different from the enjoyable but meaningless man-woman stuff we'd indulged in previously—but it wasn't the sort of thing you could talk about without spoiling it.

"Yeah," I said. "Nice. Be careful, doll. We don't know what we'll be running into on shore."

This was a lie, of course. I knew—or hoped I knew—exactly what we'd be running into: a professional killer named Holz. But I couldn't warn her further, no matter how nice it had been. I just turned away and squeezed between the parked cars to the camper and checked on Hank. There wasn't time to let him out for his morning airing. The first cars were already driving off the ship, including, I noted, an old white Plymouth station wagon.

I told the pup to hold everything, closed the door on him, and took a quick look under the truck to see if any bombs had been added or any brake lines or steering linkages removed in my absence. I checked the engine compartment. Even commercial vehicles are encumbered with a lot of Mickey Mouse gadgets these days—that big, rugged, powerful truck engine was decorated with a cute little automatic choke, for God's sake! Apparently modern-day truck drivers are considered too stupid and feeble to pull a knob out of a dashboard. But there didn't seem to be any gimmickry that hadn't been there before.

Well, I didn't really think the Woodman would go the sabotage or explosives route. There are guys who like to see guys blow up or fall off cliffs by remote control, and then there are guys who prefer to have them die, if they must die, with neat little personalized holes in them. Having studied his dossier carefully, I'd come to the conclusion that Holz, like me, belonged in the latter category.

Still, I was glad when the engine started without extraneous fireworks. Presently I was driving away from the ferry slip in the misty morning twilight, in a slow-moving line of cars winding along the shore, headlight to taillight. At the first suitable spot, I pulled out and turned the pup loose.

Libby's car passed without slowing up. Pete's station wagon was somewhere up ahead in the parade. The converted Ford delivery van rolled by with two up front, but the visibility was too poor for me to make out whether young Smith or his bearded partner was driving. Where the rest of the boyscouts were—the ones who were supposed to be keeping tabs on me and anyone who approached me—I didn't know or care, as long as they stayed out of my way. I had to admit they'd done a pretty fair job of it so far. Their moral attitudes might be childish, but their tailing techniques seemed to be adequate.

I let the pup sniff and explore happily along the stony beach, wet with the night's rain. He'd been locked up on shipboard a long time and deserved a run. It was chilly standing there on the shore—after all, these were Arctic waters. Ahead were the lights of the town of Haines; behind was the ferry dock. As I looked that way, the *Matanuska* pulled out and headed up the bay for Skagway and the end of her northward voyage. I was on my own once more, doing my own navigating. When Hank had fired both barrels and become thoroughly reacquainted with terra firma, I loaded him back into the camper and cruised through the sleeping town in the vague, slowly growing light.

Watching the rearview mirrors, I saw Pete's station wagon pull out from behind a darkened filling station and fall into place close behind me. Apparently he was going to stick to his open-surveillance routine, hoping it would make me mad or scared or guilty. It was too bad. I mean I admire loyalty as much as anybody, but the guy was overdoing his devotion to his defunct comrade. He was crowding me.

The delay had let the cavalcade of cars from the ship pull ahead of us. We had Alaska pretty much to ourselves as we pulled out of town on a paved two-lane highway that followed the bank of a sizeable river upstream. I could see the water gleaming through the trees, an odd, murky, milky, light blue-green color, rippled with current eddies. I jacked up the speed as civilization, such as it was up here, dropped behind us, and looked for a suitable spot to teach friend Pete that tailgating is bad driving.

What I needed was a reasonably sharp curve, and a reasonably steep drop-off on the left, or river, side of the road. I found just the right spot after a few miles. I took the curve fast, hit the brakes just beyond, switched on the right-turn signal, and veered over as if to park.

Pete, rounding the curve right behind me, had no real choice. He was too close to stop; he had to swing around me, or try. Maybe he even thought I was actually parking. As he came up, I threw the long shift lever from fourth to third, the real acceleration gear. I put my foot down hard, and all four barrels of the big carburetor opened wide, and all two hundred and forty horsepower—truck horsepower, remember—came in with a roar. The pickup leaped forward just as Pete drew abreast.

He tried to make it clear, but he didn't have a chance. The old station wagon had neither the power nor the gears. He couldn't get past me and he was going too fast to drop behind. I put my cab door even with his front wheels and, slightly ahead of him like that, holding it there, moved deliberately left across the highway. He didn't even try to ram. I guess the big truck-and-camper rig towering over his flimsy passenger job looked just too massive and invulnerable, and maybe it was. Anyway, trick driving was apparently not his specialty. He just let himself be herded across the road and over the bank. It was finished in an instant.

I looked into the left-hand mirror. . . . He could have ridden it out alive, but I saw no reason to go back and look.

Some sixty miles farther on, I came upon the little white Canadian customs-and-immigration building that marked the international border. The geography up there is pretty scrambled, with a strip of U.S. territory—the Alaska panhandle, so-called—running down the coast for hundreds of miles and Canadian real estate inland. Since there are no roads along that rugged shoreline, we now had to leave the U.S. and head across the Canadian interior, through British Columbia and Yukon Territory, to pick up the northern end of the Alaska Highway, which would then lead us back across another international boundary into Alaska proper.

The customs man had apparently just got out of bed. The office was open, but there was a line of cars still waiting to be processed through. Libby's convertible was parked at the side of the road a little back from the mob scene. I stopped the truck behind it, and she came over and joined me in the camper, reacting in typical feminine fashion to Hank's muddy feet and affectionate tongue.

"You really ought to teach that dog some manners," she said, wiping a smudge off her corduroy pants.

"He's just being friendly," I said. "Down, Stupid. The lady doesn't like dogs."

"You can say that twice," Libby said. "My God, that poodle they saddled me with in Seattle! The idiot bitch was carsick all the way to Pasco and back, and I was a total wreck by the time I got rid of her—well, you saw me."

Her voice was a little challenging. We were proving something. Perhaps we were demonstrating that, even if last night meant something, I was going to have to take her as she was. She wasn't going to be a hypocrite, no matter how nice it had been. She wasn't going to pretend to be a dog-lover, or anything else, to please me.

When I didn't rise to the challenge, or come to the defense of our four-footed friends—even my own four-footed friend—she sighed and said in a different tone: "I was beginning to worry about you, darling. What kept you so long?"

"Why, Hank had a lot of business to attend to, after two days on shipboard," I said. "And then there was a slight accident down the road."

"An accident?" After a moment, she glanced at me quickly. There was an odd, savage, expectant little gleam in her eye that I'd seen before. As I've said, she wasn't the gentlest lady I'd ever slept with. She licked her lips. "That man you called Pete? I saw him waiting for you at that filling station as I drove by. Is he . . . is he dead?"

"I didn't stop to check," I said.

"What do you mean, you didn't stop to check?" Suddenly her voice was harsh. "You fool, if you made a try at him and he's still alive——"

I said, "Sweetheart, you are the damndest girl for just

wishing people dead. If you feel all that homicidal, why don't you get out and do a little murdering on your own?"

I grinned as I said it, but she didn't smile back. Her voice remained angry as she said, "But now that you've confirmed his suspicions by trying to get rid of him, he can ruin everything!"

It had been a mistake, after all, not to go back, or at least to tell her about it. I'd forgotten that this girl didn't know, as I did, that whether or not Pete's suspicions were confirmed didn't really matter, since he'd already communicated them to somebody else, who was acting on them or soon would be.

She didn't know, and I was not authorized to tell her, that this was just the way my assignment had been planned a long time ago—well, it seemed a long time ago. She was thinking of a different operation with a different objective, and I couldn't put her straight. That Mr. Smith and his people and his counterespionage mission were just a cover I was using for a totally different job wasn't information I could entrust to anybody, certainly not to a girl who claimed to be working for Smith.

To cover up, I had no recourse but to get nasty. I said, "With all due respect, Miss Meredith, I'm just a little tired of your trying to use me as a lethal weapon—and then complaining when I fail to pile up the corpses in large enough heaps to suit your bloodthirsty taste!"

She looked at me coldly. After a moment, without speaking, she rose from the dinette seat in a dignified manner—at least it would have been dignified if the camper had had about six inches more headroom. The crack on the head didn't improve her temper. She just glared at me and pushed past me and went out of there fast. I heard her, outside, running around the rig to her car. The forward window, giving a view ahead through the cab and windshield, showed me the Cadillac lurching away to join the diminishing line at the customs office.

I drew a long breath and turned back to the stove. After a little, I noted that she'd been checked through. Obviously still mad, she was out in the left lane, highballing it past the slower traffic before she was out of sight. Well, that might be all right on smooth U.S. pavement, but

the Canadian roads up here, I'd been told, were very much unpaved and had to be treated with respect, particularly if you were driving a vehicle designed for glamour rather than durability.

But that was her problem. I really had no business worrying about it. It was time for me to remember once more the maxim of the profession: *What happens in bed has absolutely no bearing on what happens elsewhere.* No matter how nice the night had been, it was daytime now.

I sat down to eat. Afterward, I went through the border formalities and, alone on the road, headed toward the Alaska Highway a hundred miles away, thinking about Holz and just how he might be figuring to take care of me, now that he had me available in open, empty country instead of on a crowded ship.

At least that was what I was supposed to be thinking about.

25 INLAND, IT WAS A FANTASTIC country. The stuff along the coast was picturesque enough, but I was brought up on mountain scenery, and it takes a lot of rock to impress me. The real experience for me came when I climbed out of the coastal cliffs and canyons and topped out on the endless roof of the world, bright in fall colors. I'd seen something like it once before, in northern Europe at the same time of the year, but that kind of landscape doesn't grow old very fast.

The road was just as lousy as I'd been promised it would be, making the total impression even more memorable. There's something kind of insulating about asphalt and concrete. In order to appreciate a country fully, you've got to dodge the rocks, smash into the potholes, weave along the ruts, splash through the puddles, and taste the high-flung mud blown in through the open window. . . .

My next—and last, thank God—pickup wasn't scheduled until early this evening, at the final border crossing at a small town called Beaver Creek, only some three hun-

dred miles ahead. It was still early. I had plenty of time to make it if I didn't get in a hurry and break something, so I just cruised easily along the twisting gravel road—gravel, in that part of the world, means anything from chicken-gravel to head-sized boulders—across the gaudy tundra, if that's the proper term for the terrain I was viewing.

There was no human habitation and no traffic for a good many miles beyond the border. Then I passed a single car, a fellow straggler from the bunch off the morning's ferry, judging by the shiny paint and the California plates. It was a big new Lincoln carrying a middle-aged couple obviously reluctant to get their expensive sedan bent or dirty; the man was driving very cautiously, picking his way along the rugged road like a lady trying to cross a wet street late at night without ruining her party shoes.

Five miles farther on, I saw another vehicle approaching from ahead. As it drew closer, I realized that I knew it, even though it was going the wrong way and had got pretty muddy since I'd seen it last. It was the lab truck, as young Smith had called it. It was heading back toward Haines for some reason, and the boys weren't sparing it a thing the road could dish out. They were really coming, hammering over the washboards and sliding through the curves. As they neared me, I pulled over to give them plenty of room, since they didn't seem to have the situation altogether under control.

The man at the wheel—whichever one of them it was—flashed his headlights at me and slammed on his brakes. He skidded to a halt well beyond me as, in answer to his signal, I stopped my rig more sedately on the other side of the road. It seemed like a hell of a place for a conference, out in wide-open country where anybody within a five-mile radius could see us together; but it was their mission and their security, and if they wanted to blow it, it was their business. Actually, considering what Holz probably knew or guessed by this time, there wasn't much left to blow, but they weren't supposed to know that.

I got out. The driver of the panel job got out. I saw that it was Smith, Junior. He came running toward me

across the muddy road. Something about his approach didn't strike me as friendly. I moved clear of the truck to give myself maneuvering room, and checked on the bearded partner I'd seen on shipboard. He was just coming around the pseudo-delivery-van, too far away to be an immediate threat. Young Smith ran up to me, breathless.

"You killed them!" he shouted wildly. "You damn crazy murderer, you killed them!"

He swung a fist at my face. I stepped back. As he started to bring the other fist into action, I kicked him between the legs, quite gently. Castrating him might not have been a bad idea, but it's not for me to say who should, and who should not, be permitted to perpetuate the race.

Young Smith doubled up and went to his knees. I looked at the other man, who had his hand inside his zipper jacket.

I said, "I'm not the world's greatest quick-draw artist, friend, but when I pull it, I shoot it. Don't wave anything at me you don't plan to use."

He brought his hand out empty. After a moment, he came across the road and looked down at his kneeling associate and up at me.

"You didn't have to do that," he said.

"No," I said. "I didn't have to. I was just feeling magnanimous. The routine response to that windmill attack involves a karate chop and a broken neck." I drew a long breath. "Who are you?"

"Davis," he said. "Lester Davis, sir."

I regarded him for a moment. He was a chunky, powerful-looking young man, wearing jeans, a heavy sweater, and the zippered windbreaker. His beard was reddish and so was his hair, which was fairly long. It had to be a disguise. His chief, Mr. Washington Smith, would just naturally take a dim view of hair, attributing all kinds of high moral values to razor blades and clippers.

Personally, I'm not all that sold on the virtues of barbering. I just like to be able to tell the boys from the girls, but in this case no confusion was possible. Hair or no hair, whiskers or no whiskers, I rather liked the rugged appearance of Lester Davis. At least he didn't have the

hungry look of fanatic self-righteousness that seemed to run in the Smith family.

"Are you going to break down and tell me what this is all about?" I asked him. "Does your friend make a habit of going ape in the middle of the public highway or does he have some particular reason for flipping his wig today?"

"Ronnie's upset," Davis said. "We just got word that a couple of our friends have been shot."

This information, imparted under these circumstances, made no sense at all. At least I couldn't see how it applied to me—and the idea of having friends in this business was fairly outlandish anyway.

I said, rather helplessly, "Honest, *amigo,* I haven't shot anybody all day."

"They were shot by an Indian called Pete," Davis said. "Ronnie seems to feel that you're responsible, sir."

I blinked, trying to figure out what might have happened, but the only answer I got was so incredible I didn't want to believe it. Before I could speak, a car appeared on the road, far away, approaching from the direction of the coast. Davis stepped forward to grab one of young Smith's—well, Ronnie's—arms; I grabbed the other and we straightened out the casualty and leaned him against the truck, more or less surrounding him sociably until the tourist couple in the big Lincoln had passed. By that time, he could stand by himself.

I looked at the red-bearded man. "I don't get it," I said. "I suppose the friends you mentioned are the agents who've been watching over me and spotting all the people with whom I made contact——"

"That's right. They've been switching operatives and cars on you pretty frequently on this job, sir, but these two are the ones who made the ferry ride up from Prince Rupert with us."

"Sure," I said. "I figured some of them might be along, but it seemed best not to look for them too hard. But they were supposed to be keeping an eye on *me.* How the hell did they get mixed up with Pete, for God's sake!"

Davis started to speak, but it was Ronnie Smith who answered indignantly: "They couldn't just leave the man

to die by the roadside after what you'd done to him, could they?"

I stared at his gaunt young face and at his eyes burning with anger and idealism, if that's what it was. Sometimes I have an uneasy feeling that the rest of the world operates on a different wavelength from the one to which Mac and I and a few other hard-working agents are tuned.

I mean, back there near Haines were a couple of presumably well trained and carefully briefed operatives who'd been given a job to do. It had undoubtedly been impressed on them, as on me, that the safety and welfare of their country depended on their doing it right. But instead of minding their assigned business, they'd wandered off to perform a totally irrelevant rescue of a totally irrelevant gent in a wrecked car!

All right, if you want to get technical, Pete wasn't completely irrelevant to the mission. Nevertheless, he was a known quantity. The work on Pete had all been done, or should have been. They'd had a week, more or less, to study up on him, circulate his description, and arrange to have him grabbed when convenient. They had absolutely nothing to learn, nothing to gain, by meeting the guy face to face, and they could lose the whole ball game if their mission of mercy misfired. Apparently, they'd gone right ahead and lost it.

Ronnie said harshly, as if sensing the direction of my thoughts: "You ran him off the road and drove away and left him. *Somebody* had to go down there!"

"Why?"

"You can't just leave a human being pinned in the wreckage of——"

"He can't have been pinned very hard," I said sourly. "At least he seems to have got an arm free to shoot with. Your friends could have figured on that. Why the hell do you think I went off and left him? Because I don't tackle any wounded grizzlies unless I have to, certainly not when I've got important work to do. You people did say this job of yours was important, didn't you?"

Ronnie started to speak angrily, but drew a long breath and decided against it. He glared at me instead and turned away. Walking a little stiff-legged, he marched to the lab

truck and got behind the wheel, slamming the door hard. He cranked down the window and stuck out his head.

"Come on, Les!" he called. "We aren't getting anywhere with this guy. Let's go!"

"Just a minute." Davis looked at me and said, "Actually, the man wasn't in the wreckage, according to the report we got. He'd crawled off into the bushes a little way and was lying there with his gun, waiting. When the boys started looking for him, he let them come in close and shot them both. One was hit in the face. He was unconscious for quite a while afterward. When he came to, both his partner and Pete were dead. He managed to struggle back to his car and raise us on the two-way radio."

"And now you're hurrying back to hold the poor guy's hand?"

Davis flushed. "He's badly hurt, sir."

I glanced at my watch. "At nine this evening you're supposed to take some important material off *my* hands at a place called Beaver Creek. You'll never make it if you drive clear back to Haines, particularly if you get tangled up with doctors and cops."

"I know. That's why we stopped, sir. To ask you to hold things up until tomorrow morning. There's nobody to cover you now and see who slips you the stuff, and we need that lead to the commie cell operating up here. You'd better pass up the evening rendezvous altogether, on one excuse or another, and use the alternate contact at breakfast instead."

"And where do I make contact with you afterward?"

"We'll set up an emergency drop down the road. Stop for coffee at The Antlers Lodge, east of Tok, Alaska. That's where you check back in through U.S. customs and immigration. The road divides, one branch going to Fairbanks and one to Anchorage. Turn left toward Anchorage like you're supposed to anyway. It's fifteen or twenty miles to the lodge. Try to make it as soon after nine as you can. We'll be waiting. Run the dog as usual before you go into the cafe. I'm told there's good cover east of the main building. Give us fifteen minutes and turn him loose again for a bit before you take off. After that, we'll handle the Anchorage part as originally planned, and tie it

all up with pink ribbons. Okay?" The horn of the Ford blared impatiently. Davis glanced that way and called, "I'm coming, Ronnie."

I said, "Okay, but there's one thing you'd better keep in mind."

"What's that, sir?"

"Pete wouldn't have burned down just any two Good Samaritans who wandered down there. Since he shot your boys, that means he knew who they were. Maybe, not realizing their warm and friendly intentions, he thought they'd come to finish him off. Or maybe he was just doing the best he could to strike a final blow at me. But the important thing is that he knew them; and that therefore the two of you could be known, too. So watch your steps, every damn one of them. Now you'd better go before your friend blows a gasket."

I watched them drive away; then I got back into the truck and headed toward Haines Junction, where the ferry cutoff from Haines joins the Alaska Highway. As I drove, I tried to dream up a plausible way of killing a few hours so I'd be late for tonight's contact without being obvious about it. I needn't have bothered. The excuse I needed was ready and waiting for me.

A good fifteen miles before the junction, I came upon a muddy Cadillac convertible stopped in the road. It was kind of slumped toward the left rear, like a bogged-down horse, and that wheel—not only the wheel and tire, but the brake drum and part of the axle—lay in the road nearby.

As I approached, a slender figure in yellow-brown corduroy jumped out of the crippled car and waved me to a halt.

26 THE TIMING WORKED OUT AS
well as if I'd planned it that way. It took a couple of hours to get Libby's car towed into the town ahead: a handful of buildings bunched around the bleak and lonely highway junction. Then we had to arrange to have replacement

parts sent out from Anchorage. By the time all the necessary phone calls had been made, it was plenty late enough in the afternoon that I could start driving again without any fear of arriving at my destination on time.

We reached Beaver Creek well after dark. The Canadian officials checked us out of their country, leaving us in a kind of international limbo, since we wouldn't be officially admitted to Alaska until the corresponding U.S. authorities had looked us over in Tok, over a hundred miles ahead.

The border community we'd just entered was no bigger than Haines Junction, if as big: just a few businesses scattered along the road to keep the customs shack from getting lonely during the long winter nights. We had no trouble at all in finding the motel, since it seemed to be the only one around. Like many of them up there, it looked as if it had been concocted by a house-trailer manufacturer and trucked here in sections, and maybe it had. In other words, it was a long narrow, railroad-car kind of building, of typical mobile-home construction, covered with ribbed, white-painted metal.

The room to which we were shown had two beds, a heater, a chair, and a tiny dresser, all crowded into a space barely adequate for a clothes closet. However, it was clean and warm and we were happy to have it. It had been a rough day, and we hadn't really slept much the night before. When the proprietor had left us, Libby tossed her trench coat on the chair and started to unbutton her jacket. I went to the door.

"Where are you going?" she asked.

"I've got to feed the pup, give him some air, and lock up the truck. Which bag do you want?"

"The same little one. . . . Oh, hell, if it's any trouble, never mind. I can sleep in my undies, and I hope to God you're not feeling masculine and virile, because I'm not feeling a bit feminine and seductive. God, what a drive! If you insist on eating dinner or something, be quiet when you come in, because I'll be asleep."

It was almost like being married again. I grinned and went out, stirred up a bowl of food for the pup and, while he was eating, took her suitcase and mine and shoved

them inside the motel-room door. When he was through, I turned Hank loose briefly, then locked him up and walked slowly toward the part of the building that served as a café. There were cars parked in front of the units of the long motel, and suddenly I found my glance drawn to a mud-covered, beat-up-looking little two-door job that seemed vaguely familiar.

At least, the sloping rear deck reminded me of a car I'd seen before and so did the fancy wheel-covers simulating wire wheels, although one of these was now missing and the rest were so dirty that no hint of chrome was visible any more than the original color of the car could be determined in the dark, through the coating of mud. There was a star-shaped crack in the windshield and a broken headlight; the kind of mementos one tends to pick up during, say, a fast thousand-mile dash along a wilderness road full of loose stone and gravel.

I stood there only a moment; then I moved on into the café and ordered a hamburger, and a beer since they served nothing stronger. *The damn little fool,* I thought. *I told her to go home; what the hell does she think she's doing up here?*

But that was a silly question. Obviously, Pat Bellman had trailed me clear to Alaska to take revenge for the friends I had killed; or she still had her eye on the dog collar that, properly filled, was worth fifty grand to a Chinese gent called Soo.

27 *I WAS AWAKENED BY SOMETHING* wet and cold applied to my face. I sat up in bed, wondering how the hell the pup had got into the motel room. Then I remembered that I'd brought him in last night. It had been one of the times when there were obviously a million precautions that should have been taken, but that had been the only one I could think of.

As I sat there, yawning in the half-darkness, Hank put

his forepaws on the bed and tried to give me another slobbery lick. I pushed him away halfheartedly.

"Down!" I whispered, glancing toward the other bed where Libby was sleeping soundly. "I get the message: you want out. Just hold your goddamn little black horses."

I glanced at my watch and found that it was later than it felt: six thirty-five to be exact. My alarm clock was set for seven—I reached over to switch it off—and I had an appointment outside the cafe at seven-fifteen sharp.

I got up and went into the bathroom. Threats to the contrary notwithstanding, Libby hadn't slept in her undies: she'd washed them and hung them on the shower rod to dry. It was another homelike, wifely touch. Fighting the early-morning battle of the nylons—well, just brassiere and panties in this case—reminded me again, nostalgically, of the comfortable state of matrimony from which I had resigned, or been fired, a long time ago.

When I got outside, there was enough light to see by, but yesterday's fine weather was gone and rain was falling: a slow misty drizzle. Hank thought it was great. He was a water dog; he liked rain. He took off happily through the puddles to transact his morning business while I zipped up Grant Nystrom's ski jacket against the cold and pulled down Grant Nystrom's Stetson to shield my face from the dripping moisture. Waiting, I checked the truck, and nobody'd been at it. I checked the parked cars, and the hard-driven little Mustang with the stone-cracked windshield was missing from its slot.

"Excuse me," said a male voice in my ear, "excuse me, but isn't that a Labrador retriever? He's a beauty. What's his name?"

I turned to look at a plump man in his early thirties. His rather citified hat and plastic raincoat proclaimed him a tourist, as did the rubbers he was wearing over his city shoes. Behind him stood a similarly plump woman almost totally wrapped in waterproof, semi-transparent plastic, except for her lower legs, which displayed very tight green pants ending just below the calves. Her bare ankles looked unbearably cold, and her low shoes were too flimsy to serve adequately as anything but bedroom slippers, which was exactly what they looked like.

I spoke to the man. "Yes, he's a Lab," I said. "His name is Hank."

"No, I mean his full name. He's pedigreed, isn't he?"

I said, "His registered name is Avon's Prince Hannibal of Holgate."

"Thanks," said the man and turned to the woman, "See, I *told* you that was a pedigreed Labrador, dear."

She said, "I'm getting wet. Let's grab a cup of coffee and get going before this whole miserable country melts and runs away. Whose bright idea was it, coming to Alaska, anyway?"

They went into the café. I checked the time surreptitiously. Ten minutes later, I whistled in the pup and locked him up in the camper, since he was pretty wet and Libby had made it abundantly clear that she didn't even like dry dogs very much. Exactly fifteen minutes from the time the plump dog expert and his unhappy wife, if that's what she was, had gone through the door, I went in after them.

Inside, the tiny café looked pretty much like a railroad dining car, with booths on either side and an aisle down the middle. My people had the middle booth on the right-hand side. They'd finished their hasty coffee and were just leaving. There was no competition; I had no trouble establishing myself in the same booth, after first letting them go by.

I ordered coffee, orange juice, eggs, and bacon, and went to work on the canned juice and the coffee while waiting for the main event. Only after the plate was put in front of me did I reach for the salt cellar. Seasoning my eggs carefully, I palmed the wafer of tinfoil stuck to the bottom of the cheap glass container, and contact number five was completed—but it still seemed like a silly game for grown-up men and women to be playing.

When I returned to the room, Libby emerged from the bathroom, fully dressed, to greet me. She retreated hastily as Hank romped forward to say hello.

"Damn that mutt!" she snapped, brushing at herself. "Why does he always have to put his great big dirty feet on . . . ah, hell! Come here, you black monster. I didn't mean to hurt your damn little feelings."

She held out the back of her hand to let Hank sniff it and give it a couple of licks; then she scratched his ears forgivingly and laughed.

"What are a few paw prints between friends?" she said ruefully. "After yesterday, I look like I'd been sweeping out the stables anyway; but I didn't see any sense in putting on something clean until we get out of this mud and dust. If we ever do." She glanced at me quickly, as if only now remembering what I was supposed to have been doing this morning. "My God, I forgot! How did the contact go? Did you get it?"

"I got it," I said. "I thought, as my self-appointed partner in this caper, you'd like to see it stashed away; that's why I brought the pup inside. Hank, sit!"

Obediently, he plunked his fanny on the floor, and I bent down to remove his collar, then stopped. There was a long silence as I looked thoughtfully at the black, metal-studded strap around his neck. It was the right color, and it had the right number of decorations of roughly the right shapes in roughly the right places. It even had the right, slightly faded, well-worn look. But it wasn't the dog collar I'd come to know and love.

I stood there for a long moment, thinking back; but I already knew the answer. The collar had been right yesterday. This morning it was wrong . . . .

"Is this what you're looking for?" Libby's voice said softly behind me. I turned, and there it was, in her hand. She smiled. "As your self-appointed partner, darling, I thought you were being just a little careless, letting him run around with all that priceless NCS information around his neck. So last night, after you were asleep, I just switched them to show you how easily it could be done."

I drew a long, slow breath. "Where'd you get the duplicate?"

"I've had it right along. It was an obvious thing to bring, just in case. Here. Take this one." I didn't move at once, and she looked at my face hard. "Matt!"

I said, "Damn it, the name is Grant."

"To hell with you, Matt! You really thought. . . ! Don't you ever trust anyone?"

170

"Sure. And I can show you a scar for every damn time."

"After . . . after everything, you really thought I . . . you really thought I'd *stolen*. . . !" Her voice was choked. "Oh, damn you, Matt Helm! Damn you, damn you, *damn* you! Here, take your precious strap!"

I ducked as it came flying at me. She grabbed her coat and suitcase and marched out the door. It was a great performance.

All her performances had been great, I reflected grimly. She was a real trooper, a real pro, and I was full of admiration for her. I mean that. There wasn't any resentment in me, any indignation, any feeling of wounded pride for the way she'd fooled me. I respected and admired her, and I was sorry she'd been given such a lousy script to play, because she deserved better. Holz and his associates should have been ashamed of themselves, to give such a fine actress such crummy material.

I mean the richbitch routine with which she'd started out had been unconvincing enough, but the U.S. secret-agent line she'd had to fall back on had been a real turkey. Yet she'd put it over, selling me the farfetched notion that not only was she working for Mr. Smith, but that that gentleman operated his respectable government agency in a peculiarly complicated and two-faced manner. I must have been in an impressionable state when I bought that one, but bought it I had, at least provisionally.

She'd been good all the way. As a pro, I thought with real pleasure of the casual way she'd treated security, to make me believe she was really pretty amateur after all. As a man who'd had a lot of approaches tried on him with sinister motives, I couldn't help recalling fondly the infinite variety of her treatments of the sex theme.

Of course, she'd made some mistakes; we all do. Her worst ones had been with the pup. Well, she'd had a difficult problem to solve. To forestall suspicion, she'd wanted to give me the idea that she hated and feared animals and wanted nothing to do with them, while at the same time she'd had to gain Hank's trust so his collar would be available to her when the right time came.

I should have spotted the inconsistency at once, when

he started putting his paws on her. A trained hunting dog does not jump on people unless actively encouraged—you don't want sixty-odd pounds of retriever hitting you in the chest while you're holding a loaded shotgun. Hank might lick my face when it was within his reach, in bed or in the camper doorway, but he'd never dream of expressing his joy at seeing me in the undisciplined way he'd suddenly started greeting Libby. She must have taken advantage of the morning they'd been alone in the camper, on shipboard, to get across to him what she wanted, so that later she'd have an excuse to put on her I-hate-dogs act for me.

On the whole, however, her performance had been very, very good. She'd overcome the handicaps of a poor script beautifully. In the end what had betrayed her was a faulty intelligence system. She'd gambled and lost because nobody had informed her of the one thing she was bound to know if she was the trusted agent of Mr. Smith she claimed to be. She hadn't known about the lab truck; she hadn't known that we U.S. troops had, right along, been playing tricks with the stolen NCS data as we intercepted it. She hadn't known that the stuff in the pup's collar not only wasn't priceless any longer, but was stuff we'd be happy to get into enemy hands. No matter how secretive Mr. Smith might be, he would have confided such essential knowledge to a trusted operative working for him on the sly. But Libby hadn't been aware of it.

I drew another long breath. My next move was obvious. Now that I had her spotted, now that I could guess how, or at least through whom, Holz planned to move against me, it was clearly up to me to act totally stupid, trusting, and fondly bemused, until I could see what kind of deadfall she was supposed to lead me into. That meant reassuring her by letting her have what she wanted—the real collar—regardless of how this would louse up the careful plans of Messrs. Davis and Smith.

I picked it up where she'd thrown it, filled the last stud, gathered my belongings, and followed Hank outside. Libby was standing in the slow rain with the hood of her superspy trench coat pulled up to cover her hair. I guess she was realizing that the trouble with dramatic exits is that you've got to have somewhere to go afterward. I

walked around to the rear of the truck and opened it. Hank jumped in without being told.

I said, "Throw your bag in here if you're coming."

Libby approached stiffly and set her suitcase inside the camper without looking at me or speaking to me. I closed the door and went forward, unlocked the left-hand cab door, got in, and pulled the latch across the way so she could join me. When we'd driven a little way, she tossed back her hood and unbuttoned her damp coat. She fastened the seat belt across her lap.

"Here," I said. She looked at me and at the metal-studded strap I was holding out. I said, "It's the genuine article. Check it if you like."

"What am I supposed to do with it?" Her voice was cold.

"You don't like it on the dog. Where do you like it?" I tossed it into her lap. I hoped my voice sounded convincingly petulant as I went on. "There it is, all deliveries complete. You don't approve of the way I take care of it, so hide it yourself." I grimaced. "What I mean is, if you're so smart, partner, you take charge of the lure until we've used it to hook the last little fish in Anchorage and can put it back in the tackle box where it belongs."

She hesitated before she picked up the collar and looked at it. There was a brief silence; then she said in a changed tone of voice, rather uncertainly: "Matt, you don't have to . . . I didn't really mean . . ."

I said irritably, "*Now* what's the problem, doll? First I catch hell for not trusting you and then I get a big song and dance when I do . . . "

She said, very softly, "Darling, it's all right. You hurt me, you really did, with your crazy suspicions, but it's all right now."

As I say, she was good. Busy driving, I never did see what she actually did with the damn dog collar. An hour or so later we hit smooth black pavement. A sign featuring Smoky the Bear welcomed us to the state of Alaska and begged us not to set fire to it. At the moment, it was difficult to see how anybody could ignite any part of that soggy landscape.

By the time we reached Tok, however, the rain had

stopped. The U.S. customs-and-immigration man asked a few questions and passed us through. In smooth, quiet, dry comfort we rolled down the paved highway. After a while we encountered, on the right-hand side of the road, a big sign proclaiming the nearness of The Antlers Lodge. I pulled up at the gas station below the main building, which was constructed of peeled logs and located on a wooded knoll a little back from the road. Near the door labeled "Coffee Shop" stood a muddy Ford van.

Libby said, "My God, look at all the horns! What's that big mounted one, a moose?"

"The one with the fancy shovels sticking out front? No, that's a caribou," I said. "Reindeer to you. The snooty white one with the swept-back stickers is a Dall sheep. Are you hungry?" It seemed a safe question. She never ate much before lunch.

"No, but I could use a rest room."

As she moved off to find it, I got out of the cab and went back to release the pup, telling him to stick around. I would have preferred to leave him locked up, but I'd turned him loose at practically every previous stop, and I didn't want anybody watching to think there was anything different about this one.

I'd been tempted not to stop at all, since there was nothing to be accomplished here without the proper collar. However, I didn't know how carefully young Smith and his red-bearded friend would be watching the highway. If they missed seeing me go by, they might hit the panic button and betray themselves, or me, by running back and forth looking for me when I failed to show up. This way, seeing me stop and go on without making the prearranged contact, they'd know something was wrong and, I hoped, proceed cautiously.

A sudden animal howl of fright and pain spun me around where I'd been standing, ostensibly watching the man fill the gas tank, actually watching the corner of the station around which Libby had disappeared and wondering what she might be up to. I realized belatedly that Hank, despite orders, had taken advantage of my preoccupation to slip away. His cry had come from up the hill, near the main lodge.

I ran that way hastily as the half-choked canine call for help came again. I was honestly worried. On this trip I had learned that it takes a lot to hurt or scare a Labrador seriously enough to make him open up and tell you about it. I pounded up the hill and around the corner of the lodge, where the brush was thick, and slowed down, drawing a breath of relief. There was an old barbed-wire fence running through the bushes, and he'd just got himself hung up on it, that was all.

"Okay, pup," I called. "Take it easy. I'm coming."

He stopped fighting it as I came up and awaited me, trembling, suspended half off the ground. I reached for the substitute collar he was wearing, caught in the rusty wire. With his weight on it, it was impossible to free it, so I unfastened the buckle to release him before tackling the wire. Only then did I realize that it would have been practically impossible for a dog just running into some loose fencing to get himself so badly entangled in the brief time he'd had.

As the thought came to me, there was a movement behind me, and I knew that I'd found the elusive Mr. Holz at last, or he'd found me. Pain went through my head, and the world turned blazing white, then glowing red, then black . . . .

28 I AWOKE IN FAMILIAR SURROUND-

ings. Somehow, even before opening my eyes I knew I was lying on the floor of my own—well, the late Nystrom's—camper. It seemed to be proceeding along a reasonably well-paved road at moderate speed.

I lay there, tied hand and foot, rocked back and forth gently by the motion of the rig. Without moving, I sent my mind on a quick perimeter check, so to speak, and detected no gun-bulge under my belt and no knife-bulge in my pocket. Well, that figured. I thought about my colossal, sentimental stupidity, since there wasn't much else to think about, except the pain in my head. I reflected

bitterly on the philosophical truth that no matter how hard a man tries to be inhuman, or superhuman, he never quite makes it.

On this job, I'd managed to be tough and professional and heartless practically all the way. To be sure, in just one instance, to cut down on the bloodshed that seemed to be getting out of hand, I'd taken the calculated risk of releasing somebody who perhaps should have been silenced instead—the returns weren't in on that—but otherwise I'd killed ruthlessly as required. I'd refused, as it had turned out quite correctly, to let humanitarian considerations, or any other considerations, send me back to see about the driver of a car I'd wrecked. The best efforts of a clever and beautiful woman had failed to make the slightest dent in my armor of suspicion.

And then, I reflected grimly, and *then*, knowing that the critical moment of the mission had to be close at hand, I'd let the frantic howling of a year-old pup send me rushing blindly into an ambush any first-year trainee could have avoided in his sleep.

"Grant. Grant, are you all right? Can you hear me?"

The voice was familiar, perhaps too familiar. Rather surprised to hear it here, I opened my eyes. As I'd figured, I was stretched out on the camper's narrow floor, between the stove and the sink cabinet. My head was against the door. My feet were under the dinette table.

Avoiding them with her own bound feet was Libby, still in her open trenchcoat, somewhat awry, and the natty pants costume that was now, as she herself had pointed out this morning, just a bit the worse for several days of strenuous wear. Her hands, like mine, were tied.

Apparently Holz thought he was being clever, sticking her in here dramatically bound hand and foot to share my misery, keep an eye on me and, perhaps, learn something from me that somebody wanted to know.

I felt a little stir of hope. If Holz did want something from me—and if not, why wasn't I dead?—then I still had a chance. And the more carefully I played my attractive companion along, the better that chance would be.

"Greetings, doll," I whispered. "Don't say it. I goofed."

She was tactful enough not to comment on that. "Your

dog got away," she said. "They tried to catch him, but they'd already scared him so badly he wouldn't come near them."

"Good for old Hank," I said sourly. I was glad to hear of his escape, but I'd expended quite enough sympathy on him for one day. "How did they catch you?" I asked Libby.

"I ran up there right behind you when I heard him screaming. A man stepped out from behind a tree and put a hand over my mouth and a gun in my back. Afterward, he made me walk back down with him and pay for the gas and drive the truck up the hill so they could load you aboard without attracting attention. Darling, what are we going to do?"

"Could you tell which way we turned from the lodge?" I asked, ignoring her question because I had no answer to it.

"Yes, I can see pretty well out the front here. We're still on the same highway, heading toward Anchorage."

"How long have I been out? Specifically, how long have we been driving?"

"Well, I'm not in the best position to keep checking my wristwatch, but it's only been a few minutes."

"Who's up front?"

"A couple of real characters. There's a woman, plain and plump, in a plastic raincoat and green pants. Why is it that the fatter the fanny, the tighter the trousers? Then there's a plumpish male type who looks as if he'd just stepped off a rainy city sidewalk. He's even got galoshes on, for God's sake!"

I said, "Be charitable. I think it's a disguise. Who's driving?"

"The man. The woman keeps rubbernecking to make sure we're not setting fire to the bus or rolling out into the road." A round, unpretty face I'd seen before appeared at the forward window of the camper, looking back at us suspiciously. When it had vanished, Libby said, "You see what I mean."

"Keep talking," I said. "How many more?"

"It's a real caravan, darling. There's an older couple, middle-aged, driving a big car——"

I asked wearily, "It wouldn't be a Lincoln, by any chance?" I was remembering the large, slow-moving sedan I'd passed and repassed on the Haines cutoff. It seemed likely, now, that after seeing me on my way, the tourist-appearing couple had turned back in pursuit of the lab truck. Judging by this morning's events, the pursuit had been highly successful.

"Yes," Libby said, "yes, it's a Lincoln. And then there's a kind of boxy delivery van. The guy who gives the orders is driving that, a man they all call Mr. Wood."

"Mr. Wood, eh?" I kept my voice casual, wondering if the boys in the van were still alive, and if so, for how long. Well, they weren't my boys. "What does Mr. Wood look like?" I asked.

He wasn't very subtle, I reflected, or maybe he was just arrogant. Maybe he thought nobody knew enough German, up here in the benighted wilderness, to remember the English translation of "Holz."

"He's kind of a tallish man," Libby said. "Not a bean-pole like you, but probably about the same weight, since he's broader. He's got metal-rimmed glasses, slick black patent-leather hair, and a silly little black moustache, but I have a hunch there's some dye involved. Nobody's got hair that black. And I don't think his real name is Wood. It's probably Rubinsky or Kubicek or Ivanoff or something. I know a Slav when I see one."

It was my man, all right. She had sharp eyes, or she'd been told exactly what to say in order to gain, or maintain, my confidence, probably the latter. The fact that Holz's name wasn't Holz at all was fairly common knowledge, but we'd never learned the real name and likely never would. Maybe he'd forgotten it himself; he'd been Hans Holz so long. They often go in for Teutonic or Anglo-Saxon labels, I guess because these days, over here at least, people tend to look a little more closely, in cases involving security, at anyone named Vladimir, Ivan, or Olga.

Thinking along these lines, I found myself wondering just what might be the real name of the lady known locally as Elizabeth Meredith.

She asked, "Do you know him, darling?"

I shrugged. "Not under that name. Do you?"

"No, but I can tell just by looking that he's not a very nice man. In fact, he scares hell out of me. Darling, what are we going to do?"

I still had no answer to that question, and if I'd had one I wouldn't have confided it to her. I asked, not because it mattered, but because I'd be expected to be concerned about it, "What about the item I gave you to take care of?"

"It's safe. They didn't get it. They must think the one the dog was wearing is the right one."

"Where is it safe?" I asked.

She hesitated. "I don't think I'll tell you right now. I mean, that way, if things get tough, you can say quite honestly that you don't know."

"Thanks," I said. "That's sweet of you. But suppose we get separated; how do I find it?"

"You'll find it," she said cryptically, smiling a bit. "You'll need some help, but you'll find it."

"Sure."

I didn't press it. Except for the material I'd picked up this morning, which might or might not be genuine, the collar wasn't worth much to anyone. Certainly, it had served my purpose: it had brought me within reach of the man I'd come to Alaska to find—not under the most favorable circumstances, granted, but still within reach.

I was no longer in the dog-collar business, and if anyone really yearned for the lousy strap, I could probably locate it, assuming that she'd really hidden it where she'd hinted. There was, after all, only one place she'd been where I, a man, would need help to find it: the room marked LADIES, back at the filling station.

The woman up front looked in on us once more, giving us a careful scrutiny this time to make sure we hadn't changed positions suspiciously, or tampered with our bonds. I lay there, trying to figure things out. The timing was important. The ropes around my wrists and ankles posed no real problem, since a trick belt with a sharp-edged buckle—well, sharp if you know how to get at it—is part of the standard equipment. The question was whether to use it now or wait.

I decided to wait. At the moment, the risk of detection was too great, and according to Libby's census, the odds were five to one against me, six to one if I counted Libby herself, and there was no good reason not to. It seemed better to let the situation sort itself out a little. Maybe I could somehow, eventually, separate my bull from the cows and steers.

The truck slowed down suddenly, made a sharp left turn, and started bumping over the ruts of a very rough road, little more than a track by the feel of it, leading away from the highway.

"What do you see?" I asked Libby.

"Just trees," she said. "We seem to be in some kind of mountains. The car ahead is stopping in a little clearing. That's the Lincoln. There are some horses, four of them."

"Horses?" I said. "I didn't know they used horses up here. I thought they all traveled by bush plane and dog sled."

The truck stopped. The camper door opened. Somebody reached in, grabbed me under the armpits, dragged me out, and stood me on my feet to face a tall, solidly built man dressed for the woods in boots, wool pants, a heavy lumberman's coat, and a cap—the kind with earflaps—of the same reddish plaid material. Among all this rugged clothing, the little black Hitler moustache and the gold-rimmed glasses looked lost and effeminate.

29 I DIDN'T LOOK AT HIM TOO HARD

or too long. There's a kind of telepathic recognition that sometimes passes between people in our line of work. Maybe a couple of artists occasionally feel the same odd little tingle of kinship when they meet, or a couple of auto salesmen. I wouldn't know about that.

I only know that I can often spot one of my fellow specialists, even at a distance; and I didn't want Holz to spot me or guess my real mission. As long as he thought I

was just a dim-witted counterespionage type, I was much more likely to keep on living.

He looked me over for just a moment, giving nothing away; then he indicated a nearby log for the man behind me to park me on. Libby was hauled out of the camper and set down beside me. She tossed some displaced hair out of her eyes and shifted position uneasily.

"He might have picked a drier log," she murmured.

"I don't think Mr. Wood spends a great deal of time worrying about preserving the seats of our pants. Quite the contrary," I said, with a meaningful look toward the horses. "I don't know where he intends to take us, or why, but how are you at riding with your hands tied behind you?"

She said, "Ugh. If there's any animal more objectionable than a dog, it's a horse, if only because it's bigger and stupider."

I refrained from making a face at her, but I felt like it. She was back on her antilivestock kick and to hell with her. Probably it would turn out that she'd taken the equestrienne gold medal at the last Olympics. As for me, I've held down a saddle or two in my time, but I'm still the kind of rider who requires some cooperation from the horse.

The little clearing was fairly crowded. The Ford delivery job had pulled up behind the camper. Ahead a ways was the Lincoln, the four-horse herd, and, half hidden in the brush at the end of the opening, another sedan with a big cattle trailer hitched on behind. I saw the younger man, the citified one with galoshes, who'd given me the password in Beaver Creek—the one who'd just dragged me out of the camper—head that way on some unknown assignment.

Holz had attacked the Lincoln. Helped by the younger woman, now without her plastic covering, he was dragging horse gear and other equipment out of the rear seat and trunk. I noted four scabbarded rifles, one for each horse. Two were strictly nothing-guns. They were the movie-cowboy, bang-bang rifles; the short, flat little lever-action carbines that, although handy to slip under your leg when

riding, don't have much more range or accuracy than a good revolver.

The other two I couldn't make out in detail since their scabbards were equipped with leather hoods for full protection, but they were obviously longer and heavier, real big-game guns, bolt action rifles with telescopic sights, suitable for serious marksmanship if properly assembled and prepared. Since they were presumably Holz's guns, I thought they'd probably be tuned pretty well. Maybe one was even the weapon intended for his next assignment, down in the Lower Forty-Eight, right after election-time— the date I was supposed to prevent him from keeping.

The old woman, the one I'd seen riding in the Lincoln the day before, wasn't visible anywhere. Her companion, the older man, was leaning against the truck watching over Libby and me. He had no weapon out, but there was a hint of armament under the armpit of his civilized overcoat; not the most convenient place in the world, but plenty available enough under the circumstances.

After Holz and the lady in the green pants had worked between the Lincoln and the horses for a while, the galoshes gent came out of the brush beyond, a changed man. Now instead of city shoes with rubber protection, he was wearing well-worn cowboy boots. There was also a pair of greasy jeans, a faded denim jacket that reminded me of Pat Bellman, who'd favored a similar garment, and a wide-brimmed hat that had real character, obviously seasoned by years of Alaska weather and a multitude of campfires. Even his walk had changed to the rolling gait of the horseman, and he was lugging a saddle with each hand. Well, he'd never made a very convincing city slicker.

He moved across the clearing to where Holz was now adjusting the cinch of a bony-looking chestnut gelding.

"All right, Mr. Wood," I heard him say. "I'll take care of this."

I saw Holz glance my way and I heard his voice: "Better lengthen the stirrups on the little mare. The man has long legs."

"So his knees bump his chin today, who cares? Tomorrow he'll never feel it."

"Lengthen them, Jack."

"Sure, Mr. Wood."

It was a revealing exchange, in more ways than one. I watched Holz come across the clearing toward us, accompanied by the unattractive female in the tight pants. He passed some sort of signal to the man guarding us, who walked back to the lab van and returned with the older woman: a sturdy, gray-haired lady in a tweed skirt, cotton blouse, and cardigan sweater. She stuffed a small automatic pistol into the pocket of her skirt as she came up.

Holz spoke to the three of them: "I want you to tie up the loose ends. The first thing is the dog. We couldn't wait around for him just now; Jack and I have a long ride to make to reach the lake before dark. Besides, he was too excited. He'll have settled down by this time. I want one of you to stay here to guard our guests in the van while the other two go back and dispose of him quietly and privately."

There was a brief silence. I noted that Holz was carefully not looking my way. You might have thought he was a little embarrassed about giving orders to kill my dog, right in front of me. It didn't seem in character, but on second thought I realized I didn't know the man's character. All I knew was his record. I'd made him up a personality to fit that record, in my mind, but it didn't have to be the right one.

The man with the overcoat asked, "And what if the pooch won't be caught."

"Do what you can without attracting attention. I'd rather not leave him around. He's obviously a valuable animal. Even without a collar, he might be traced. But leave him if you have to; don't stay so long that you can't be back here by, say, two o'clock. How are our young friends in the van?"

He looked at the gray-haired woman as he asked the question, and she said, "Red-Whiskers is all right. The other one is feeling sorry for himself. I took his gag out, but he moaned so loudly I had to put it back."

Holz nodded. "Well, you know where to stage the wreck. Give them the injection—you know which one— just before you send them through the guard rail. We

don't want any miraculous survivals. You know where to turn in this camper. The people there have instructions for burying it. Take the Lincoln back to Anchorage. When Jack and I come back, we'll dispose of the horses and trailer and meet you there. You know where."

The man with the horses called, "All ready here, Mr. Wood."

"All right, Jack." Holz looked at the three in front of him. "Any questions? Very well, untie this pair and bring them over . . . Wait a minute." He turned to look down at Libby and me. "Miss Meredith or whatever your name may be," he said, "and Mr. Nystrom or whatever your name may be, you undoubtedly realize that you are scheduled to die. . . . No, no, Miss Meredith, let me finish. It was one of the risks you assumed when you embarked on your missions of deceit and impersonation; it should come as no surprise to you now."

Libby said quickly, "You're making a mistake. You wouldn't listen to me back there, you were in such a damn hurry . . ."

"What is my mistake?"

"I'm working for the same people as you are. I have credentials——"

"Whom you're working for is yet to be determined, Miss Meredith. We know that in Seattle you identified your companion, positively, as Grant Nystrom. For your information, Jack over there was well acquainted with the real Mr. Nystrom and guided him on two hunting trips. Jack says that this man is no more Grant Nystrom than he, Jack, is Sophia Loren. Yet you identified this impostor as our courier, your lover. What does that make you, Miss Meredith?"

"I can explain——"

"You will be given an opportunity to try. But not here. There isn't time."

"You'd better listen to me right here!" she said hotly. "You're making a bad mistake. You'd better check and check carefully or you're going to be in real trouble, Mr. Wood or whatever *your* name may be. I'm working for some important people in San Francisco, people you know very well, and they gave me a message to deliver. . . ."

"Where is the message?"

"I'm not authorized to give it to you. I was told to deliver it only to a man named Anson, George Anson. There were some corny words we were supposed to say, as usual."

Holz smiled faintly and gestured toward the middle-aged man in the overcoat. "This is George Anson . . . Say the corny words, George."

The man leaned down and whispered in Libby's ear, and turned his head so she could whisper back. He straightened up and nodded.

Libby said triumphantly, "Well, are you satisfied? Untie my hands so I can give him the message."

It was Holz's turn to nod. The man called Anson worked briefly at the knots. When the ropes fell away, Libby sat rubbing her wrists for a moment; then reached well up under the front of her high-necked sweater and brought out a tiny cylindrical object which she handed to Anson. She smoothed the brown sweater down once more.

Anson produced a slip of paper and tossed aside the capsule in which it had traveled. He said, "Just a minute, Mr. Wood. It seems to be in code."

Nobody spoke or moved as he bent over the hood of the truck, writing with a small gold pencil he'd fished from inside the overcoat somewhere near the shoulder-holstered gun. I didn't look at Libby, or at Holz. They had me baffled. Together, they were putting on a great show, apparently for my benefit, but the purpose escaped me. Well, it would become clear eventually, I hoped.

Anson straightened up. His face was expressionless. He walked over and gave the paper to Holz, who read it and looked at Libby.

"Well?" she snapped.

"Would you like to hear the message you brought so many thousand miles, Miss Meredith?"

She licked her lips. "Yes, of course."

"The communication, decoded, reads: BEARER IS TRAITOR—LIQUIDATE."

"No!" Libby cried. "No, you can't. . . . It's a mistake."

Holz shrugged. "Perhaps. If so, it seems we're all making it, both here and in San Francisco. I'm afraid you're

just going to have to live with it—and die with it, Miss Meredith. What I started to say earlier was that while your execution and that of Mr. Nystrom is inevitable, I have been instructed to learn certain things about you, both of you, before I carry it out."

"What things?" Libby demanded.

"I am supposed to determine who you really are, both of you, and how much damage your treachery has done, so that steps can be taken to repair it. Unfortunately, there isn't time to perform the necessary research here. Your presence indicates that the scheduled drop in Anchorage has probably been compromised. We have therefore canceled it and set up another meeting some fifteen miles back in the wilderness where we're not likely to be disturbed."

I said, "In other words, we ride."

"Exactly, Mr. Nystrom. The immediate question is, *how* do you ride. This is rough country, and fifteen miles is a long way on horseback, even for someone unencumbered by ropes and bonds. Furthermore, I prefer to have us look as much as possible like a bona fide hunting party, just in case a stray bush plane comes over. I will therefore let you both start out with hands and feet free. Your horses will be the two slowest; the rifles on your saddles will be unloaded. I am a good rider and an excellent shot. Jack over there is an excellent rider and a good shot. The information in your heads is of interest to us, but it is not valuable enough to save you if you should try to escape. I hope I make myself perfectly clear." He turned and walked away.

Libby called after him desperately, "I tell you, it's all a horrible misunderstanding."

Nobody paid any attention to her. After a moment, she shrugged and turned to me with a wry grin. "Well, hell, darling," she said, "at least I tried."

30 *I WAS UNTIED AND HERDED TO-*
ward a shaggy little brown mare with an independent, mulish look that proved to be an accurate indication of her character.

If I'd had any foolish notions of making a break for it and galloping off wildly with Holz's bullets whistling around my ears, that little mare would soon have disabused me of them. She made it abundantly clear that she wasn't galloping wildly anywhere. In fact, without a stout switch I'd never even have got her moving. All she really wanted was to stop and eat the willows and other green stuff along the way.

Libby's bony chestnut seemed a little more willing, but he was one of the worst equine stumblebums I'd ever seen, forever half falling over his own big feet. To consider a fast escape over broken country on such a shaky plug was obviously suicidal. By way of contrast, Jack, riding ahead, had a fine, leggy buckskin that obviously wanted to go; while Holz, at the rear of the parade, was mounted on a powerful bay with a ground-eating stride that kept it nipping at the moth-eaten tail of my reluctant transportation.

Not that it made a great deal of difference. Even if we'd been mounted on registered thoroughbreds, we could hardly have made a race of it. It wasn't that kind of country. The first stretch was wooded and mountainous, up a rocky trail that also served as a bed for a small stream, then over a fairly rugged pass, and finally down into a tremendous open basin by way of another running brook.

The high ground was bad enough, but the lowlands were worse. Except for my one previous Arctic venture in Europe some years back, I'd never seen such wet country. When we weren't actually splashing through puddles and streams, we jolted along to the steady squelching made by the horses' hoofs sinking in the black ooze beneath the low

brush and rank, hummocky grass that covered the landscape whether it was wooded or open.

It started to drizzle once more as, working our way around the edge of the great basin, we swung northward, entering a long, gradually narrowing valley running up toward some snow-capped mountains. The ground got no drier and the trail got no better. Toward the end of the afternoon, with mountains slowly closing in on us, we came to a swampy little brown-water lake surrounded by soggy-looking evergreens on all sides except one, where an avalanche or landslide from above had left a bare and rocky shoreline.

The horses picked their way through the jumbled rocks, crossed the small inlet of the lake, and presently forded a large creek or small river. The water here was the same milky blue-green color that so many streams seemed to be up here. We rode up the river for about fifteen minutes, crossed once more, and came to the camp: three more or less white wall tents and some grazing horses in a meadow that was edged with trees and overlooked by the towering mountains that formed the east wall of the dwindling valley up which we had come, still several miles wide at this point.

The largest tent, in the middle, was equipped with a stovepipe, from which smoke was rising. An elderly, wrinkled, brown-faced gent, who could have been the father, or maybe even the grandfather, of the late Pete, came out to meet us.

He took charge of Holz's horse. Jack dismounted and came over to hold mine. Covered by Holz, who'd produced a small Spanish automatic, I slid stiffly from the saddle and, since there was no reason not to be a gentleman, limped over to Libby and helped her down. She was heavy in my arms. It was a moment before she could stand unsupported. I thought her weariness was genuine. It had been a long hard ride for anybody, even an expert horsewoman concealing her talents, if that's what she was. I still hadn't made up my mind about it.

"Take them to their tent and tie them up," Holz said. "I'll question them later. . . . Oh, just a minute." He turned to face us. "Let me first make the situation quite

plain. You will find your accommodations rather basic, I'm afraid: merely a roof over your head, and a canvas roof at that. You will have noticed that the afternoon is already growing cool; the temperature will probably drop well below freezing tonight. To combat the cold, it helps to be well fed. A ground cloth and blankets are also useful. Everything is available at a price. Do I make myself clear?"

I managed a grin. "And the price is information? That's pretty childish, isn't it, Mr. Wood?"

He shrugged. "I see that you are a strong man, probably accustomed to hardship. What does the lady think? Am I being childish, Miss Meredith?"

She stared at him dully, but didn't speak. She'd been ahead of me during the ride, and although I hadn't seen much of her face, I'd thought she was making it all right, but now I was shocked at the way she looked.

I don't mean just the fact that she was rather spectacularly wet and muddy; I was by this time no sartorial masterpiece myself. What disturbed me was something dark and ugly and broken I thought I could see in her eyes. I'd seen it before, in people driven beyond their personal limits of endurance. It's a hard thing to fake. I didn't like it.

I took her arm and helped her to the tent that Holz indicated with his pistol. It was, as he'd warned, no palace. The floor was bare, if you want to call it that; actually it was dirt, softly and damply carpeted with a mixture of old spruce needles, humus, and decaying leaves. While Holz covered us, Jack tied us up, and propelled us inside. I landed pretty hard. When I'd caught my breath, I heard an odd little whimpering sound beside me. Libby was crying helplessly.

There wasn't much I could do to comfort her with my hands tied. I said, "Take it easy. We're still alive."

"I . . . I'm sorry," she gasped. "I c-can't help it. It just isn't *fair!*"

"What isn't?"

"This wilderness kick. It's just not my *thing,* that's all! I'm very g-good in cars and bars and penthouses, but that goddamn lousy b-bastard of a *horse* . . . God, I've got

blisters, darling! And then it has to *rain* on top of everything. I'm filthy and soaking wet and my nose is running and I'm cold clear through . . . Look, I don't intend to freeze to death in here, I'm warning you. I'm just not going to do it. I've had it. I'm through!" She sniffled. "I'm sorry, darling, b-but that's the way it is. For b-brave little frontier heroines, you'll have to apply elsewhere."

"Spell it out," I said. "Just exactly what are you through with, Libby."

"I mean it!" she said defiantly. "To hell with the old school tie and all that jazz. I'm copping out, darling. They just picked the wrong girl for this pioneer bit. Anything it takes to get some food and blankets I'll do, even if it means telling everything I know about everything. Even about you!"

It was, of course, exactly the line she'd take to put pressure on me to talk if she were working with Holz. I warned myself that, judging by past performance, she was a good enough actress that there was no reason whatever for me to believe in her words or her tears. Nevertheless, I was aware of a new feeling of uncertainty. There had been too many odd, unexplained bits of behavior. Suddenly the reasoning by which I'd proved, to my own satisfaction, her guilty liaison with Holz, didn't seem quite as convincing as it had back in Beaver Creek this morning.

However, it really made very litt. difference whether she was now going to spill her guts through weakness, or whether she'd already betrayed me to Holz because she was working for him or with him. In either case, the man knew or soon would know all he really needed to know about me: my name. It made me feel no better to remember that I'd supplied her with the information, at a time when it didn't seem particularly important.

So far Holz had given no sign that he recognized me, but that could be just part of the cat-and-mouse game they like to play. My dossier was in files to which he had access, I was quite sure. With the name, he'd be bound to make the connection, if he hadn't already. Knowing for whom I really worked, he'd know what I'd been sent here to do.

"All right. Up, you!" It was the man called Jack,

190

sticking his head in the canvas doorway. He was address-
ing me.

I said, "Sure, if you tell me how."

He knelt to untie my ankles. "All right, come along and
no funny business!"

The big tent to which he took me was warm and
comfortable, with a fire crackling in the sheet-metal stove.
The elderly Indian was busy cooking something that reminded me I hadn't eaten since early morning. At the rear
of the tent, some planks had been laid across impromptu
trestles to form a table. The chairs were just chunks sawed
off an eighteen-inch log. Jack kicked one of these up to
the table and wrestled me down on it with unnecessary
force.

I was beginning not to like the man very much, but I
had to admit that, despite the plump appearance I'd noted
this morning, he was no weakling. Besides, he didn't look
nearly as soft and flabby in the rough clothes he was
wearing now. I decided that he wasn't as much plagued
with incipient obesity as he was simply built round to start
with.

Holz was sitting on the other side of the table, on
another improvised stool, or chopping block. In front of
him lay a number of exhibits: Grant Nystrom's .357 Magnum revolver and holster, the Buck knife I'd picked up in
Prince Rupert, and two black dog collars. There was also
some other gear, including a fine, scope-sighted, bolt-
action rifle and a box of 7mm Remington Magnum cartridges. They're all Magnums these days, rifles and pistols
both.

"Well, Mr. Nystrom?" Holz said.

"Is that a question?" I asked. "If so, rephrase it, and
I'll decide whether or not to answer it."

Jack swung a hard fist to the side of my head and
knocked me off the log. I picked myself up with some
difficulty, since my hands were still tied. Jack slammed me
back down on the primitive chair.

"Don't talk like that to Mr. Wood," Jack said mildly.

I didn't say anything. Holz waited a little; then said,
"These are the collars we got from the dog and from the

two boys in the delivery truck. They are worthless, as you doubtless know. Where is the real one?"

"I don't know," I said.

Jack knocked me off the log once more, and I went through the routine of getting up and being rammed back into my seat.

When he was through, I said again, "I don't know."

Jack started to raise his fist. Holz shook his head. "No," he said, "that'll be all, Jack."

"But, Mr. Wood . . ."

"That'll be all."

Jack shuffled out reluctantly. The Indian at the stove continued his cooking, oblivious of the rest of us. I faced Holz across the table, remembering that he'd killed, among a lot of other people, a colleague of mine called Kingston—but I hadn't been fond enough of Kingston for it to matter here. Holz's soot-black hair and moustache looked phonier than ever. Then I realized they were supposed to look that way. It wasn't a question of deceiving anybody now, it was a matter of preventing anybody from recognizing him later.

Shave the toothbrush from the upper lip, wash the dye and stickum out of the slick, shiny hair, throw away the silly, gold-rimmed, schoolteacher glasses, and you'd have a different man, one nobody who'd seen him in Alaska would find even slightly familiar. He had the dead-white, coarse, rather thick-looking skin with large pores that often seems to grow in eastern Europe. His eyes were a slaty gray color. They watched me steadily across the table. Abruptly and surprisingly, he gave a little laugh.

"Well, Mr. Nystrom, are you satisfied?"

"Satisfied?"

"That was the type of interrogation you expected, was it not? I didn't want to disappoint you." When I said nothing, he went on, "Of course, we are no longer interested in the dog's missing collar. We know that all five studs contained nothing but substitute messages. Four substitutions were engineered by the young men in that very interesting mobile laboratory, and the last one by me. I, of course, took personal charge of the real information from the final drop. From the young men in question, I

got the material from the previous drops. They'd kept it in an ingeniously hidden safe in their van, the location of which they were persuaded to disclose to me."

He drew a small white envelope from the pocket of his heavy wool shirt and shook five tinfoil disks into his hand, answering one question posed by Mr. Smith's compulsive secrecy. I'd never been told exactly what juggling tricks were being performed in the fancy lab van, but apparently it had been a simple disk-switch routine that you'd think could have been performed in an ordinary family sedan—if you didn't know the way things worked in Washington. After a moment, Holz replaced the wafers in the envelope and put the envelope back into his pocket.

"Persuaded," I said. "As a matter of curiosity, which one did you persuade?"

Holz smiled faintly. "That is a stupid question. You know perfectly well that the young fellow with the beard was the tough one of the pair. It was easy to determine. Any captive who wastes his breath telling me what I cannot get away with is obviously a fool and probably a weak fool. The bearded one kept his mouth shut; the other one babbled dire threats and promises of violent retaliation. So we started with him. It did not take long. He soon told us everything—well, almost everything."

"What didn't he tell you?"

"He didn't tell us about you, Mr. Nystrom. His principles were at stake, it seems. He could be persuaded to tell us about things, inanimate objects, but he wouldn't betray, as he put it, people." Holz laughed shortly. "They draw all kinds of high-principled lines, these foolish young men." He raised his slaty eyes to study my face. "Are you going to be afflicted by principles, Mr. Nystrom?"

"Hell, no," I said. "I lost my last ones years ago. What do you want to know?"

"The collar. Just out of curiosity, I would like to know where it is."

"I honestly don't know," I said, which was technically true. I might guess, but I didn't know.

Holz stared at me for a full minute. Then he shrugged

his heavy shoulders. "Very well. I'll accept that. Will you give me your real name?"

"Sure, why not?" If he didn't get it from me, the way things were, he'd get it from Libby. I might as well get the credit for frankness. "The name is Helm, Matthew Helm. Cross-filed under the code name Eric."

"Ah. I thought there was something familiar . . . "

He stopped. There was a lengthy silence. Well, it was about time he made the connection. As it was, my professional pride was hurt. I'd thought I was better known in the circles in which Holz moved than his reactions had indicated.

"Yes, I've heard of you," he said at last. I didn't say anything, and he went on slowly: "What are you doing here? If I remember the dossier correctly, counterespionage is not your line."

"Another organization had a dead man to match," I said. "They needed to borrow a trustworthy agent, six-four, a hundred and ninety, blue eyes, white hair. The personnel computer doubled up in agony and vomited up my name. The hair was bleached, and here I am, Grant Nystrom at your service."

Holz heard me out, but he didn't seem to be listening very hard. His eyes, narrowed, were studying me intently, and I knew that he knew, instinctively, what I was there for. I also knew, suddenly, that he wasn't going to act upon this instinctive knowledge because he, too, had his professional pride.

The sensible thing for him to do was to pull out his little Spanish gun, or load up the big 7mm, and shoot me through the head right now. But if he did that, right after being informed of my identity, I might, in my dying moments, have thought he was afraid of a fellow pro named Matt Helm. Or *he* might have thought he was afraid of me, and that would not do. So, to reassure both of us, he was going to behave toward me exactly as he'd planned from the start. Well, we all have our weaknesses, dogs or pride or whatever.

"And the lady?" Holz said at last.

I gave him the story Libby had given me, watching him to see what it meant to him. "She works for the same

department as the bearded guy you got and his talkative friend, the people who drafted me for this play acting. She was planted on your San Francisco people some time back, I gather. She recruited Nystrom for them—the real Nystrom—and gave him the sex treatment, and he responded very well. She had him under perfect control and pumped him for information at will, whatever information she couldn't get herself as a member of the cell in good standing. She was probably the one who recommended trying this impersonation when he got killed, but I don't know that for sure. She did come along north to give me a hand in playing the role, and as you know I found her especially useful in Seattle."

"Yes," Holz said, "but that man of ours, Stottman, was apparently not deceived."

"No," I said. "But it took him a little time to get his message across to the rest of you by way of Pete. I can't tell you the lady's real name. She never told me."

Holz nodded, apparently satisfied. After a moment, he smiled faintly. "For what you are, you were remarkably easy to catch, Mr. Helm."

I shrugged. "I got careless, I guess."

He said a strange thing then. He said, quietly, "It's a lonely life, my friend."

I didn't know what to say to that. He didn't speak for a little, and I could hear the night breeze going through the trees outside. The canvas of the tent stirred and subsided. The old Indian shoved a couple of sticks of wood into the stove, and juggled some pans to catch the heat exactly right.

Holz said, "I was in prison once, Mr. Helm. Well, I have been there more than once, but this time it was intentional. I was assigned to reach and silence a certain prisoner. First they put me in a cell alone, for observation. It was not a very clean or well-run place. There were, among other things, rats. One in particular considered my cell his territory. As the weeks went on, I made friends with him. It was something to do. One day the guard came in unexpectedly. My rodent friend had lost, to some extent, his fear of man; also he'd learned that visitors usually meant food. He came too close, and the guard stamped his

195

boot, once. It was what the man had come in for, to deprive me of that bit of companionship. I killed him."

I didn't say anything. Holz waited a little and went on: "I couldn't help myself, Mr. Helm. I struck once and he was dead. It was a blow that, in my role as prisoner, I should not have known. It blew my cover instantly. It wrecked my mission and almost caused my death. All for a small, dirty, brown rat."

There was another silence. I didn't speak. Anything he wanted to give me, I was happy to take. He'd already given me more than he should have. He'd given me the clue to his sad, soft way of talking. He'd told me I was dealing with a man who'd been in the business too long.

He said gently, "I am explaining how I knew you would come to the cry of the dog, after traveling with him for a week. It is a lonely and dirty business. We take what friends we can get, do we not, Mr. Helm?" After a moment of silence, he went on more briskly, "Jack will escort you back to your tent. You will live, if you do not try to escape, until the plane arrives tomorrow afternoon. There may be some further questions they'll want to put to you or the woman. This impersonation of yours has worried them greatly. They may even take one or both of you away with them alive, but I would not count on that. Good night, Mr. Helm." He waited until I had reached the door, where Jack had appeared as if summoned. Then he said, "Oh, just one more thing."

I watched him rise and come to me. He was smiling faintly. He said, "Now I remember the dossier more clearly. I think I will take that belt. Since you are going nowhere, you should have no trouble keeping up your trousers without it."

Well, it wasn't unexpected. These days the belt trick is only good for amateurs anyway, and for all his sadness, he was no amateur. Back in the tent, I told Libby as much as she needed to know. We were fed and given a tarpaulin to lie on and a couple of blankets to wrap up in. Huddled together for warmth, still in our damp clothes, we lay and listened to the rain start up again, pattering on the canvas above us.

"Matt?"

"Yes," I said.

"Did he ask about the collar?"

"Yes. I told him I didn't know where it was."

She sighed. "I suppose he'll question me in the morning. I'm not looking forward to it. Have you got any bright ideas for getting us out of here."

"No," I said. "Not any."

I didn't, either, now that the belt was gone. There should have been some way I could take advantage of the weakness Holz had shown me, but I couldn't think of an appropriate lever.

I lay beside Libby, wondering who the hell she really was. I mean, there in the big tent just now it had been clearly established that she had not been in communication with Holz, after all. I was as sure as I could be of anything that my name had come as a real surprise to him tonight; yet she had known it for the better part of a week.

I must have gone to sleep. The next thing I knew, something energetic had burst into the tent like a cyclone and my face was being licked by a cold, wet, affectionate tongue.

31 THE PUP WAS CRAZY WITH HAP-

piness at having found me. He was all over me—all over both of us. Libby woke up with a gasp.

"What——"

"Shhh!" I hissed. "It's just Hank. . . . Easy now, Prince Hannibal. Relax. You'll have them all rushing in here. . . ."

"You mean he's followed us all this way?" Libby sounded incredulous. "My God, how could he? We must be forty or fifty miles from that filling station. . . . Ouch, can't you keep him off my face?"

"Hank, down!" I whispered. "Lie down, boy. Quiet, now!"

It was a wonderful thing. He'd been left at least twenty

miles back along the highway. He'd trailed the truck along those twenty miles of pavement to the horses, and then he'd tracked the horses another fifteen miles through the wettest, soggiest country in the world, over mud, running water, and bare rock.

It was Faithful Fido's Fortunes, or Rover's Revenge. It was Lassie with bells on. It was beautiful and touching, man's best friend at his best and friendliest, a real tear jerker. I didn't believe a word of it. I wouldn't have believed it even if he'd been a bloodhound trained on a convict a day; and he wasn't a tracking dog at all but a goddamn bird dog. But if anybody wanted to fall for the gag, I wasn't about to disillusion them.

"Hey, what's going on in there?"

It was Jack's voice. I heard him come charging toward the tent. There was only a moment to make the decision. I sat up as best I could.

I said softly, "Dead bird, Hank. Dead bird."

There's no command for telling a retriever just to get the hell out of wherever he may be, say a confined space in which he can easily be cornered and killed. You've got to send him *for* something, but even in the dark I could tell that the pup was looking at me oddly, wondering just what the hell kind of dead bird he was supposed to be fetching from inside this nine-by-twelve tent. Jack's footsteps were almost at the door.

I said, "Go get it. . . . *Hank!*"

He'd been trained to go on his name, and he went, charging off the way I had him pointed, right out the tent door, just as Jack came pounding up. I heard the man stumble and swear.

Holz's voice shouted: "What's the matter over there? Jack?"

"It's the dog, Mr. Wood! It's that damn dog we——"

"You're crazy. No dog could have followed——"

"Well, it's too big for a squirrel and too small for a wolf, sir. Look over there by the woodpile. If that isn't that same black mutt, I'll eat it!" There was a little pause. "By God, he must be quite a dog, coming all this way to find his master! Do we have to kill him?"

The Lassie syndrome was at work. Even the hard-

198

boiled Jack was falling for it, taking for granted that any loyal dog could perform any kind of a TV miracle to find the man to whom its loving canine heart belonged. Holz didn't answer at once. I had a sudden hope. Maybe I'd found the lever for which I'd been looking.

"Well," Holz said at last, and I could tell that he was remembering a small brown rat in a jail cell, "well, let's see if we can't catch him. But first get your rifle and check the prisoners. It could be a trick. Wake up the cook to give us a hand."

Jack stuck his head into the tent and shone a flashlight at us briefly and disappeared. What followed had a lot of the elements of slapstick comedy; at least the sound effects were ridiculous, considering that they came from a bunch of sinister conspirators who'd kill a man as soon as look at him. But this wasn't a man; it was a miracle dog, and you don't shoot Lassie or Rin-Tin-Tin.

As I'd hoped, once out in the open, away from the tent, Hank proved as elusive as an eel. These were the same people who'd manhandled him before—some of them, at least—and hung him on a fence to choke. He obviously recognized them and would have no part of them, even when they tried to lure him within reach with a nice, juicy piece of meat.

When the chase got really lively out there, I wormed my way out of the blankets and back to the rear wall of the tent. I rapped my bound hands against the canvas lightly.

"Anybody there?" I whispered.

"Here, sir." I recognized the low voice. It went with a red beard. "Watch out, I'm going to cut the tent."

"Are you alone, Davis?"

"No."

"Well, tell Ronnie——"

"It isn't Ronnie, sir. They worked Ronnie over pretty badly; we had to leave him with the lab truck. It's a girl, Mr. Helm. She knocked out the woman they'd left guarding us and cut us loose. She'd picked up the dog where you'd left him. She says you know her. Her name is Pat."

There wasn't time to ponder the implications of that

news. I heard the whisper of a knife slicing through canvas.

"All right, sir, stick your wrists out the hole and I'll cut you loose. . . . There you are."

"Thanks. I'll take the knife, if you don't mind. Tell Miss Bellman to keep an eye on the circus and warn me if anybody starts this way. What's the weapons situation?"

"Well, they got ours, but I took a little pistol off the lady guard."

"Hang onto it, but don't shoot unless I give the word."

I heard Holz's voice: "Never mind, let the dog go. He won't leave the neighborhood as long as his master's here. Just don't let him back in the tent."

"Watch out!" Pat Bellman's voice hissed. "The man with the cowboy hat is coming this way. I think he's going to take another look at you."

"I'll handle him," I said. It was about time I handled something. "Let him come in. Get down and keep quiet."

I dropped beside Libby and flipped the blankets over me, holding the little knife. It was a boyscout model, which seemed appropriate: the kind with a screwdriver, can opener, awl, and bottle opener, but no corkscrew because scouts aren't supposed to associate with *that* kind of bottle. The blade was between two and three inches long and not very sharp. I thought regretfully of the fine Buck knife, carefully sharpened and oiled, that I'd last seen lying on the table in the cook tent.

Then Jack yanked back the canvas door and aimed his flashlight at us. In spite of the glare, I could make out that he was holding a scope-sighted rifle in his left hand; a fine weapon but not very suitable for work at night or at close range.

He frowned at the heap of blankets with the two heads protruding from the far end; then he stepped forward, reached down, and snatched the blankets away for a good look—and I kicked him hard in the pit of the stomach with both feet before he could get the rifle up. He lost his breath with a bellowslike sound and sat down hard. I was on top of him and had his throat cut before he knew he was dead. Outside, somebody was rushing toward the tent.

"Shoot that man, Davis!" I yelled.

A little pistol cracked three times and I heard something fall. I grabbed the rifle Jack had dropped and went out the tent door fast, to stumble over a dead body. Even in the dark I could see that it wasn't the man I wanted but the old Indian cook. The vanishing American seemed to be going fast these days.

A shape recognizable as Holz showed at the dark door of the cook tent, carrying a rifle that seemed to be the twin of mine. Holz threw his weapon to his shoulder as I took aim, or tried to take aim; but in the dark, in that powerful telescope, I couldn't find my target. I couldn't even find the cross hairs. Desperately, I threw myself flat as the other gun fired. The bullet came nowhere near me. Apparently Holz couldn't see his sights any better than I could.

I was trying to line up the fool gun by feel and instinct, without using the sights. I saw that Holz was doing the same thing, but the range was too great—about forty yards—for that kind of trick hip-shooting. We'd both handled firearms too long to do much blasting without a reasonable chance of success. Holz reached inside his coat for a pistol, a better weapon under these conditions; then Davis' little gun cracked, and Holz winced. He turned and ran for the nearest horse, his own, as Davis emptied his undernourished weapon in that direction without any further reaction from the target.

Holz yanked the rope loose, leaped astride like a stunt man, and galloped off bareback toward the head of the valley. I tried once more to get him in the fancy telescopic sight, but there was simply not enough light coming through all that glass. I lowered the gun, watched him disappear among the trees, and turned to see young Davis standing over the dead cook. His face, where the beard didn't cover it, was pale in the darkness.

"He . . . he didn't have a gun. But you *said* to shoot."

There was accusation in his voice. I said, "That's what I said. You did fine."

I couldn't help thinking that tonight the boy- and girl-scouts had done a lot better than the old pro, me; or even the old pro, Holz. All I'd managed was to cut one man's

throat with a dull knife somebody'd handed me. Holz hadn't even accomplished that much. He'd just managed to escape with his skin, slightly damaged. A couple of inexperienced youngsters and a black dog had done the real work. I patted the pup as he came up, a little guiltily, to lick my hand and tell me he hadn't been able to find the dead bird I'd sent him for. There had been distractions.

"It's okay," I said. "There wasn't any bird, *amigo*. I was just kidding you." I looked up, frowning. "Where'd the girl go?" I asked Davis.

She answered for herself. "Over here. Come on, give me a hand with the horses so we can go after him."

"In the dark?" I said. "To hell with that. We'd either fall into a swamp or run into an ambush."

"You mean you're going to let him go?" Davis' voice was accusing once more.

I said, "He's not going anywhere."

"What do you mean? I didn't wound him badly, I don't think."

I said, "Never mind. He'll be around. We'll wait for daylight."

I thought of Hans Holz, wounded, out there on a horse without a saddle, with his fancy gun, the one designed, perhaps, for killing a brand-new president-elect. But before that he had another job to do. He'd been assigned to cover this espionage operation and to make sure the goods were delivered—the goods he carried in his shirt pocket. He wouldn't ride off and leave the job unfinished; he wouldn't let the people he was expecting fly into a trap.

It was time for the old pro, me, to show that he could do something besides lie around to be rescued by a couple of kids and a dog. I started thinking my way into Holz's mind. It wasn't hard, since it was a mind very much like mine, but I was interrupted by an indignant female voice from the nearby tent.

"Matt, for God's sake! Are you going to leave me tied up in here all night with a corpse for company?"

Davis started that way. I said, "Hold it. Untie her feet, take her to the cook tent, and tie her again, securely. Make sure the stove is nice and warm and she's got plenty of blankets."

"But——"

I was annoyed with him and with Libby. I was trying to read Holz's mind at long range, and they weren't being a bit of help.

"Do it," I said.

"But I thought——"

"How much security clearance has she got with your people?"

"Well, none, but——"

"And none with me," I said. "So leave her tied. Okay?"

So much for our mystery woman. She could remain a mystery, a hog-tied mystery, until I had time to bother with her.

32 IT WAS WARM AND PLEASANT IN

the big cook tent with the fire crackling in the stove and a kerosine lantern throwing a yellow light over the table on which lay, now, just one exhibit: a businesslike 7mm Magnum rifle equipped with a six-power telescopic sight. One collar was back on the pup; the other had been tossed aside. Grant Nystrom's revolver was back under my belt, which had been returned to duty, and the Buck knife was back in my pocket; but neither of these was apt to do me much good in this mountainous country, dealing with an expert and well-equipped long-range rifleman. Holz was no fuzzy-faced boy with a woodchuck gun. If I could stalk within two hundred yards of him without getting shot, I'd be doing well. But first I had to find him.

Libby said angrily, "Matthew Helm, if you don't cut me loose this minute, I . . . I'll . . ." She was so mad she couldn't finish the sentence.

I looked at her where she'd been bedded down comfortably near the stove. Her hair was mussed and her face was pink and lovely among the rough blankets.

I said, "You're warm and dry. You couldn't go anywhere even if you weren't tied up. Now shut up and let me figure something out, will you?"

"But I don't understand! It's so damn unreasonable, darling. You can't think I——"

"Look," I said warily, "at the moment, strange as it may seem and unflattering though it may be, I don't have time to think about you at all. That's why you're tied up, so I *don't* have to think about you. When I've taken care of Mr. Wood, I'll deal with you. Maybe I'll apologize. Maybe I'll even bend over and let you kick me hard. Okay? In the meantime, just be quiet."

"Well, I don't know what you expect to accomplish by just sitting there staring at that silly rifle——"

I drew a long breath and took a handkerchief from my pocket. It wasn't very clean. I twisted it to form a loose rope, deliberately.

"If you insist," I said, "if you absolutely insist on being gagged as well as tied——"

"Matt, you wouldn't dare!"

I started to rise, but settled again as Pat Bellman entered the tent. She had a yellow cartridge box in her hand, and for a moment I was hopeful, then I saw that it was too small to hold the long Magnum cartridges.

"I found this box of thirty-thirties in the little tent," Pat said.

"No seven emm-emms?"

"Nothing," she said. "If you saw a box here, he took it with him."

I sighed. "Okay. At least we can load up the two carbines, one for you and one for Les. How's he doing with the horses?"

She laughed. "Well, just between you and me, he's a nice guy but a horseman he isn't. I'd better go out and help him before he spooks them all clear above the Arctic Circle."

"Sure." As she turned away, I rose and followed her outside. It was frosty and dark out there but a hint of dawn showed in the sky over the east rim of the valley. "Pat," I said.

She stopped and turned slowly to face me. I couldn't make out her expression, only the tousled blond hair and the long, slim, half-boyish figure.

"Yes?" she said warily.

"Thanks," I said. "I don't know why you did it, Skinny, but thanks."

"Go to hell," she said. "It was something to do. For kicks. You were so damned experienced and ruthless and professional. I got a big bang out of helping the great man out when he got himself all loused up like an ordinary human being."

"Sure."

"I still say it's all a big, bad joke. One side is as good as another, yours and that of the guy who just rode out of here. Or as bad. But I drove clear to Alaska to find some action, and your side happened to be where it was. I just took a piece of it, that's all."

"Sure," I said again.

"Besides, I did owe you something for turning me loose back there. I don't like being in anybody's debt. Now we're even. . . . I'll see if I can't round up some of those nags." She started to turn away.

"One more thing," I said, and she stopped. "How much help was the pup, really? I'm curious."

I saw her look back at me and grin. "Well, he found us two coveys of ptarmigan and one bull moose," she said. "No, actually he did help, but it wasn't a hard trail to follow, four horses in all that soft stuff. But he made a swell diversion when we got here, didn't he? I kind of figured on that."

She was quite a girl. I watched her go off toward the open meadow. Holz had taken the only horse that was tied. The rest had been hobbled and turned loose, and you'd be surprised at how well an experienced wilderness horse can get around with his forelegs roped together. Well, that was her problem.

I went back to mine, which was very simple. The big Magnum rifle held three cartridges in the magazine. It could have held a fourth in the chamber, but Jack hadn't put one in. He'd been riding, and you don't carry a rifle in a saddle scabbard with a live round under the firing pin unless you're stupid, optimistic, or suicidal. Nor do you chamber a round in camp unless you're planning to shoot something right away. Apparently, he hadn't really expected trouble.

Three cartridges ought to be enough, with a properly sighted-in rifle. The question I had to answer was: *Had* Holz sighted in this gun carefully, and was it still on target? Presumably he had his number-one weapon with him. This was just his spare rifle, lent to Jack. Just how careful had he, or Jack, been about seeing that it shot where it looked? If I made the stalk and found a mark to aim at, would the bullet go where the cross hairs indicated?

I sighed. I was just kidding myself, trying to convince myself that I didn't have to waste any of my precious three cartridges. There's only one way to find out if a rifle is shooting right for you, and that is to shoot it, no matter what kind of a genius-marksman fired it before you. To go hunting a fellow specialist like Holz without first checking my weapon would be sheer lunacy on my part.

Waiting, I cooked some breakfast and listened absently to the wheedling and abuse put out by Libby, on the floor. It didn't bother me, now that I knew what I had to do. When there was clear daylight at the tent door, I bent down and kissed her.

She said, "Damn you, Matt."

"You're a lovely thing," I said. "You just talk too much. Be good."

I took the rifle and went out, cut a round white blaze in the bark of a nearby tree, and paced off one hundred yards. I lay down and adjusted the rifle sling to my measurements, chambered one third of my ammunition supply, and took careful aim. When the cross hairs were absolutely steady on the improvised target, I let the piece fire. Then I walked over there and looked at the result: a little black hole just three inches above my point of aim, exactly where it should have been to keep the bullet on a man-sized target out to roughly three hundred yards. Well, now I knew.

I pulled the bolt to eject the empty case, worked a fresh cartridge into the chamber, and set the safety carefully, as Davis came running up with Pat right behind him.

"What is it?" Davis panted. "What's the matter? Did you see Mr. Wood? Why did you shoot?"

"I was just checking the gun," I said. "It shoots fine."

"Just checking . . . but you only had three cartridges!"

"And now I have two, but I know what they'll do when I fire them," I said. "Well, it's about time I was on my way."

"Where are you going?"

"Up there." I pointed. "That spot up there on the mountainside above the little lake we passed. You crossed the rockslide if you were following our trail. Mr. Wood is sitting right above it this minute. He's got to be. From there he can watch this camp—he's probably got his scope on us right now, and he's wishing we were about a mile closer. But he's not going to come after us, because we're doing him no harm here. What he's got to make sure of is that none of us gets back to civilization in time to pass the word about the plane that's coming in this afternoon."

Pat said, "You're sure there'll be a plane?"

"He was sure," I said. "And that's why he's not going to play Indian in the brush; one of us might slip out while he was doing it. He's just going to sit tight at the head of the rockslide where he can watch the camp and cover the only trail out of here—the only trail we know. From there, he can keep us from leaving, and at the same time he can pick us off if we try to interfere when the plane does come. At the last minute, he'll scramble down the rocks, jump aboard, and fly off with the NCS material in his shirt pocket."

Pat was watching me closely. She said, "So you're standing in the open and waving your arms to tell him exactly what you're going to do."

I grinned. "He knows what I'm going to do, Skinny. He knows I'm coming after him. That is, he's almost sure. But if I'm real obvious about it—sighting in my gun where he can see me, and pointing out my objective dramatically—he may get a few doubts. He may just start wondering if I'm being tricky, and if so, how. The suspense will do him good." I looked at the two of them. "Stay here. Don't take any chances with Mr. Wood. You can't do a thing to help me with those damn little hundred-and-fifty-yard carbines, so don't try. And don't take any chances with the lady in the tent, either. She may just be

the greatest, sweetest person in the world, but . . . wait a minute. Les, how well do you know your chief?"

"Mr. Ryerson? Ronnie's dad? Well, he's not the palsy-walsy type of boss. I wouldn't say any of us really knows him, even Ronnie."

"Ryerson, eh?" At last I could stop thinking of them as Smith, Junior, and Senior. "Then you wouldn't be really startled to learn that he was running another organization parallel with yours, only much more secretive and uninhibited?"

Lester Davis frowned. "You mean . . . you mean you think he's just using us as a screen, a cover, for another. . . ?" He stopped, and considered the proposition. Then he shrugged. "I really couldn't say, Mr. Helm. Of course if he were doing that, we'd be the last to know, wouldn't we?"

"That's right," I said. "Well, Libby Meredith claims to be one of his super-secret, lower-level operatives. Or upper-level, depending on how you look at it. A colleague of yours, no less. Maybe she is. It remains to be proved. In the meantime, she stays tied. You get the horses rounded up and wait for me."

Pat Bellman hesitated. "How long do we wait?"

I said, "Until you hear some shooting up there, and about half an hour longer. If I'm not back by then, I won't be back, and you'll be on your own. . . ."

33 *IT WAS A BEAUTIFUL MORNING,*

which was too bad. Yesterday's rain and mist would have been useful, but what I had was a clear blue sky, bright sunshine, and endless visibility. Since I had it, there was nothing to do but make use of it. With my nose to the ground, like Hiawatha on the trail of his winter venison, I let myself be seen marching off on foot in the direction up the valley that Holz had taken on horseback some hours earlier.

If Holz was where I thought, watching from high above

and far away, and if he wanted to think I was tracking him, that was all right. It was more or less what I was doing, and I couldn't prevent him from anticipating it. But if he wanted to think I just wanted him to think I was tracking him, that was all right, too.

For instance, if he remembered the part of my dossier that said I was pretty good in the boondocks, he might start worrying about whether or not I could be trying to get back to civilization for official help by way of a different trail or no trail at all. A worried man can't sit still nearly as well as an unworried one; and a moving man is easier to spot than one who holes up in a bunch of rocks and stays there. I'd rather play mountain tag with the man than try to dig him out of hiding.

It was pleasant to be walking, working the soreness out of the riding muscles that had taken a beating yesterday. I could have been better dressed for the work, particularly in the matter of footgear—the cowboy boots of my Nystrom role were a bit slick-soled for climbing and a bit noisy for stalking—but on the whole I didn't feel that I was operating under any serious handicaps. At least I didn't have a bullet in me, and Holz did. And I wasn't brooding heavily about what a sad and lonely job I had, either, even though I'd once been a sucker for a dog in trouble.

I could hear the pup for a long time after I could no longer see the camp behind me. He didn't like being tied up and ordered to stay put, and he was telling the world about it. Finally, a shoulder of the mountain cut off the sound, and I was alone with the whisper of the fitful early-morning breeze that would have caused me a lot of worry if I'd been after moose or caribou.

As a matter of fact, the first sign of life I encountered was the crashing and thumping of a big cow moose taking off through the timber ahead after catching my scent. I found that hard on the nerves; and a bunch of white-winged ptarmigan flushing noisily didn't help my peace of mind either. Even my first glimpse of Holz's horse, tied just at timberline, was mildly nerve-wracking. I mean, when you're after game that can shoot back, you react violently to anything that moves, even a horse's tail.

I considered the question of the horse for several minutes, crouching among the sparse trees halfway up the mountain. It could be bait for a trap, of course, but the likeliest explanation was that Holz had left the animal there simply because he was heading up into terrain no horse could handle. At last I moved forward cautiously. The big bay was happy to see a human being. I untied him and let him go. He'd probably wander into camp sooner or later, and Holz would probably see him and know I'd got this far. Then he would, I hoped, start wondering just why I'd made a point of advertising the fact.

There hadn't been much of a trail to follow up to now. The ground had been frozen when Holz had come this way. I'd stumbled on the horse more or less by following the shape of the country and guessing at the route a rider bound for a certain spot might pick at night.

But now, heading upward from there, above timberline, I had nothing whatever to guide me: it was all rock and rubble on which no tracks showed. It took me an hour to work my way up to a notch that let me cut around behind the mountains overlooking the camp and the lake. The going was rough and steep, and the country was wide open. From up here I could see that what I'd thought, yesterday, to be autumn snow on the faraway peaks was actually a series of permanent glaciers.

Some small white spots on a mountainside ahead, that I also took for snow at first glance, turned out to be mountain sheep that scampered out of sight when they spotted me, moving as easily as if they'd been running across a level meadow instead of a forty-five-degree slope of loose rock. The bad part was, of course, the fact that, crossing the open slopes myself much less rapidly and gracefully, I made a beautiful target for a man with a scope-sighted rifle waiting anywhere above; but no shots came.

Playing it by ear, or by instinct, I made a very wide circle, much wider, I hoped, than Holz had made to reach his vantage point above the lake, if that's where he'd really gone. Then I scrambled back across the rocky spine of the mountains into what I hoped would be the big valley I'd left. It turned out to be a small, steep side

canyon instead and I had considerable trouble working my way down into it. I'm willing to hike all I have to, uphill or down, but I'm not much of a mountain climber, particularly in cowboy boots.

I finally got to the bottom of the gorge by sitting on, and sliding down, a steep sheet of rock, to the detriment of Grant Nystrom's slacks. Picking myself up, I fought my way down a little stream, over fallen trees and jumbled boulders, until the country opened up ahead, and there was the pond for which I was looking, far below me and off to the right, just where I wanted it. I stopped to check the rifle and prayed that it had taken less of a beating than my hands and knees, not to mention my shins and tailbone.

The rest of the approach just took time and caution. I stayed low, where the timber covered me, until I was directly under the point I'd decided to reach—as close to Holz's probable hiding place as it seemed safe to go. I took off the high-heeled boots, kind of wedged them under my belt, and made the final climb through the rocks in my stocking feet—when I used my feet at all. Mostly I was on hands and knees and sometimes, when the terrain required, on my belly.

It was hard work, but when I got to the preselected spot, I found that I'd made a good choice. Sheltered in a little hollow there, with a scraggly bush and some tufts of tough-looking grass for additional cover, I could watch the lake and the rockslide and the crumbling stone outcropping at the head of it, near which I figured my target would appear sooner or later. It was about two hundred and fifty yards away, within easy range of my borrowed weapon. I couldn't see the camp for the curve of the mountainside, but unlike Holz, I had no reason to watch that. At least I thought I didn't.

Nevertheless, when the break came, after over two hours of motionless waiting, it came from the camp I couldn't see: a single gunshot report, echoing off the mountainside. I reached for the rifle beside me, a futile gesture considering the range. I had a sickening sense of failure. Again, as with Libby, it seemed that my elaborate reasoning had been haywire. Apparently Holz hadn't behaved

the way he should have—the way I'd thought he should have.

Instead of waiting obligingly where I'd wanted him to, he must have sneaked back to camp as I'd been sure he wouldn't. Now he was disposing of the easy part of the opposition, secure in the knowledge that I wouldn't be around to bother him.

I started to rise, but checked the movement. I'd made a certain investment of time and effort in this hiding place. To move now would be to throw it all away. I couldn't reach the camp in time to be of any help anyway, so I just lay there listening, and heard more shooting: this time a rapid-fire fusillade of five reports so close together that they sounded like a burst from a submachine gun. That was no slow bolt-action rifle with a maximum capacity of four rounds, I realized; that was a lever-action carbine worked by an expert.

I drew a long breath and lay there waiting for something that would give me a clue to what was going on. There was no more shooting, and for a while nothing moved, either below or on the high slopes I was watching. Then I saw a distant horseman fording the river below camp—a horsewoman, rather. I couldn't actually make out the face or the sex at the distance; but the rider was dressed in a yellow-brown outfit. Pat Bellman had been wearing her familiar denims when last seen. Davis had been in jeans and a dark green windbreaker; Holz in his checked wool lumberman's rig.

Watching Libby approach along the trail, wondering how she'd worked it, I almost forgot the man I'd come several thousand miles to meet. I was warned by a hint of movement at the very edge of my vision, high up around the mountainside where the stony slope ran up against a perpendicular wall of solid rock. Looking that way intently, I saw nothing for several minutes; then Holz came into sight once more, moving diagonally toward me. Obviously he'd been hiding high above the spot I'd expected him, just a little too far around the curving hillside to see me as I sneaked into place. Maybe my psychological warfare had had some effect after all, making him too nervous to stay in the one place. .

He was using his rifle as a crutch, cautiously, as he made his way downward, limping. There was a bloody handkerchief bound around his right thigh. He was in a hurry now, taking few precautions, angling down across the rocky stuff toward the spot I'd figured he'd choose, but still too far away for a good shot. Besides, with only two cartridges, I wasn't about to monkey with a moving target. Sooner or later he was bound to stop.

Below, Libby was approaching the pond. A good distance behind her, just crossing the river, I saw Davis flogging a horse—my reluctant mare, by the looks of it—in pursuit. I didn't try to figure out what had happened to cause all this activity. I just returned my attention, and my mind, to Holz.

He slid and scrambled the last few yards to the outcrop at the head of the rockslide—and disappeared from sight. Apparently there was a hole among the rocks I couldn't see from my angle. He simply vanished, leaving me without a target. I steadied the cross hairs of the scope on the rock against which I'd seen him last, and waited.

Libby was just starting across the rockslide below him, down near the shore of the little lake. She was riding the big buckskin that had belonged to Jack. For a girl who'd claimed to have died in the saddle yesterday, she looked very good on it, erect and confident. She'd left her raincoat somewhere, and she was carrying one of the lever-action guns in her hand.

She had to check the buckskin and let it pick its own way across the rocks. I saw her glance back occasionally, apparently hearing Davis hammering down the trail behind her. There was no sign of Holz. I didn't know what he had in mind and I didn't let myself speculate on it. I'd done enough telepathy for one day. I just waited. Libby had made it across the rocks and was starting into the trees on the far side of the slide when Holz's rifle fired and the buckskin went down.

I was aware of Libby throwing herself clear and rolling aside, still clinging to the carbine, but now I was concentrating on the telescopic sight four inches in front of my eye. Suddenly my target appeared, clear and sharp in the

field of the glass. Holz was leaning over and around the rock on which I'd been focusing, aiming at something off to the right that he'd apparently not been able to cover from his safe hiding place. I realized that he'd waited until the last possible moment to take Libby, hoping that Davis would come into his view, too. Now he was reaching far around for the second target. . . .

I drew a long breath, let it out halfway, and held it. I put the cross hairs in the right place and added trigger pressure very gently, letting the piece fire itself when it was ready. There was a lot of noise and commotion. None of those Magnums, pistols or rifles, are gentle guns. Two hundred and fifty yards away, Holz lay for a moment quite still. Then, too soon for me to fire again, he slid limply off the rock out of sight. His weapon remained behind, neatly balanced on the ledge he'd been using as a rest.

I was up and running, watching the shadowed hole into which he'd disappeared. I swung high up the slope, trying to find an angle from which I could see the bottom of the crevice. Finally I found it and saw him lying there in the shadow, apparently dead. At a hundred yards I stopped and went to one knee. The sitting position is steadier and the prone steadier still; but I couldn't get down any lower and still see my mark. Kneeling, I took careful aim and fired my last cartridge.

The limp figure in the shadows moved abruptly. It rose, swaying, and emptied the pistol in its hand blindly in my direction. Flat on the ground, now, I heard a couple of bullets strike off to the left. One whined directly over me. Then Holz's gun was empty. He slumped back out of sight. I drew my own revolver and spent a full fifteen minutes making the final approach. I could have saved myself the trouble.

When I got there, he was quite dead, with his empty automatic in his hand. A guy named Kingston was avenged, if it mattered, and a more important gent, exact identity not yet determined, wouldn't be shot this fall, at least not by Hans Holz. I suppose you could call it a victory. I took the little envelope from his shirt, a box of

cartridges from his jacket, and a set of car keys from his pants. I picked up his rifle and went off, leaving him there.

34 THE COOK TENT LOOKED AS IF IT

had been subjected to machine-gun fire. I glanced at Davis and he nodded bleakly. He pulled the flap aside to let me go in. A familiar-looking trenchcoat had been tossed on the table. There was something under the blankets near the stove.

I shrugged off the two rifles I carried—I didn't need both of them, but you don't leave good guns lying around outdoors—and went over and drew back the blankets gently to look at Pat Bellman. She was quite dead, of course. I still didn't know everything about the woman who'd called herself Libby Meredith, but I'd learned enough to know she wouldn't miss.

I said softly, without looking at Davis, "That's damn good shooting for a lady tied hand and foot . . . how did she talk you into turning her loose?" Davis looked miserably at the ground and didn't speak. I said, "Never mind. Don't tell me. Let me guess. She blackmailed you. She convinced you that if you didn't untie her she was going to starve to death painfully, or wet her pants humiliatingly, right before your eyes. . . ."

Some muscles in his face twitched, telling me I'd guessed right on the second try. I started to say something sarcastic and bitter to the effect that sacrificing one girl's life to save another's kidneys wasn't really a very good bargain, and that in any case people had been known to go to the bathroom with their hands tied, but I kept it back.

So they'd turned Libby loose, all the way loose, and Pat Bellman had escorted her out behind the bushes and, of course, looked discreetly away at the critical moment, because even if you're a woman you don't stare rudely at another woman answering the call of nature. That mo-

ment of inattention had been all Libby had needed to grab Pat's .30-30 carbine, shoot once, and then spray the tent with rifle bullets to keep Davis from interfering as she ran for the horses.

I looked down at the dead pale face among the blankets and remembered a riverbank far to the south, early in the morning, and a handsome steelhead trout. I remembered a Labrador bitch called Maudie that I'd never actually seen. Well, the girl had had an accessory-to-murder charge to answer to. We'd have had a hard time getting her out of that, no matter how much we owed her, but I'd been prepared to go to work on it, or get somebody else to work on it who wielded a lot more influence than I did.

"Mr. Helm! Listen!"

I listened and heard a distant humming sound, growing steadily closer. I glanced at my watch. The hour was barely noon. Well, Holz hadn't said *when* in the afternoon the plane was arriving. It buzzed the pond twice, apparently needing some kind of signal to land. Getting no response, it flew away in the direction from which it had come, but not before Davis had made careful notes of its description and number.

When the sky was silent again, we climbed on our horses and headed out with Hank, released from bondage, romping happily around us. Soon we were passing the dead buckskin at the foot of the rock slide. The body of Hans Holz, the Woodman, was of course not visible from below, but I could feel its presence, sad and lonely. For some distance after leaving the lake we saw, from time to time, the small tracks of a woman's shoes in the trail ahead of us.

I took a few precautions, but I didn't really think Libby would try to tackle us. She'd fired six times back there in camp, and her weapon held only seven cartridges fully loaded. Like the pro she was, she'd saved one shot for emergency use, but it wasn't enough to deal with two well-armed men.

Anyway, we were not attacked, and presently there were no more footprints in the trail. Hearing us coming, she must have hidden to let us go by. Hank did act rather oddly at one point, but I whistled him to heel and kept

him there for the best part of a mile. We reached the highway shortly after five o'clock and found a welcoming committee waiting. Apparently young Smith—Ronnie Ryerson, to give him his right name—had got on the radio and called out the reserves after Pat and Davis had headed off into the bush to rescue me. Our arrival interrupted a great debate as to whether or not a second rescue mission should be dispatched.

They weren't my people and it wasn't my job they were talking about anyway. That was all taken care of. I wasn't proud of it—I'd needed a lot of luck and a lot of help—but it had got done, which was what counted. I gave Davis' people their little envelope full of ducky little tinfoil wafers, accepted their thanks and congratulations modestly, and checked my watch constantly as the talkfest dragged on. At last I cut young Davis out of the herd and choused him to one side.

"I want a car," I said. "They took the keys I grabbed, the ones to Holz's sedan over there, and I couldn't get it out of this traffic jam, anyway. Get me something to drive, quick. You can come along if you like."

"Where are we——" He changed his mind about asking questions. "All right, but if you're thinking of the Meredith woman, she's being taken care of."

I refrained from speaking my thought, which was that it would require a hell of a lot of boyscouts, young or old, to take care of the Meredith woman, however you wanted to interpret the phrase. I glanced at my watch again. Figuring roughly three miles per hour for men on horseback, as against two for a woman on foot, we might have only some forty minutes left.

"Maybe so," I said. "But I still want a car. Let's go."

It took us twenty minutes to reach The Antlers Lodge. There was no reason to think anybody would recognize the borrowed vehicle, but I took no chances and parked it out of sight. Then I led Davis into the brush at the side of the building, the same cover into which I'd charged incautiously the other day to help a howling dog.

The stuff ran down the hill to a point almost opposite the filling station rest rooms. We made our way there and lay down among the bushes on the damp moss and leaves

that soon soaked through our clothes, but I'll have to hand it to my companion, he knew how to lie still. Occasionally, like now and when he'd fired instantly on command, back in the camp, he showed real promise. It was too bad he hadn't learned to follow instructions consistently, but that could be fixed. . . .

Twenty minutes passed, and another twenty, and still another. She was behind schedule, but it had been a long, tough walk, and afterwards there would have been arrangements to make. She couldn't be blamed for being a bit slow. At last, when it was fully dark, she came.

The big car drew up to the gas pumps and she got out on the right-hand side and headed for the rest room. She didn't look good. She'd changed from the yellow-brown corduroy outfit, of course—it would have come out of the brush much too tattered and muddy to appear in public—but in spite of fresh clothes, pants and a heavy sweater, she looked tired and bedraggled. She needed a bath, a beauty parlor, and about twelve hours sleep. Nevertheless, despite the show of utter weakness she'd put on for me yesterday, complete with tears, she was by no means crippled or exhausted by her greater ordeal today. She'd eluded the posse sent out to capture her, she'd made contact with her principal somehow; and now she was completing her mission.

At least I hoped the driver was the principal for whom she was working. In the darkness, I couldn't see his face as he gave instructions to the filling station attendant and came around the car. He walked along the building to the door marked MEN. I still couldn't get a clear look at him in spite of the lights above both rest-room doors. He paused with his hand on the knob, stalling, until Libby came out of the adjacent room. She had the dog collar in her left hand, and she was shaking water off the other hand.

"Here you are, Mr. Soo," she said. Her voice reached us clearly. "Damn it, why do they make those cisterns so deep?" She started to squeeze the sleeve of her sweater, soaked at the wrist.

"You're sure these are the right ones? There seem to have been a lot of substitutions going on."

"I told you. Four of them are good. The fifth was probably never transferred—that man who called himself Wood most likely just passed a dummy at the last drop—so I wasn't able to get it. At least I don't think he'd use the real information as bait."

"Too bad. It would have been better if we could have had the complete set. But you have done well."

As the man turned, I saw the familiar Chinese features I'd known briefly in Hawaii. Everything was perfectly clear at last. Mr. Soo had hired the young interlopers for fifty thousand dollars to carry out the murder-and-impersonation job set up by the female agent, Libby, whom he'd planted in the Russian espionage cell in San Francisco. Apparently Libby's control over the real Nystrom hadn't been as great as she'd claimed, and she'd decided to have him killed and use a substitute courier instead.

But then she'd found a better substitute—me—in Seattle, and decided that she could gain my confidence and get the stuff from me when delivered. That had canceled the usefulness of Nystrom Three and Pat Bellman and their friends, who'd loused up their first rendezvous anyway. Libby, claiming revenge as a motive, had sent me out to get rid of them so they couldn't talk; and Mr. Soo had helped by giving them instructions that made it easy for me to wipe them out.

Davis stirred beside me as Libby and Mr. Soo walked back to their car.

"But aren't you going to . . . ?"

"Stop them?" I whispered. "What the hell for?"

"She's a murderess!"

"She'll be taken care of," I said. "You know what's in the collar; you helped prepare it. Do you want it to go to waste? If we can't get it into Russian hands, what's wrong with letting the Chinese have it? And what do you think is going to happen to the lady when her superiors discover, belatedly, that they've been misled by a lot of phony information supplied by her?

Davis was silent. We watched the big car drive away. I remembered a woman in a Seattle motel room early one morning, reminding me how Moscow deals with failures.

Peking's reaction would be no less violent, I hoped. Or did I?

The city of Anchorage was surprisingly large and civilized considering the amount of wilderness through which I'd had to pass to reach it. From my comfortable room high up in a very plush hotel named after the same Captain Cook I'd heard a lot about in Hawaii—that sailor really got around—I could look out upon miles of metropolis, as well as upon several empty blocks destroyed in the earthquake of some years back, now mostly converted into parking lots.

I said into the phone, "Very well, sir. I'll get right over there." I hesitated. "One question?"

"Yes, Eric."

"Now that we're through with this lousy friendship job of yours, sir, what the hell is NCS, anyway?"

Mac's voice was expressionless. "Do you have a need to know, Eric?"

I grimaced. It was the old security catch phrase, the idea being that even a fancy title and an astronomical security rating do not in themselves entitle a government employee to any classified information he does not actually require in the line of business. In some of those Washington buildings, they won't even tell you the way to the cafeteria if you can't demonstrate that you haven't eaten for six hours and really need a meal.

I said, "Go to hell, sir. I should have pried those damn disks open and used a magnifying glass."

Mac's dry laugh reached me across thousands of miles of wire. "I am merely giving you the answer that was given to me when I asked the question. I should also inform you that our late associates, while they approved of your results, felt obliged to inform me that they considered your methods deplorable. Somehow I got the impression that they will not require your services again."

"Golly," I said, "that makes me feel just terrible, sir."

"I thought it would. Well, take it easy. And if you, like the late Holz, ever start brooding about the lonely, desperate life of a secret agent, please let me know at once. You cut this one quite fine enough without that handicap."

"Yes, sir."

I made a face at the phone as I put it down. Then I told Hank to be good and took my hat and topcoat, feeling kind of strange and sawed-off in my civilized clothes and low-heeled shoes. Those cowboy boots are habit-forming. I had a taxi run me to the hospital on the edge of town—the camper rig had been returned intact, but it was being serviced after the long journey.

The nurse at the desk directed me to the room. Heading that way, I met Mr. Smith, Senior—I mean Mr. Ryerson. He was accompanied by Lester Davis.

Ryerson gave me a bleak, unhappy nod and kept on going. At the moment, he looked like a man who might have trouble handling one set of agents, let alone two at the same time. Davis stopped and said, "I'm sorry, Ronnie can't have any more visitors today, but he'll appreciate your coming."

I said, "I'm not here to see Ronnie, and I doubt that he'd appreciate a visit from me. Tell me, how was the old man, stern and understanding or stern and unforgiving?"

Davis said angrily, "Damn you——"

I said, "So Ronnie spilled his guts under pressure; why make a federal case of it? Everybody talks, given adequate persuasion. Some people can take a little more than others, that's all. There's only one way to deal with the problem: if the guy is carrying information that's truly important, you give him a death pill to take if captured. And if the information isn't all that valuable—and this wasn't—you just damn well leave him free to sing like a bird. This business of requiring everybody to be great close-mouthed heroes all the time is pure TV, and you can tell Ronnie so from me. Tell his pop, too, if you like, but he won't thank you for it." I hesitated. "Davis."

"Yes, sir."

"If you ever get tired of playing Rover Boy with these cliché-bound jokers, there's a number in Washington you might call." I gave it to him.

He looked at me for a moment. "I suppose I should be flattered," he said slowly, "but I'm not. If this world is to be saved, Mr. Helm, it's going to be saved by people who

still retain a few illusions, not by people like you. I'll stay a Rover Boy and a boyscout, if you don't mind."

Well, I'd asked for it. I grinned. "Sure. Your choice, *amigo*. But watch those illusions. The last one you had killed a girl very dead, remember?"

It was unfair and I shouldn't have said it. I walked away quickly from the stricken look on his face. The room I wanted was down the corridor. I knocked on the door. A feminine voice answered. I went in. It wasn't as bad as I'd expected. Mac had said she'd had a real rough time.

"Hi, Justellen," I said. "A guy in Washington asked me to bring you some flowers, but I forgot them. What the hell happened to you after you left the ferry at Petersburg, anyway?"

The small, brown-eyed, blonde girl whom I'd known briefly as Ellen Blish sat up painfully in her bed as if to prove she could. She said, "We were right. They did suspect me; that's why they sent me to make contact with you on the ship. Apparently something we did there proved something to them about me. Afterwards, they damn near killed me."

"So I see."

She had a tremendous black eye, puffed almost shut. The whole side of her small face was swollen and discolored. One arm and shoulder was covered with bulky bandages. If there was other damage, it was under the covers where I couldn't see it.

We faced each other for a moment in silence, sorting out the questions that could be asked and answered from the ones that couldn't. There was, of course, no eager comparing of professional notes on the job just past. I didn't inquire as to precisely what her mission had been, or even whether or not it had been successfully completed. My hunch was that, in spite of having her cover blown, she must have managed to pull it off somehow, whatever it was, or Mac wouldn't have sent me here to cheer her up. He wasn't much fonder of failures than Moscow or Peking.

Ellen gave me a lopsided grin. "It's all right. I'll get over it, they tell me."

I said, "In about two weeks, I hope."

"Why two weeks?"

"I'm going hunting," I said. "But I'll be back."

"Hunting!" She sounded shocked and at the same time amused. "Talk about your busman's holiday! Or do you mean you've got another job——"

I said firmly, "Hunting, like with a shotgun. I have a friend, a black, four-legged friend, who's earned a reward for services rendered. I——" I stopped and cleared my throat. "I'm going to have to give him back pretty soon. I'm hardly in a position to keep a pet. But in the meantime . . . well, he's a damn nice pup, and he's had a long, dull trip. And while you may turn on with beautiful music, or LSD, he turns on with ducks. I've got nothing against birds, these days, but if ducks are what he wants, ducks are what he gets. Okay?"

She gave me her crooked smile again. "Okay. Two weeks. I'll try to be presentable by that time. . . . Oh, Matt."

"Yes."

"I shouldn't ask, but I did work on it, and I feel I deserve . . . I mean, after all, it almost got me killed. Just what is the Northwest Coastal System, anyway?"

I put a stern look on my face. "Do you have a need to know, Miss Blish?" I asked and grinned as she stuck out her tongue at me.

Then I stopped grinning and her face grew serious and we studied each other for a long moment, knowing exactly why we'd been brought together like this: two agents, male and female, after a tough assignment. It was Mac's idea of safe rest and rehabilitation for both of us—simpler, cheaper, and less obvious than turning the wig-pickers loose on us; and more effective if it worked.

It worked.